THE

BRIGHTWOOD

CODE

THE
BRIGHTWOOD
CODE

MONICA HESSE

Little, Brown and Company

New York Boston

Content Note: *The Brightwood Code* **is a work of historical fiction, and touches on many issues that remain all too prevalent today, including misogyny, grief, PTSD, bullying, and sexual assault.**

Little, Brown and Company
Hachette Book Group
1290 Avenue of the Americas, New York, NY 10104
Visit us at LBYR.com

First Edition: May 2024

Little, Brown and Company is a division of Hachette Book Group, Inc. The Little, Brown name and logo are trademarks of Hachette Book Group, Inc.

The publisher is not responsible for websites (or their content) that are not owned by the publisher.

Little, Brown and Company books may be purchased in bulk for business, educational, or promotional use. For information, please contact your local bookseller or the Hachette Book Group Special Markets Department at special.markets@hbgusa.com.

Library of Congress Cataloging-in-Publication Data
Names: Hesse, Monica, author.
Title: The Brightwood code / Monica Hesse.
Description: First edition. | New York : Little, Brown and Company, 2024. | Audience: Ages 14 and up. | Summary: A cryptic message forces eighteen-year-old American Edda to investigate what secrets followed her across the ocean, even as she tries to make sense of her time as a telephone operator on the French front lines of World War I.
Identifiers: LCCN 2023035236 | ISBN 9780316045650 (hardcover) | ISBN 9780316045711 (ebook)
Subjects: CYAC: World War, 1914–1918—Fiction. | Americans—France—Fiction. | Telephone operators—Fiction. | Ciphers—Fiction. | LCGFT: Historical fiction. | Novels.
Classification: LCC PZ7.1.H52 Br 2024 | DDC [Fic]—dc23
LC record available at https://lccn.loc.gov/2023035236

ISBNs: 978-0-316-04565-0 (hardcover), 978-0-316-04571-1 (ebook)

Printed in the United States of America

LSC-H

Printing 1, 2024

For Mazie

THE CODES CHANGED EVERY DAY. *That was the point of them, the entire point. Each night we received two pages of code names to memorize. The next day we sat down at our switchboards, and when a caller asked to be connected to Montana or Buster or Wabash, we would know that they really wanted to be connected to the Third Infantry, maybe, or to the Thirty-Fifth Division or to General Pershing's chief of staff. We drilled one another to make sure we knew the information cold. We drilled through wailing shrieks of air-raid sirens; we drilled through the vibrations of shrapnel. In English and in French, drilling.*

Our job was not in itself complicated: Answer the line, match the code name to a number, insert the right plug into the right jack, connect the telephone call.

Number, please? I must have asked that a thousand times a day.

But we were on the front. It was so hard to understand that later: that two hundred American girls had not been merely sent to France but sent to the bloody, bloody western front of the Great War.

We were doing the job while bombs rang in our ears. We were doing it while working twelve-hour shifts. My old classmates were still celebrating our high school graduations, and I was in France, where the German Army was sometimes close enough to intercept our ground wires, and I was listening for the dull thud signifying a compromised line, and I was remembering two pages of daily codes so that if the line had been tapped, listening spies couldn't make sense of what they overheard.

I would eventually learn what had happened. I would live in fear of being discovered.

But in the moment what I knew was that it was 1918 and I was just five months beyond my eighteenth birthday and I was a telephone operator with the American Expeditionary Forces and the ocean separating me from home was dark and deep salt water.

And it is possible for lives to be lost in ten seconds. It is possible for a life to be ruined in ten seconds. It is possible for a life to be ruined and to realize the story you thought you were telling was a different kind of story. I knew that, too.

Brightwood.

Brightwood.

Brightwood.

1

JACK ALBERTSON

NOVEMBER 1918

"Edda. Your blouse."

Miss Genovese's voice behind me pierces through my head-set, and I know the rest of her lecture before she begins it: Here at Central switchboard, if we wear dresses, they must be black or navy, and if we wear skirts, our blouses must be white. Mine today is yellow, my last clean one, excavated from the crumpled piles on my wardrobe floor and pale enough that I'd hoped it would go unnoticed.

"This is your third infraction this week," my supervisor

continues, wedging herself in between me and the operator next to me. Helen manages a sympathetic peek before turning back to her own switchboard. "I don't enjoy disciplining my girls, but it's a matter of dignity. Every day, you are representing not only Bell System, but all girls like yourself who are trying to prove that this is a respectable profession for respectable girls. Dignity is the—"

In front of me a small electric bulb, one of hundreds on the board, lights up and I lunge for it with relief: The only thing that will put an end to Miss Genovese's lecture about the seriousness and dignity of the job is me actually doing the job.

"Number, please," I say in the syrupy voice they taught us in the training I was forced to go to even though I'd already been trained by the United States Army. *Num*-ber, comma, *please*. The army had wanted to make sure I could remember complicated instructions, in English and in French, while translating information crucial to the war. Bell wants mostly to make sure I can use my voice to smile.

"Say, didn't I talk to you last week?" asks the staticky voice on the other end of the telephone line—young, male, swaggering.

"What number, please?" In my right hand I ready a long cord, preparing to plug it into the corresponding jack for whichever telephone number I'm given. Miss Genovese has folded her arms over her chest, clearly meaning to monitor this call to make sure my infractions don't extend beyond my wardrobe.

"No, I'm sure I talked to you," the boy on the line says. "I can tell when the voice belongs to a pretty girl. What's your name? Is this your usual shift?"

"You could have spoken to any number of operators. There are hundreds of us working around the city. What's the number you're trying to reach?"

I can see a frown out of the corner of my eye; Miss Genovese is trying to figure out how I must have encouraged this conversation even though she's heard all the words coming out of my mouth. She can't be more than a few years older than I am. What she lacks in age she makes up for in sourness.

"Yes, but if I wanted to make sure I got you next time, how do I reach you?"

"May I place a call for you now?" I ask a bit desperately.

"My friend and I have a theory about the kind of girls who become telephone operators. It's—"

"Tremont 4246?" I blurt out the string of numbers as if I'm repeating them. "Please hold."

"Wait now, I didn't—" The caller begins to protest, but he's too late; I'm already jamming the other end of the cord into the corresponding jack for the telephone number. I didn't pull it from thin air; I connect to it at least twenty times a day. When I hang up my line, the boy will find himself talking to a taxicab company.

That call dispensed with, I turn toward Miss Genovese again and hope that my face doesn't reveal my deception. Deliberately misdirecting a call would not be an infraction, it would be grounds for dismissal.

"That call could have been directed more expediently." She frowns.

"You know that sometimes they just want to make conversation."

Flirting boys call every day, less often on Sunday nights like tonight, the slur of gin in their voices. But we also hear from widows or shut-ins or schoolchildren, each of them calling to ask whether we know the correct time, or the capital of Idaho, or if we can connect them to the lobster restaurant they ate at two weeks ago, the one they can't remember the name of. Some older women call in every day to ask about the weather, so they know if they should wear their furs.

"Conversation isn't protocol," Miss Genovese says. "There is still a war going on. We must be disciplined."

Under my workstation I ball my hands into fists. As if any of us need reminding about the war. As if I, especially, need reminding about the war.

But instead of saying anything I nod my head. I need this job. I'd thought that the war might allow me to find a different profession, but even with thousands of boys overseas, most employment advertisements still specify that applicants must be men. A girl like me can expect to be a teacher, a nurse, or now, this new job of telephone operator.

Once Miss Genovese leaves, I feel the soft nudge of Helen's

sleeve against mine. Our workstations are narrow enough for this clandestine communication; we all had to pass weight and height exams upon hiring to make sure we fit in the chairs.

Her eyes staring straight ahead, Helen jiggles her arm so I know the brush was intentional. "I have a navy cardigan in my locker. You can borrow it at the break." She speaks in the same pitch of voice she uses for callers and keeps one hand on a cord so that anyone watching her would think she was connecting a call.

My knee-jerk reaction to Helen's earnest, missionary-daughter kindness is often unearned irritation, but this time I'm grateful for her concern. I bob my head up and down—*Yes, thank you, I'd appreciate that.*

"Some of us are going out for breakfast at the end of shift," Helen continues, and then pauses to answer a call. "*Butterfield 6937? Please hold.* Tillie found a diner."

It's not hard to imagine the relationship Helen thinks we ought to have: two eighteen-year-old girls living in Washington, borrowing cardigans and hairbrushes, drinking sodas at the end of a shift. I think I used to do that sort of thing once. Now it seems unfathomable. Seven months ago, Helen was attending her high school graduation and seven months ago I'd skipped my own to run to France under some misguided notion that I was proving something. I'd been home for two months and had spent them all praying that nobody would learn what I'd done.

Brightwood.

No. I shake my head enough so Helen can see it. I can't go out for breakfast.

Then I nod meaningfully toward my switchboard, trying to convey that it requires my full attention.

What must she and the other girls think of me? Showing up to my shift late and without stockings (infraction number one) and then showing up with untidy hair and dark eye circles (infraction two), refusing their attempts at socialization, nodding off in the retiring room while the other girls drink coffee or crowd around the piano. She must wonder what makes me so tired; she must assume that my off-work hours are exciting or scandalous. And maybe that's what explains her determined friendship, the idea that I need help or saving.

How disappointed she would be to see my room at my aunt's boardinghouse—a perilous stack of tinned peaches and corned beef hash, a nest of an unmade bed. My only visitors are my aunt or Theo, borrowing something or returning something.

In my peripheral vision Helen bites her lip. "I'll check in later in case you change your mind."

. . .

Evening creeps into the quiet, foggy hours of midnight. The night shift means fewer calls, two hundred an hour instead of three times that during the day. This is how the night shift was sold to me when I was hired a month ago: slower pace, fewer calls, and a promise to be moved to day work as soon as I could handle it.

But while the calls are fewer they can sometimes be sadder, odder, less routine. During the day, telephone calls are meant for business: banks and couriers and department stores and the post office. But nights can mean frantic calls for the police, or for an ambulance or the hospital. Each of us has a paper posted at our workstation containing the numbers for these emergency services so that when we're asked to patch someone through, we don't have to think twice.

I still find my hands shaking at random times, stilling them after my shift with a cigarette and then passing out unconscious. The job guarantees that I'm awake for at least eight hours at a stretch. Otherwise I would sleep twenty-three hours a day.

At one a.m. we get our midshift break, which is still called lunch even though it's in the middle of the night. I retrieve Helen's cardigan and then flop onto the retiring room sofa while the girls around me eat sandwiches and exchange glances over my prone body. Someone makes an announcement about a birthday cake; someone else makes an announcement about keeping our lockers tidy.

This last announcement feels pointed directly at me so I slide off the sofa and open my assigned locker. It's not just mine. I share it with two girls I've never met, other random girls on opposing shifts whose names come where mine does in the alphabet, our hats and coats hanging in turn in the slim wooden cubby. On the floor of the locker the only mess is mine: a broken bootlace, a hatpin, and a scrap of paper with handwritten text, which I bend to pick up.

Join you at Bell.

My body recoils. My hand flings the paper back to the ground as if it were filthy. Even when the letter fragment is back on the floor of my locker my hand still feels the filth, the invisible sick on my fingers. It crawls up my arm.

It's a piece of the reference letter used to gain my job here. The one I showed Miss Genovese in my interview. I didn't even know I'd kept it—*why did I keep it?*—but of course I kept it. Miss Genovese would have immediately handed it back to me after reading it, because if I didn't get a job at this dispatch location I would have needed the reference letter to show to another supervisor in another job interview. I must have torn it up in my coat pocket after my interview and then done my best to forget about it. I must have knocked a fragment of the letter loose onto the locker floor when I started my shift last night.

I should throw it away now.

If I don't pick up the paper again, it's just going to be in my locker at the end of my shift, and then be there still tomorrow. But I can't. I can't pick it up, because I can't think about why I am working here and why I have this letter and why I am not in France.

Just pick it up, I instruct myself. *Pick it up, it's only paper.*

But then the bell rings, signifying the end of my break, and I leave the paper fragment closed in my locker.

I am very good—expert, really—at leaving things closed in locked-away spaces.

The rest of the night is uneventful. I don't get requests for ambulances from injured people, I get requests for taxicabs from partygoers. I get giddy couples asking for champagne delivery, and apologetic businessmen telephoning home to announce their delayed arrivals, and tired mothers searching for all-night chemists to provide cough syrup for sick children. Tiny emergencies in the lives of people having them, but not really emergencies at all.

Number, please. A young woman with tears in her voice ringing a little after two a.m. to a private number in Cleveland Park. A call to her mother, I imagine, seeking comfort after a broken engagement.

Number, please. A collection of men, middle-aged, calling at a quarter to three: the dialer on the line asks whether there's a pair of us available to be dates at a dance, while others guffaw in the background.

Number, please. The caller at four thirty wants to know if I have any good cobbler recommendations and without even bothering to answer I recite the Tremont exchange and connect that caller to the taxi company.

At 4:45 a.m. my collarbone is hurting from the heavy weight of the mouthpiece that rests there. Over the drone of the operators on my shift in this room, I can hear the chatter of the girls on the next shift as they arrive and empty their belongings into the retiring room lockers, the only small overlap our belongings will ever have in the shared cubbies. At 4:55 they'll line up single file and enter the control room, church-mouse quiet, and stand behind each of us at their assigned stations. At 5:00 a.m. on the dot, we'll slip off our chairs to the right and they'll slide in from the left, a ballet we're required to practice dozens of times in training, so there's not even five seconds of time in which a station is left unmanned. I can't wait to leave even though I have nowhere to be except my bed. It's Monday morning. My nights off are Fridays and Saturdays, so Monday morning means I have four shifts left until my weekend.

At 4:59 an electric bulb in front of me lights up, the last call of my shift.

"Number, please?" I croak. As always, my voice is sandpaper by the end of the night; I long for a throat lozenge but instead pick up my cord for one last transfer.

"Help," says the voice.

"What number, please?"

"Help."

I sigh. So I'll end the night with one of those calls. *What restaurant did I eat at / What's the distance from Nova Scotia to British Columbia / Do you know the time in London?* Briefly, I scan the room; Miss Genovese is nowhere to be seen.

"I cannot help you," I say testily, "if you don't have a number."

"You have to tell the truth. The fa—"

"Tell the truth?" My irritation builds; this person is clearly drunk. "I'm not lying when I say that I *cannot help you if you don't have a number.*"

One day I'll be fired, and probably not long from now, and I wish I could bring myself to care more, the way I wish I could bring myself to care more about everything.

Behind me, the line of fresh operators steps forward en masse; the girl who will take over my shift is already sliding in at my left, reaching for the cord in my hand so she can complete this annoying transfer. The voice is slipping from my headset, my headset is slipping from my ear.

"You have to tell the truth before it's too late," the voice says one last time, and then, in a final insistent shout: *"Brightwood."*

2

Carmen Barbosa

"Wait!"

I claw desperately at my headset but it's already being ripped from my grasp, halfway onto the bobbed hair of the new operator. She pauses uncertainly, baffled by my lack of protocol as I rise from my chair and reach again for the wire headpiece.

"Give me back the headset. It's an emergency," I bark. "I need to finish that call."

Hastily, she hands me back the headpiece, her mouth hanging open in surprise.

"Hello?" I call into the headset. "Hello, I'm here."

But there's nothing on the other end of the line, a silent chasm of nothing. The caller is gone.

"Did you disconnect this line?" I demand, shaking the unplugged cord in the replacement operator's face. "Did you?" She reels back and then draws herself up again.

"If I did it was an accident."

"Then where did they go? Where did the call go?"

"They must have hung up," she says.

"But they telephoned for help."

She gives me a look, half-puzzled, half-pitying, which says, everyone who dials us needs help of some kind; that's why they're dialing us. *Brightwood.*

"If it was a true emergency the caller will ring again," she says. "They probably have already, and reached another operator."

Immediately my eyes scan the long rows of operators at their workstations. I don't know what I expect to see. All through the high-ceilinged electrical room of Central, all I see are girls in black and navy and white, manning their switchboards, doing their jobs.

The replacement operator holds out her hand expectantly. "I need to get to work." She says this through clenched teeth. We've wasted at least thirty seconds, and every second that passes increases the danger of us being caught out. Miss Genovese is bound to swoop in at any moment. "Your shift is over."

My world is pulled out from under me. I am gasping for air, drowning in the middle of a bank of telephone operators. I am thousands of miles away in France, but somehow I am still here in Washington, and I have no choice but to run home.

. . .

"Edda?" My aunt's voice drifts out from the kitchen as she hears my footsteps pounding the stairs. "Is that you?"

"It's me," I tell her, not slowing as I reach the second landing, hoping I can disappear without further conversation.

"It's Monday. Did you write your letter this weekend?"

"I will," I call down.

"You know I hate having to remind you. But."

But that was the deal struck upon my return from France. I could come and live with my aunt in Washington instead of remaining home in Baltimore only if I promised to find employment and to write to my parents once a week. It had seemed a small price to pay at the time.

"I'll write the letter," I say again, certain that my voice is coming out in a strangle. From the second landing I can see my aunt pause, trying to decide whether to press the issue. She believes young women are capable, deserving of independence, but she's still my father's younger sister, still responsible for me. *Don't come up*, I repeat to myself, willing Aunt Tess to stay where she is. *Don't come up. Don't come up.*

Eventually the footsteps below retreat and I stumble the rest of the way to my room.

My aunt's boardinghouse is a tower of red stone in Dupont Circle: large and airy rooms for the ground-floor parlor and dining room, well-appointed guest rooms on the second, basic but cheerful guest rooms on the third. By the time you get to the fourth, it's all leaning ceilings and postage-stamp windows, what used to be live-in servants' quarters and what are now rented to anyone who can't afford rooms on the other stories.

I wedge myself into my room, stumbling toward the bureau without even bothering to close my door, over piles of books and tissues, past the lamps I keep turned low and the curtains I keep drawn closed. Reaching my bureau, I peer into the mirror and then squeeze my eyes tightly shut. I squeeze them shut the way you do when you're not sure whether you're awake or dreaming and you hope that when you open your eyes it will be dark and you'll be in bed.

Maybe I dreamed it. Is there that possibility? That I dreamed the last phone call, the entire shift? That I never made it to work, that I'm still asleep?

But when I open my eyes it's not midnight, it's morning-colored pink outside. I'm still standing at the bureau, I'm still wearing Helen's cardigan sweater. I dip my hands into the basin and scoop water onto my face.

"The lady is awake."

I whirl around, water droplets sliding down my collar. Theo leans in the open doorway, knuckles still poised for the knock he didn't need to deliver.

"Of course I'm awake." I try to steady my voice, hiding my sheet-white face by scraping a cloth over it. "Why wouldn't I be?"

He raises an eyebrow high enough that it nearly meets his

dirty-blond curls. "Because usually when I knock on your door, you look like you've been dragged out of a sarcophagus, and that's if you answer the door at all."

There's no point in pretending he's wrong. Even from here I can see the strands of my hair on the pillow, and the narrow indentation running lengthwise down the mattress. I've spent so much time there that the mattress is less a flat plane than a trench.

"What do you want?" I ask.

"Why aren't you sleeping?"

"Cigarettes are in my coat pocket," I say, attempting to buy time while I decide whether I want to answer. "On the hook."

But when Theo starts rummaging through my duster I realize his hand is in the wrong pocket. Instead of producing my silver cigarette case, he produces my velvet coin purse and my heart stops for a moment before I launch across the room to snatch it out of his hands. "That's mine."

"Seeing as you just told me to pull it from your pocket, I had an inkling," he says flatly. "Jumpy, Edda?"

Grabbing my coat now, I dig through the other pocket, fishing out the cigarette case and tossing it to him. "Just don't take my last one, all right?"

He catches the case and takes out a cigarette, tucking it behind his ear but remaining in my room instead of leaving. "So *why* aren't you sleeping?" he asks again.

"Why aren't *you*?" Impromptu visits from Theo aren't unusual, but it's barely six o'clock in the morning and I know his first class doesn't start until half past eight. "You're so—dressed." Theo is wearing not only trousers and a jacket but also an outdoor coat.

"My professor is giving extra credit, which I sorely need, for coming in early and organizing his decrepit filing system. This is my diligent-student costume."

He attempts to gesture to his entire ensemble and ends up wincing, hand on his hip.

This hip injury, which he's had since I've known him, must be what kept him home from the war. It's the only reason I can think of that a boy his age would be home instead of fighting in Europe. But I've never asked. And he's never asked me about how I got here or why. Theo skims along life, all surface, no depth, simple and uncomplicated. We are the only boarders on the fourth floor under the age of eighty; our other neighbors are all widows and pensioners. Theo showed up at my door the day after I moved in to dryly inform me that my presence on the floor had halved the average age and doubled the original teeth, and by the way, could he borrow my teakettle? Since then he and I have settled into an unstated pact to ask and tell each other absolutely nothing of importance, and that is why, bizarrely, Theo is what would count as my closest friend.

"Do you want anything from the outside world?" He continues, "I have just enough time to find breakfast."

"You came to my room to offer to buy me breakfast?" I say dubiously.

"Well, no. I was so sure you'd be sleeping that I came to your room to quietly steal a box of cookies for *my* breakfast. But I'm here now."

"I'm not hungry."

"Not hungry. Not sleepy." He pauses. "Not chatty?"

I sweep my fingertips over my nightstand, raking the thick coating of dust on the top. "Something happened on my shift today," I say finally.

"Miss Genovese gave you an infraction," he guesses. He's never met my supervisor but loves to mock her. "Miss Genovese gave you five infractions. Miss Genovese ran out of infractions to give you so instead she just hung a sandwich board of shame around your neck for your entire shift."

Then he notices that I'm not smiling; I'm not even rolling my eyes. "Truly not chatty?" he asks again. This time his voice falters on the question, which has come perilously close to asking whether there's something I want to talk about, which of course, neither of us has ever asked before. Our conversations are typically built on competitive sarcasm. "Edda?" he asks when I haven't answered.

"It wasn't anything to do with Miss Genovese." I trace my initials in the dust. I trace a soldier's helmet. I trace a boat. I scrub my hand over the whole thing. "It was a caller. Someone rang in to place a call and it sounded as if—it was an odd call."

"Odd in what way?"

I shrug, a falsely casual gesture. "Just, something they said. A word."

"An odd *word*?"

"Yes."

"Just a word? What was—"

"It's not important," I say quickly. "I don't want to repeat it."

Theo clamps his mouth shut. I know the impression I'm leaving: that the word was a *bad* word, sordid in nature, that I'm too embarrassed to say it out loud to him. Let him think that. It's easier if he thinks that.

"Did they say anything else besides this—this *word*?"

"A little, but—they hung up," I say. "Or they were disconnected, I'm not sure. They were gone before I could figure out anything more. But I can't stop thinking about it, I suppose."

"Did they leave a name?"

I give him a withering look. "How often do people leave their names with telephone operators?"

"Did you recognize the voice? Was anything about it familiar to you?"

"I don't—" I'm about to roll my eyes at him again, for such a detective question, as if we're trapped in a Conan Doyle novel. But it's a decent question; it's one I should have thought about already. Now I furrow my brow, trying to remember. "I didn't even pay attention to the voice until they said the thing—the word. Before then I just thought it was someone fooling around; I've told you about the prank calls we get sometimes."

"Well, was it a man? I'm assuming it was a man?"

"It was…" I squeeze my eyes shut. *Help. Help. Brightwood.* "It was young. Like a child's voice. High-pitched, like a woman's. It could have been a girl, or a boy before his voice dropped. But also, it was over the telephone. You know the static—it's hard to tell sometimes. It can distort voices. I suppose it *could* have been an adult man, actually, now that I think about it."

Theo shakes his head. "You're not providing a lot of information."

"I know."

"Someone who could have been a man, woman, or child telephoned the switchboard and said a word so obscene you won't even repeat it," he says. "That person didn't leave his or her or their name, and they could have been calling from anywhere; they could have been calling from Los Angeles."

"Yes," I start to agree, and then catch myself with a dawning realization. "I mean, no. They couldn't, though. Be calling from Los Angeles. It was a local call."

"How can you be sure?"

I hold my hand up, asking for quiet while I let my brain catch up. Our switchboards have only enough jacks and plugs for Bell subscribers who live here in Washington. Someone calling from a long distance would have to dial their local central switchboard.

An operator there would patch the call to a nearer city with which it shared cables, and then to another after that. A call coming from California would be routed first to Phoenix, I think, or somewhere in Nevada. And then Denver, then Wichita, and then Chicago and then Columbus and on and on. Placing a long-distance call requires being on hold for up to five minutes sometimes, as a network of operators across the country snake the call to its destination.

"It wasn't a long-distance call," I repeat. "It wasn't another operator connecting the call, it was someone placing the call directly."

"Someone here in the city," Theo affirms.

"Yes."

Here in the city. Saying that out loud sends a tingle down my spine. *The call was made by someone here in the city.*

"Do you want to report it?" Theo asks. "It might not be the kind of thing the police would investigate, but we could try. We could—"

"No," I cut him off abruptly. "I don't want anyone else to know. And you should go; you're probably late."

Theo reluctantly checks his wristwatch; he can't argue with my assessment on the time. Before leaving entirely he stops and turns around once more. "Obviously, I'm not an operator. But I am conversant in telephones. I know how they work, as a caller. And I know that when I lift up the receiver, an operator is already there on the other end, ready to help place my call."

"Yes, genius boy, that is how the technology works."

"What I'm *saying*," he continues, "is that when I call, I have no

21

control over which operator is on the other end of the line. I couldn't request one in particular. I couldn't reach specifically you if I tried. So whomever this person was—this cretin? You'll probably never have to worry about them again."

He waits, hand on the doorframe. "I'm right?"

"You're right," I say, more to get him out the door than for any other reason.

Theo leaves and without him my room seems even quieter than ever, even stiller than ever. He has to be right. Of course Theo has to be right. There is no way to choose your telephone operator. It's random. The profession is entirely random.

Theo must be right, but he is wrong. I fear it in my bones. I don't know how, but he's wrong. *Brightwood.* Telephone calls are entirely random, so why am I so certain that one was for me?

3

Gerry Champlain

"*Pouvez-vous voir assez bien?*" my escort asked as I followed the dim blue light of his lantern down the narrow stone street. "*Je suis désolé, mais nous comptons sur des lanternes.*"

"Yes, I can see well enough," I managed in the French that still tasted new on my tongue, and then tried to figure out what else a competent, sophisticated girl might say in response. "There is no need to apologize for the lantern; I understand the streetlights are dimmed to protect the city from German planes."

Since that was about all I understood of my current situation, I clamped my mouth shut and didn't say anything more.

"It's not a long walk," my escort told me. "It's nearly three o'clock in the morning. I am sure you are tired."

For the rest of the walk he spared me the pressure of trying to sound intelligent, addressing me only to point out loose stones or other hazards of the street made invisible by the dark. My boots were army-issued and rubbed against my heels. I had no way of knowing whether they were actually ill-fitting or whether this was merely how boots fit; I had never worn anything so heavy and drab on my feet before. A searing blister had erupted on my right heel—a bloody, foreign kind of pain that I'd been afraid to mention to anyone because I didn't want to look too tender.

I wasn't tired. I was terrified.

The other girls had arrived weeks before. I hadn't been with them because I hadn't made the cut. Not initially. The army needed 200 girls and in the exams I must have ranked 201.

But then one of them came down with an illness, or maybe they got married, or maybe it was as simple as nerves. All I knew was that I had been summoned after I thought I had already been dismissed. Every step of my application had felt like a dare, an endeavor I'd taken on because graduation was approaching and my preference for parties over academics had left me with poor grades and no plans. Because I'd forgotten to go to three volunteer sessions in a row at my mother's club, too busy with friends and frolicking, and was summarily told that the Ladies' Aid Society didn't need my aid: My job should be to smile at fundraisers, not try to plan them. Because I had parents who thought I couldn't do it and an aunt who insisted I must. Nobody was more shocked than I was by how far this dare was going, and now it was me alone arriving after midnight to walk to the Hotel Piedmont.

My escort stopped abruptly. "Nous sommes ici."

But the building we were standing in front of didn't resemble a hotel at all, not the kind I'd been picturing, where a maid might draw me a bath and the other girls and I might linger over tea service. This building was barely a hostel, and a spare one at that. A sign on the door informed me that it was run by the YMCA.

"It's not much to look at," my escort acknowledged, as if reading my mind. "But I'm told the beds are comfortable."

In the gas-lamp light of the foyer, I could finally see his face, this man who had been leading me through the streets of Paris: dark-haired, blue-purple eyes. A sinewy build, a tailored uniform, barely a few years older than I. Handsome.

"I've rung the bell so they know you've arrived," he informed me, still in French like all of our conversation. He dipped his head and started to retreat. "À bientôt."

I felt a small wave of panic—the only person I knew this side of the Atlantic, now leaving.

"Wait, you're going?"

"This is a boardinghouse for girls only."

"But what do I do now?" The refinement I'd tried to project was rapidly crumbling away.

"You go upstairs. You unpack. You sleep. You wait for your next instructions."

"When will those instructions come?"

He chuckled. "Not at three o'clock in the morning."

"But am I supposed to go somewhere? Or will someone reach out to me? How will I know how to—I'm sorry, I just—" I faltered, knowing that my stoic facade had completely crumbled. My fear outweighed my pride. "I've never done this before."

It was a ridiculous thing to say. What did I mean, even? I had never been to France? I had never been to a hostel? I had never been to a war?

But then my escort looked at me. Really looked, deep into my eyes, as if I was becoming a person before him rather than just a duty. I could see him pondering something, then making a decision. "What is your name?"

"Ed—" I started, and then realized that he was probably supposed to call me by my last name, or something else official. I ended up tapping the luggage tag affixed to my traveling valise, where Edda Grace St. James was written in my best penmanship.

He read the tag and nodded. "Edda Grace St. James, you are going to be fine," he said, catching my gaze with his own and holding it. "I'll make sure of this."

"Do you really think so?"

"You already traveled across an ocean by yourself. The other girls all had one another, but you managed entirely on your own. That already tells me something about you. You already walked this whole way with a blister, I assume, causing that little break in your step but never complaining. That also tells me something about you. That you are willing

26

to work, maybe even harder than the other girls are willing to work." He put a hand on my shoulder and left it there, the gentlest of squeezes.

The empathetic words arrived like a blanket. I clung to them. It was the first time since I volunteered for this assignment that anyone had said that to me—that instead of questioning my capabilities, or lecturing me about duty, someone was assuming that I would succeed. Someone who knew better than my parents, my aunt, my classmates. I hadn't realized how desperate I was for that kindness.

"You know, you remind me of my sister," he continued. "Her name is Grace, just like your middle name."

"Really?"

"Maybe one day I will introduce you."

"That would be nice."

He gently clucked his lips. "But in the meantime, I will be cheering for you, Edda Grace St. James. The American girls are always plucky. When I trained for this role in the capital I found the operators there tougher than schoolmarms. I followed—"

Before he could finish his sentence, floorboards on the staircase creaked. A housemother appeared, waiting to take me inside and nodding that my escort could be on his way. He straightened his posture again—he'd let it get casual in the last minute of our discussion—and then he bowed at the neck.

"Will I see you again?" I asked, a bit too hopefully.

"I am the liaison assigned to manage the Hello Girls," he said. "I would be in trouble if you did not."

"But what's your name?" I asked, and he smiled.

"Luc."

. . .

The housemother gave me my room number and then sent me upstairs. In the doorway of my assigned room on the third floor I could see the dim outline of a body in the bed closest to the door and an empty bed closer to the window. I tiptoed as quietly as I could over to my half of the room. But my suitcase squeaked when I unhinged it to unpack, and the bureau drawers groaned when I opened them, and when I went to lay out my best hair combs for the morning—mother of pearl, costing every cent of my birthday money—I accidentally knocked them behind the nightstand with a clatter, and finally the dark-haired head occupying the other bed stirred.

"For God's sake," she hissed into the dark. "Are you unpacking a marching band next?"

After that I gave up trying to unpack. I crept into the empty bed fully dressed, clutching my recovered hair combs, and then tried to quell everything rising in my stomach.

I didn't remember falling asleep, but once I did it was sleep like molasses, heavy and dark, until I was wakened by a screaming sound. And then another one, louder. An air-raid siren. Groggily, I sat up. My roommate had already leapt out of her bed. She was in a nightgown but I noticed with confusion that she was also in a cardigan, a cardigan over the nightgown as if she'd slept half-dressed.

"Well?" she asked, noticing me still sitting in bed. "Take your blanket."

"Take my—really?" I wondered whether this was some kind of hazing.

"And your pillow. Come on!"

The siren wailed again.

So I fumbled for my pillow and then I followed her out into a stairway crowded with other descending bodies, down to the basement, where dozens of young women filled the floor, makeshift beds of blankets and pillows, immediately resettling themselves for sleep. The basement floor felt rough and grainy, and then I realized it wasn't a floor at all; it was packed dirt.

"We sleep here?" I started to ask the question aloud but then watching the other girls spread out their bedclothes, underneath bundles of hanging parsnips and ropes of garlic, was answer enough. I shook out my blanket and lay on top of it, shoulder to shoulder, a row of operators like matchsticks in a box.

"Edda," I introduced myself, wondering somehow if this was all really happening, or whether exhaustion from my travels was causing an elaborate hallucination. It barely felt real.

"Yvette," said the girl to my right, and then introduced me to all the girls down the line: Jennie. Elizabeth. Ida. June. Finally, my roommate, pinched tightly against my left side: "Mae."

"Tell us about yourself," Yvette encouraged. "Brothers, sisters? Cats, cockatoos, hobbies? Where are you from?"

Somehow, despite my disorientation, my debutante training kicked in—the idea that first impressions were crucial for social currency. "I'm from Baltimore. No brothers or sisters, but I belonged to the Mount Vernon Social Club so I always had friends, and—"

"Mount Vernon like where George Washington lived?" Yvette asked, laughing.

"No, it's a social club, the waiting list is miles long and—"

"Am I the only one who wants to sleep tonight?" Mae cut in.

"Are you worried that if you don't get your beauty rest you won't be Luc's favorite anymore?" Ida teased.

"I'm really not."

"It's not her looks that make her the favorite, it's her tongue," Yvette rejoined. "Those perfect Parisian r's."

By the time the chuckles died down everyone had forgotten that they were asking about me at all.

The sirens came on and off all night long. And amazingly, all around me, the other girls started to go to sleep. Pillows over their heads, breath white and puffy into the cold, damp air, sighing and rustling in the sounds that were familiar to me from any overnight birthday party, up half the night listening to the phonograph, except this wasn't like any kind of slumber party I could have possibly envisioned. I couldn't imagine sleeping a wink; I tossed and turned, wriggling noisily in my blanket. I could feel the earth shake, and back at home my bed had a lace canopy and a clean white quilt and it was where I had slept nearly every night of my life, and now there was no lace canopy and there was no phonograph; there were sirens. I squeezed my pillow around my head like a child in a thunderstorm.

A booming sound, not far away. It wasn't a siren, it was an actual bomb, I could feel it. My heart raced in panic and I tried not to cry.

You are going to be fine.

I tried to repeat Luc's words to me, and to make them my own. I am going to be fine. The liaison from the United States Army had seen something in me that I wasn't currently able to see in myself, with his amethyst eyes and his beautiful French, and all I could do was trust that he was right. Wait for my further instructions. Trust that I belonged here.

I dreamed I was still on the sea, that I was still on the ship to France and that I was being sprayed by the salt water. In the morning I woke actually wet, and when I finally sat up in my blankets, I learned it had rained overnight and the basement had flooded. The packed dirt floor had become mud. My blanket was sopping; when I tried to roll from my spot my body made squelching sounds, suctioned to the damp floor. I should have taken the time to change into my nightgown. The clothes I was wearing were a uniform, army-issued from skirt to belt and jaunty hat. My trunk wouldn't be delivered to the hotel for another few days so I'd planned to wear this uniform again today. But now it was soaked.

"Shit," I said, the first time I could remember ever saying such a vulgar word out loud, much less in public.

Mae flashed a cool look at me.

"We are sophisticated bilingual telephone operators commissioned by the United States Army to help win the war," she said.

My face flushed with embarrassment, but I couldn't seem to stammer out an apology. In the daylight hours I got my first real look at my roommate and noticed that she, along with all the other Hello Girls, wore her hair in an unfussy bob held back with plain metal hairpins. Not a mother-of-pearl comb in sight. Mae reached for one of the pins now, shaking it loose from her hair and then holding it between her teeth while she swiftly twisted the lock back in place, a move so basic it seemed elegant, almost more elegant than anything I'd ever seen.

It's funny the way I remember my time in France: little vignettes, discombobulated, a narrative drifting along an ocean, a series of scenes that meant nothing until they meant something. The friendships I thought I was building but wasn't.

"Sophisticated bilingual telephone operators," Mae repeated. "So the word you mean to say is merde.*"*

4

AUGUST DANNEMAN

Theo goes to class, and I try to do what I always do: clamp my curtains shut with a clothespin, cocoon under my covers, and then not wake again until it's time for my next shift. This time I toss and toss until I assume it's the middle of the afternoon only to look at my clock and discover it's barely ten. When I give up on sleep and emerge from my room, it's with hunger pangs in my stomach. The cookies Theo had come in to steal didn't even exist; the tins in my room are all crumbs.

On the ground floor of the boardinghouse the parlor and dining room are empty—the boarders with jobs have left for the day. The weight of a few coins clinks in my pocket; I shrug on my coat, slipping through the parlor and out the front door.

The sun is bright and disorienting. I throw my arm over my eyes as if I'm a vampire visiting the day. I can't remember the last time I was outside in the light like this. It would have been before I started my job at the telephone company. I don't even know Aunt Tess's neighborhood except as a night-lurker, walking to and from work past shuttered businesses and empty streets.

I pass a newsstand and pause to read the headlines.

"Spanish flu claims one hundred thousand lives; Americans urged to wear masks, keep safe distance."

"Suffrage allies to meet."

"How our men are dying, told by chaplain," I read, and I pick that newspaper up.

> Nearly 120,000 soldiers have died during the course of the Great War. How American soldiers are dying in France was told the other day by the Rev. Father F. A. Kelley, chaplain of the 27th Division, who praised warmly their devotion and courage. "To begin with, none of them are ignorant, at any time, of the danger in which he stood. Too many around them were fallen—victims of rifles, shells, grenades, and machine guns. All those things played their part in bringing—"

"How many copies would you like, miss?"

I blink at the mustachioed vendor, who stands with his palm outstretched.

"Pardon?"

"I assume you want to buy the newspaper you're holding. We ask that customers don't handle the newspapers unless they plan to purchase one," the vendor continues, pained. "Would you like something to go along with it? A croissant, perhaps? It's a French—"

"I know what a croissant is," I interrupt. "I don't want one. I'll take a bun. And I don't need the newspaper."

Where to now? I have hours until my next shift begins.

And that's all I'm doing. Killing time before my next shift. That's why I wasn't able to sleep, why I left the house, why my feet took me automatically in the direction of Central. Because of the voice on the phone.

Laundry. That's how I should occupy my time. I accrued last night's infraction because my last clean blouse was the wrong color; it's not as if I've magically acquired more white ones since then. Maybe I could just buy a new blouse? It's a temporary solution, since buying a blouse today will leave me in the same kind of trouble tomorrow. But I can think of that problem tomorrow.

Hecht's department store is about a mile away. I walk, first down Massachusetts Avenue and then down Sixteenth Street, toward the White House: gated, fenced, and with a parade of protesters slowly circling in front. MR. PRESIDENT: HOW LONG MUST WOMEN WAIT FOR LIBERTY? reads the simplest sign. The most complex one is considerably longer and is laid out like a letter: KAISER WILSON, it begins, likening the American president to a German dictator.

The protesters are suffragettes, out rallying for the Susan B. Anthony amendment. Aunt Tess is probably among them, hatted and gloved, waving a sign that would have embarrassed my parents.

Are you trying to break your mother's heart? my father had asked me. *Running off to live with Tess, the woman who gave you this cockamamie Hello Girl idea to begin with?*

But what could they do? Refuse to let me go to Washington? I wasn't asking them for money. They had no power over me, not technically. My future had already gone off the rails, even if they didn't realize it; I had already gone to France.

• • •

Hecht's is four stories tall and takes up an entire city block— all carved stone and ornate glass. Inside the cavernous marble hall, neatly pressed clerks stand behind waist-high display cases. I used to come to stores like this with my mother for party dresses and afternoon tea. Now I drift over to the counter displaying boring shirtwaists: rows and rows of white blouses with every imaginable variation of button or no button, lace or pleating.

"These have been selling very well," the clerk enthuses, taking a delicate, ribboned silk blouse out of the tray in front of her.

"I think I'm interested in something more basic."

She nods, her fingers deftly producing a shirt with little brass buttons shaped like anchors.

"Even more basic," I tell her.

She leans in and lowers her voice. "If you're on a budget, you might be surprised by how economical this one is. It only *looks* like silk, but really it's a very practical sateen."

"It's not about the money," I explain. "I need something that isn't distinctive. I'd like to buy as plain a shirt as you have, so that I can wear it for several days straight and never have someone question whether I'm wearing yesterday's clothing."

The clerk suppresses a look of horror before reaching for the tray on the very bottom rack. She pulls out a basic white blouse with bone buttons and a narrow, pointed collar. "Like this?"

"I'll take three of them."

Next, I should go to the skirts department and pull the same trick, buying three identical wool skirts in navy. And a dark cardigan like Helen's could be thrown over my blouse every day and save me the trouble of—

"Edda!"

I whirl around, at first convinced that the clerk somehow knows my name, and then wondering whether it's Helen herself, or one of the other girls from dispatch.

But it's neither.

The figure is still halfway across the department store but approaching me quickly, parcels spilling out of her arms.

Mae.

Her hair is longer than the last time I saw her, long and dark and pulled off her neck.

Mae.

Why is she here? She should still be in Paris; they should all still be in Paris except for me.

Behind me the clerk wraps up my blouses, unhurried, making a neat crease in the brown paper.

"I'll take them," I mutter.

"I'm just making sure they're not—"

"*I'll take them,*" I insist, sweeping the packages off the counter.

"Edda?" the voice calls again.

Something is off.

The woman I thought was Mae isn't coming nearer to me; she's still crossing the store. Her hand is aloft but it's waving to someone else. Another woman, her own hand raised. Was the first woman even saying "Edda" at all, or was it Hedda? Edna?

Mae's hair *couldn't* have grown so much in less than two months. My own is barely longer than a bob. None of the girls I worked with could now have hair long enough to wrap into a bun.

Just as I start to let out a breath, out of nowhere the grand front door to Hecht's flies open, so forcefully that the doorman leaps back. A gust of wind flies in and then two women run in, disheveled and out of breath.

"It's over!" one of them shouts. Tears are streaming down her face. "It's over!"

Her friend is carrying a stack of newspapers; now she flies around the store, pressing copies into shoppers' hands, depositing them on top of the glass cases.

"I already saw the news today," I stammer, backing away from her bright, glassy eyes.

"Special edition," she gasps. "It's over!"

The headline is in all capital letters, inches high, marching across the entire top third of the newspaper.

ARMISTICE.

"Is this true?" I ask one of the women passing out papers. "Are you sure?" Just last week, the *New York Herald* had accidentally printed that the war was over; we learned later that the streets of Manhattan had rained with ticker tape, exploded in celebration before the newspaper could correct the error.

"It's true," she cries. "We came from the White House. Wilson himself spoke from the Rose Garden balcony."

A flute of champagne is pressed on me by an invisible hand, probably from the store's mezzanine café. Dazed, I lift it to my lips and finish it in one pull, and then clutch the stem of the glass, fragile and sharp in my hands. When I look down, the glass is filled again somehow. I lift the second glass and finish that one, too.

The war is over. It's over.

Everyone will come home now. Everyone will talk.

5

CHARLES DANNENBERG

The whole city is a party.

In just a few minutes, the office buildings surrounding Hecht's have opened, lawyers and secretaries pouring out bareheaded and barehanded, the decorum of hats and gloves forgotten as the inhabitants of F Street office buildings leave their desks to celebrate in the streets.

I'm outside, too, carried out by the Hecht's throng, holding wrapped-paper parcels in my arms that I'm vaguely aware I didn't pay for. But nobody will care about what I did or didn't pay for.

The war is over and everyone will know.

This is such a selfish thought, such an unspeakably selfish thought, and I know this even while thinking it. But that doesn't stop my brain from repeating it as I fight my way through the crowds and the chaos and the celebration. The champagne I'd gulped down has begun to take effect, sloshing in my empty stomach, making my steps unsteady and my brain feel too light.

I make it back to my aunt's house without really being aware of how I got there. The front door is thrown open and I can already hear the sound of the phonograph, spilling George M. Cohan through the rooms. Inside, the parlor is a thicket of people—all the boarders of the house and even more: My aunt's suffragette friends are here, and the washerwoman who comes for the bedclothes.

Through the parlor in the dining room I spot Theo, glassy-eyed, with a bottle in his hand that he uses to fill champagne flutes and scotch tumblers and any other glass that gets passed his way by the crowd surrounding him. I fight my way through the parlor crowd, trying to make it to the stairwell.

"Edda!" Theo has spotted me. My name works its way out of his mouth in a tangled knot.

I look at the glass he's trying to offer me, a clear liqueur, but when I take it, waves of nausea roil my stomach.

"Peppermint schnapps," Theo explains. "We drank all the reasonable liquor already."

I push the glass back toward him, turning my head away from the medicinal odor wafting out of the glass.

"I can't drink this." Only then do I realize that my own voice is as tangled as his was. The room feels hot and close and spinning. How many glasses of champagne did I drink back at Hecht's?

Before Theo can remove the glass from my hand someone jostles my arm. The entire contents spill onto the floor.

"Whoopsie," Theo says, taking the cup from me to refill.

"Stop." I swat his hand away. "I need to—I need to—I need to get out of this room." I press on as the walls around me begin to spin. Did I just have the two glasses of champagne or was it three? It's rolling in my stomach, wetly, mixing with the awful, hideous odor of the peppermint schnapps. "I need to go somewhere."

A cheer rises up, and then, over the phonograph, the steady thrum of a cakewalk. Someone has removed the Cohan song and started playing dance music instead. Around us people begin to move, a swirling eddy of bodies rubbing our shoulders, beckoning us to join in. My head is pounding; I'm even more disoriented than I was outside.

"I need to get out of this room," I say again. "Somewhere private," I slur.

"Somewhere private?" Theo repeats, scanning the packed parlor as if a secret remote nook will somehow appear between the perspiring bodies.

My stomach heaves against itself. And then I vomit. In the middle of my aunt's parlor, onto the rug, spilling out champagne and guilt and self-loathing.

"We should get you out of here," Theo says, finally latching on to what I was trying to tell him, marshaling me toward the stairwell.

I manage to make my way up the first flight of stairs and then the second, until at last the party downstairs is a buzz instead of a din and we're at my bedroom door.

I step inside and before I can tell him not to, Theo follows me. My mouth tastes sour. I swipe at it and then look around for a handkerchief to better do the job. *Handkerchief.* As if I would have anything so civilized. When I turn back around Theo is helpfully holding up a pair of my bloomers, scavenged from the swamp of my floor, indicating that I should wipe my mouth.

"There you go!" Theo slurs brightly, handing me my own underwear, with obviously no clue what he's holding in his hand.

I swipe at my mouth with the undergarments, nodding in vague thanks.

"They're coming home. Can you believe it?" Theo continues, wonder in his voice. "Everyone who got sent over there is coming back *here*."

It's so odd to hear these words coming out of his mouth, the same words I had thought myself, but filled with celebration instead of dread.

"Everyone whose name was called—it can all stop, finally," he continues. "All of it can all just be...done."

"Theo, I—"

"I'll get you a glass of water," he suggests abruptly.

"I don't need—"

"I'm getting you water," he insists, backing out of my door and disappearing toward the bathroom down the hall.

Once he's gone I pace, tiny steps that cover my tiny room, but my steps feel unsteady so I move to sitting on my bed. I wonder if I could and should do what I always do. Sleep it off. Sleep through it. Curl under the covers and hope everything goes away. From three flights below a raucous cheer arises, a new song on the gramophone.

Theo had left my door open when he went to get water—*how long does it take to get water?*—but when I get up to close it I see something unexpected: Theo in silhouette, partway down the hall- way. A filled water glass sits on the floor beside him. Theo is leaning against the wall, forehead pressed against the wallpaper, the muscles in his back working as he exhales all the air from his body.

My brain is too fuzzy for me to fully make sense of what I'm seeing. All I know is that I am watching Theo and he doesn't real- ize it, and he reaches up to brush a hand—smudged with graphite, precise architect hands—across his cheek. Next he laces his fingers behind his blond curls and, mouthing something, looks up toward the ceiling. I realize now that his eyes weren't merely glassy from drink downstairs but shiny from tears.

He looks so still, so somber and sincere.

I can't bear this serious version of him. I can't bear the way that this version of him makes me feel about my own selfish feelings about the end of the war—me, the only person in the country who isn't celebrating and who is instead terrified of what the war's end will mean for me.

My head is on fire and I need to make my way to my bed. That was the right instinct after all.

In the hallway Theo must have realized I'm standing at the door. I hear a rustle of movement and when I look over again he's scooping the water glass from the floor. When he straightens to standing he throws his arms up in a sheepish shrug. "Too much schnapps! I nearly passed out in Mrs. Pettibone's doorway."

And then I no longer know what I saw. Whether Theo was overcome with emotion or just overcome with alcohol, whether he was crying or just sweating. I only know that I can't manage anything else right now, that I am overcome myself and barely hanging on, and I don't want someone else in my room while I unravel. I don't want someone else in my room at all.

"You should go," I tell him before he reaches the doorway. "I don't need the water."

"What?"

"You should *go*."

"Edda, is something wrong?" he asks, but doesn't stop coming toward my door.

"I can't tell you."

"Of course you can," he offers. "I speak English and understand most words under three syllables." He lifts the water glass now, but all that my brain registers is that the clear liquid looks like it could be peppermint schnapps, and Theo is taller than me by half a head, and he's still coming closer to me after I told him to go, and it was definitely three glasses of champagne that I had, drunk in quick succession.

"Theo, I told you to *leave*."

I back into my room again, heaving the door shut on Theo's surprised face. Then I lean against the door and close my eyes. Breathe in. Breathe in and out.

"Edda?" he begins from the other side of the door.

"You got me upstairs," I mumble through the oak, sliding down to the floor. "I don't need any more help."

"You don't seem—"

"I don't need your help."

"Edda," Theo says, voice low. "Is this about the word?" he asks. "The dirty call you told me about this morning?"

I don't say anything.

"He said something else, didn't he?" Theo continues. "Some other nasty thing? Just—out with it, Edda. You'll feel better when it's all out in the open."

"I won't feel better," I tell him bitterly.

"You *will*." Theo is on the other side of the door but I can still feel him pressing, pressing at a button I don't want pressed. "For pity's sake, Edda, it was just a call; this can't have been the only time that a lecherous man—"

"It was not *just a call*."

"Really, Edda, it—"

47

"It wasn't—Jesus, it wasn't a—Theo, you have *no idea*." The words pour out of me now, uncorked and furious and drunk. "I went overseas. During the war I went overseas."

"I know that," Theo says through the door, and I think I hear him stammer a little, taken aback by my fury.

"As part of the war effort, as part of the American Expeditionary Forces."

"Edda, I know *that*, too. The trunk at the end of your bed has an AES stamp on it; I assumed you were a Hello Girl."

"Oh, you know *everything*, then." For some reason it's the past tense that bothers me. I *was* a Hello Girl and now I am here, a hermit in a boardinghouse, protected by a disheveled fortress of my dirty clothes and empty tins, and Theo knows absolutely nothing.

"The codes changed every day," I spit. "Did you know *that*? We had codes to remember. Platoons and bases and generals and— basically anything to do with the war was in code."

"They changed—" Theo tries to follow along but I don't let him.

"The reason I came back early from the front was—one day near the end of my shift, I received a call from headquarters ordering me to place a call to Brightwood, and that was the code that day for Baltimore's Forty-Eighth Regiment."

Suddenly I am back there in that tent, that muddy, sweaty temporary military tent on that muddy, sweaty horrible day, and now I'm not telling the story to spite Theo, I'm telling the story because

I can't stop telling the story, because it's coming out in a desperate race.

"But I couldn't do it. For more than thirty seconds—for almost a minute—I could not remember the code. The officer who telephoned in asking me to make the connection was urgent at first, and then he was angry and then—then he sounded scared, which was the worst of all. But I couldn't do it. I couldn't remember the code."

"I'm sure it happened all the time, Edda," Theo says, with compassion but also, I think, a touch of impatience. "You can't have been the only operator to make that mistake."

I'm already shaking my head, impatient myself at his lack of understanding. "It *didn't* happen all the time. Or it did, but not like this. Because the call—it wasn't something routine, like requesting more horses or more helmets. It was that the Forty-Eighth Regiment had advanced beyond the front and they didn't realize it—they didn't realize how exposed they were. Some of them were already on a boat. The call was an emergency order for them to turn around and fall back immediately. Only they didn't. They couldn't. Because I didn't patch through the call. Because I couldn't remember the code."

"What happened next?" Theo asks.

"Another operator took over my switchboard. She saw that I was—she saw that something was wrong and she took my headset, she took over the call."

"And what happened to the boys?"

"What happened to the boys?" My voice rises, incredulous. "What do you *think* happens to young men in wars who are behind enemy lines? They died. They died. *They died.*"

The story is finished. I'm finished. I'm wrung out. Meanwhile the door has gone silent. I wonder if I've lost him.

"Theo?" I say. My voice sounds small, both desperate and dreading to hear his response. "Theo, are you even still there?"

"I'm sorry, I'm still here." His words come out halting, tripping. "I'm just trying to figure out what to—they died?"

I don't think he's drunk anymore. I don't think either of us are. I think it's the fact that even sober, even after two years of war, it's difficult to fathom this concept. Thirty-four of them. Thirty-four, whom I memorized in alphabetical order after reading about them in newspapers. Jack Albertson. Carmen Barbosa. Gerry Champlain. August Danneman. I always imagined August Danneman was the last to die—that the boat was hit, and August helped the others find life preservers to grab on to, and then there was nothing left for him to grab on to.

"Edda," Theo says finally. "I'm not saying this just to make you feel better, but it is—it was—a *war*. Hundreds of people were dying every day. You forgot the code. Another operator remembered it one minute later."

"It made a difference," I insist. "I know it did."

"But how does this relate to—you said this was something to do with the telephone call you received at work. The one with the vulgar word?"

"The word the caller said was Brightwood."

Brightwood.

Brightwood.

"Couldn't Brightwood mean something else?" Theo asks, still trying to sound reasonable. "A restaurant or business?"

"No," I say firmly. "There are no taxicab companies or hospitals or streets named Brightwood in Washington. It's not the name of a restaurant. It's not the name of a nearby town; it's not an exchange, like Butterfield or Chester. There is no reason for someone to call dispatch and say that word. Not unless they were trying to reach me, and tell me they knew what had happened."

"But Edda, who would that be? Presumably everyone else who knows what happened is still in France."

He's right about that. The technology of long-distance calls is getting more impressive every day, but there is still no way to telephone someone across an ocean.

"This doesn't make any sense," Theo says finally. "Is there anything you left out?"

Is there anything I left out.

Of course there is. Of course there are things I left out. But nothing that would excuse any of my behavior. Nothing that would make this story make any more sense. Boys were dying on the front. My job was to answer telephones. My only job was to answer telephones.

"What do you mean, something I left out?"

"Was one of the boys...special to you?" he asks.

"Special?"

"Did you know one of them personally? Did you have a personal relationship with—Edda, you know what I mean."

I do know what he means. I know exactly the question he thinks he is asking—a romance specifically with a boy from the Forty-Eighth—and that narrow specificity is why I am able to say, convincingly, "I didn't have a romantic entanglement with one of the boys who died on the boat."

"But—but why would someone do this? What do they want? Blackmail?"

For the first time since the switchboard call, instead of trying to escape from the memory, I close my eyes and try to take myself back to it. The end of my shift. Eyes bleary. Helen next to me. Headpiece heavy over my ears. "They told me I had to tell the truth," I say suddenly. My eyes fly open. How could I have forgotten that part of the conversation? "Before they said the word, they said I had to tell the truth."

Theo shakes his head, as if clearing water from his ear. "Tell the truth to *who*?"

"I don't know," I say, miserable that I've remembered something else, but not anything helpful. "I don't know, I don't know. They started to say something else—another word that started with an *F*, maybe an *F-A*, but I got impatient and interrupted them."

Why had I interrupted? What if they were about to explain more, explain everything?

"*F-A?*" Theo asks. "*Face? Facts?* Maybe it was a *P-H*—could they have just been saying *phone?*"

"Theo, could you leave now?" I ask. My head is swimming and spinning. I need to go to sleep.

"No, Edda, I think we should talk more about—"

"Could you go back to your room? I'm tired."

"I don't—"

"I'm *tired*, Theo. And I'm asking you to please leave."

He waits one more beat, still, before leaving. Finally, his footsteps pad away, softer and softer, until he opens and closes the door to his own room. Tucking himself inside.

Theo didn't say anything, but I know what he must be thinking. He must be thinking either that I have presented him with a mystery with an impossible solution or that the whole thing is entirely in my head.

6

Silas DuBois

A plain room. Wood floor, no windows. In the middle of it, one solitary switchboard stall, and in front of it, a single stool. The soldier who ushered me into the room stepped out and closed the door behind him.

I opened my mouth to call out for assistance but then thought better of it. Presumably I was to wait for a superior officer to come in— a final training, or at least a debriefing of instructions before I was assigned a permanent duty station. My uniform was clean, at least; I'd managed to wash and mostly dry the muddy one, but my hair was still damp. Feeling self-conscious about the elaborate mother-of-pearl comb I'd planned to wear today, I'd left my hair unadorned entirely and now I worried that it made me seem even younger than I was.

I stood near the door, trying to look professional, when suddenly a light went on in the switchboard. Insistent, flickering. I glanced one more time to the door, praying for someone who knew what they were doing to walk through it—what if the incoming call was important?—before realizing that if the call was truly important, I needed to answer it myself. I was the only one there.

I went to the stool and, sucking in a breath, I reached for the jack.

"Hel—number, please?"

"Allo, allo?" The barking voice on the other end of the line spoke in rapid-fire French.

"Allo," I repeated. "Je vous ai—"

"Connect me to headquarters in Lyon," the voice interrupted in French, and while I was still translating that in my head, it continued. "Get me Colonel Liebowitz there; tell him it is Colonel Boisclair and I need six hundred and forty-eight horses."

Frantically I searched the switchboard in front of me until I saw a notecard with dozens of extensions on it. I located the correct one for Lyon and waited for someone to pick up the extension.

"Allo," I began. "Je cherche—"

"I don't speak French!" the voice on the other end snapped. "What do you want?"

For the next ten minutes, my brain leapt back and forth as I translated the conversation: horses and gas masks that were needed on the southern front of the war, never able to catch my breath or think too hard about what I was saying, as the voices of a Frenchman and an American overlapped in my headpiece, shouting out numbers, addresses, times, crucial details.

"Finalement, téléphoniste," the first man said to me—Finally, telephone operator—"how many horses do we need?"

It was the first time since the conversation began that I was addressed directly, and I tried to remember back to the very first order I was given. "Six cent quarante-sept," I blurted out. "Non, quarante-huit!"

The feeling in my chest—it was hard to describe the blend of anxiety and elation. Because I had done it, I had done it. Frivolous Edda, and I'd connected my first call overseas.

And then, a burst of applause. Not coming from my headset but coming from the very room I sat in. I watched, incredulous, as two figures appeared from the other side of the switchboard. The man on the left had a paunchy middle and a bored-looking expression. The man on the right—and I was so relieved when I realized this—was Luc.

"Six hundred and forty-eight horses indeed," he said, clapping his hands together.

"It was a drill?" I asked slowly, still reeling from the breakneck pace of the telephone exchange and trying to wrap my head around what had happened.

"We just like to make certain, before officially placing the girls on duty."

"But, I had no idea you were back there!" I exclaimed. "Switchboards can work this way?"

"They can," Luc said, smiling. Despite his insistence at conducting his end of the phone conversation in French, despite the fact that we had spoken only in French the night before, English now rolled easily off his tongue with barely a trace of an accent.

"Your name is Colonel Boisclair?" I asked, wiping away a drip of sweat that ran down my forehead.

"I am the man who was Colonel Boisclair on the telephone," he said. "But it is a bit of a private military joke—there was a firework incident in the Fontainebleau—"

The other officer smirked next to him at this memory and Luc cut off the story of his calamity. "Anyway, my real name is Luc L'Enfant. I told you we would meet again. You are settling in?" Luc asked.

"I—I don't know. I soaked my uniform in the air raid last night," I blurted out.

"It looks dry enough now."

"I stood at the window and flapped it in the breeze for an hour this morning," I admitted. "It's still damp at the seams."

"I love this," he said, bursting into a chuckle before turning to the dour-looking officer next to him. "I told you this one had the potential to be special."

The other officer nodded in response, busy examining his fingernails, but I couldn't help but flush at the compliment. Luc thought me worthwhile enough to mention to someone else, a colleague in the army.

"You are still behind the others," Luc continued. There was caution in his voice now, something warning me not to get too excited. "Your

French is textbook and formal, which I would expect from your educational background. But the successful operators here, the ones we trust with important assignments, have more conversational experience and they know more military terms. Those terms can save precious seconds on the telephone, and you need to know them. It would take a lot of work, though."

"I can do the work," I blurted out and then tried to pare back my own eagerness. "I mean, I can learn different kinds of French, if that's what I need to do. Are there books I should read? Can you help me?"

"Perhaps." He appraised me. "I make the time for operators who are serious about their work."

I thought about Mae, casually tossing off French curse words, and about the other girls teasing Mae for being Luc's favorite.

"I want to be serious," I said. "I want to be like Mae."

"Do you?" he asked, and I thought I sensed a little doubt in his voice, as if he were too polite to tell me that there was no way I could be as competent as Mae, no way that my Parisian r's would ever float off the back of my tongue. "Then we must get to work," Luc said. "What I would propose is—"

Before he could continue, the other officer cleared his throat, the first sound he'd made since the pretend telephone conversation. "Captain L'Enfant, we're already beyond our time," he said shortly, and then extended his hand to me for a firm shake.

"This was your final exam," he said, and a jolt of excitement ran through my body. "Welcome to the Expeditionary Forces."

7

BARTHOLOMEW FAGER

Door knocking. Throat clearing, the rustling of drapes. When the sounds don't stop I finally pry my sticky eyelids open. Light from a streetlamp beams into my cavelike bedroom and reveals the source of the noise— Aunt Tess, sitting on the edge of my bed, appraising her surroundings.

"Edda," she begins. "You know that I don't hold to the idea that all women are natural homemakers. When I let you this room, it was without any specified stipulations for cleanliness. I intentionally didn't—"

"What time is it?" I interrupt her, squinting behind her to see the vague positions of the clock hands on the wall. *Can that possibly be the right time?* My brain is still foggy. Hungover, apparently. That must mean it's still Monday, that when Theo finally left and I finally went to sleep, I didn't lose another day entirely. But the clock says it's a quarter to nine. I'm about to be late for my shift again. I swing my legs onto the floor.

"—I intentionally didn't give you explicit instructions for how you would tend to the room. But I nonetheless expected—"

"Have you seen a parcel from Hecht's? White paper and tied with string?"

If I skip brushing my hair and finding anything to eat—not difficult, as my stomach feels as though it would reject food anyway—I might be only a few minutes late to work. But I'm still—*still*—in the wrinkled yellow blouse from yesterday, and I can't possibly wear it to another shift.

"Edda," she sighs. "Are you listening to me? I think we need to have a talk."

I told Theo. I told Theo almost everything.

Why would I have done such a thing? Theo, with whom I have never had a conversation about matters more pressing than which of our fellow boarders hogged all the hot water. Theo, whose entire point is that he makes life seem simple, that we never ask anything of each other.

Finally I spot the corner of the parcel sticking out from underneath my coat. I tear it open and pull on the first of my three cheap blouses, nearly as wrinkled already as the one I'm removing from my body, since the Hecht's package has been crumpled on my floor all day. But clean, at least, and sparkling white. At my bureau I splash water on my face, pull my hair back with pins.

Why did I tell Theo? What if somehow I'm wrong about this and it's just a strange coincidence? What if I'm making myself paranoid for nothing?

"Edda—" my aunt tries one more time, but I'm already jamming my arms into my coat, leaving my aunt in my room, muttering something about being a responsible employee and then slipping out the door.

The streets aren't fully mine, the way they usually are when I walk to work in the dark. There are other people, straggling revelers, giddy still with the war's end, and clogging up the streets with their unfamiliar nocturnal activities. I slide past a romantic couple walking arm in arm, unaware they're taking up the entire sidewalk, and give wide berth to another man vomiting in an alleyway. I run my tongue over my teeth. *Did I at least remember to brush them before falling asleep?*

"Come celebrate with us!" an inebriated man yells from a restaurant as I pass, patting his knee. When I don't respond, he calls louder. "Awww, come on! Just trying to have a little patriotism here!"

"I'm going to work," I call out at last, only when the man starts to rise from his seat.

"What's a young lady need a job for? I'll buy you a dress."

One of the man's companions places a hand on his shoulder, firmly propelling the man back to his seat. "Ah, let her go, John."

It's like this for the first half of my route: intoxicated revelers, loose bits of streamers, the remnants of today's celebrations. Finally, when I reach Sixteenth Street and the end of the restaurant district, things start to quiet again; nobody is throwing late-night celebrations outside of the staid federal buildings that empty out every night at five like clockwork.

I told Theo. And for what? To unburden myself? Over something I have no proof of? What was I thinking? How could I have done such a thing? Why couldn't I keep it locked up forever, in the tomb of my own body? Why couldn't I have—

And then I feel the rock. The size of a golf ball, skittering past me on the ground, coming from behind.

I whirl around, expecting to see a drunken reveler, a meandering crowd. But what I see instead makes my hair stand on end:

Nothing. Nothing but dark, empty shadows alongside the federal buildings.

Next to my ankle the rock comes to a stop.

I open my mouth with the intent to call out. *Hello?*

But before the word comes out I think better of it. I cut myself off at the first syllable. If I spoke out loud I don't think I could keep the shake out of my voice. I don't want anyone to know I'm scared.

Instead I freeze and listen.

Again, nothing.

Nothing but deafening silence.

And then, out of the corner of my eyes, in a doorway halfway down the block I think I see the quickest flicker of movement. The ripple of a cloth in the night wind. A curtain? A coat? A coat on a person?

Someone is in the doorway. Someone is watching me.

Brightwood.

Now I couldn't call out even if I wanted to. My throat is constricted, tight. There are four more blocks to go before I know I will be in another populated area—the White House, where I'm sure people will have congregated to celebrate armistice. Just four more blocks, but my shoes are held to my feet with the flimsiest of straps; my skirt allows only for short, quick steps. The restaurant district that I've already just passed is closer, only two blocks, and with it, the safety of crowds. But getting back to it would require passing by that sinister doorway.

The shadow in the doorway moves again. *Toward me?*

Without giving myself another moment to question the right course of action, I hitch my skirt above my knees and run. In the direction of the White House, as fast as I can, feet slapping against the brick street, until my breath comes out in short barks. I want to look behind me, but I'm terrified of what I will or won't see, and so I force my eyes ahead.

Finally I round the corner onto Sixteenth Street and see the signifiers of safety: the armistice banners, the bouquets of poppies, and a hazy orange glow that eventually reveals itself to be celebrants holding candles in a vigil. And then, finally, a few minutes more, the pale stone of switchboard headquarters.

By the time I slide into my workstation, I'm soaked through with sweat and my hands are shaking. I pick up my headpiece; at least my body remembers how to do that by rote.

The rock. Was it meant to hit me? Was it meant to merely alert me?

Brightwood.

"It's all right," Helen whispers, noting my panic and confusing it for mere lateness. "She isn't here."

"What?" I dab at the sweat pooling on my lip.

"You won't get a demerit," Helen spells out. "No supervisor today. There was an emergency with one of the day shift girls— *Lakewood 3729, please hold*—did you ever meet Louisa Safechuck? Miss Genovese is out managing it."

"Oh." I try to feign a look of relief, even as the back of my neck is still crawling. I have to force myself to face my switchboard, feeling as though I'm leaving my back exposed. "Lucky me."

"I heard it was another elopement," Helen continues. "With the war ending. I bet Louisa got married, just like Caroline did last week—*Number, please. Saratoga 9780, please hold*—and now Miss Genovese has to fill her position. We should take up a collection for a gift."

Was the rock thrown at me or rolled? Could it have been an accident, someone accidentally kicking it out of their path? It didn't hit me, after all. It just skidded past my feet.

But then if it was an accident, why would the culprit duck into the doorway, instead of just apologizing?

"How did *you* celebrate?" Helen asks, glancing at me with concern.

"Celebrate?"

"You did get to celebrate, didn't you? You'll come out with us at end of shift."

I nod abstractly with no real plans to join in. I tell myself I'll have an excuse for Helen by the end of shift in the morning.

But then the hours are packed full with long-distance calls placed all over the country and I don't have time to think of an excuse. Family members trying to reach one another to talk about the end of the war. Old lovers ringing up in the middle of the night, looking for a warm body to celebrate with.

A tap on my shoulder.

"Your headset?"

I yelp, but it's only the operator come to take over my shift. It's five a.m.; the hours flew by without me marking them. I look up to the narrow windows lining the perimeter of the room. It's still very dark outside; you wouldn't guess that it was morning by the inky black.

In the retiring room I stand at the open door of my locker, breathing heavily, unable to pluck my coat off the hook, knowing that putting it on means navigating the same dim streets that brought me here.

The floor of my locker is clean. No scraps of paper like there were during my last shift when we were warned to keep our lockers tidy. My invisible lockermate must have had to clean up my mess, and the primary feeling I have is relief. I didn't have to touch that horrid reference letter—*Join you at Bell*—and now I'll never have to see it again. It's forgotten in a bin or an incinerator.

"Are you coming?" Helen asks from her own locker a few doors down. She's waiting with a few other girls—Tillie and Rose, I think, already bundled in their own coats. I make a split-second decision that forced collegiality with my coworkers is preferable to a dark walk alone.

"Yes."

Thirty minutes later I'm sitting in the mahogany booth of Teddy's, sandwiched between three of my coworkers as the diner begins to fill with patrons.

As reluctant as I was to come out, this is what I needed: the bright antiseptic light of an all-night diner; the grubby din of laborers coming off shifts or preparing to start them, yawning over their cups of coffee. I order a plate of biscuits and hash and then stare at them when they arrive, unable to remember the last time I ate in public, in a restaurant with other people.

"*Chin-chin*," Helen says, raising her cup of tea in a toast. "To the end of the war."

"Chin chin," we all repeat, and by the time the cup reaches my lips it's almost steady.

"Well, my ears are about to fall off," Helen says, rubbing her earlobe. "Or my larynx is about to fall out. I don't think I've ever connected so many calls in one night in my life."

"I had one woman"—Tillie starts collapsing into chuckles before she can continue—"who just kept saying, *Connect me to the PRESident.* I told her the best I could do was connect her to the White House switchboard but she just kept saying, *I'll only speak directly to WOOD-row.*"

"At least she knew who the president was," Helen says. "The other day I had a poor old man demanding to have a word with Teddy Roosevelt." The other girls laugh, and I try to manage at least a smile, to behave as one of the group.

"Gawd, what a job we have." Tillie picks up her mug of coffee. "Do you think we'll keep them? When the boys come back? Or will Bell want our jobs for the soldiers who served in the war?"

"Oh, men don't have a gentle enough demeanor," Helen says. "That's why my parents let me take the job. This is women's work."

"This is chimpanzee's work," Tillie replies. "Any returning soldier with half a functioning brain could figure it out, I'm sure."

At Tillie's comment, a fork clatters onto the table and then the floor. When I turn toward the sound, Rose—a slender, mousy girl who has heretofore been mostly silent—is still poised with her hand in the air, fingers now emptied of cutlery. She has a pale, drawn expression on her face.

"*Excuse me,*" she says quietly, before dropping her napkin onto the table and sliding out of the booth. Her heels scrape on the floor as she rushes to the lavatory while the rest of us watch.

Tillie's hand flies to her mouth. "Oh hell," she says. "I completely forgot."

An awkward silence hangs in the air for a few seconds before Helen turns to me and finally explains. "Rose's fiancé. He came back from Austria-Hungary four months ago and his brain was—well, it wasn't the same. He doesn't speak; it's not clear how much he understands. That's why Rose had to get this job." She lowers her voice. "Honestly, I'm not even sure whether she still considers them to be engaged."

"And me talking about functioning brains." Tillie buries her head in her hands. "I'm the one whose brain isn't working."

"Well, you didn't mean to," Helen tells her. "Hopefully she'll realize that."

"Do you think I should go after her?"

Helen hesitates. "Let's give it a few minutes and see if she comes back on her own. It's an awful situation, obviously, and—*and my flapjacks are very good, does anyone want to try one?*" She finishes in a voice half an octave too high, and I know this means Rose must be returning from the bathroom.

I slide over to make room for Rose as she lowers her small frame into the booth, placing her napkin on her lap again and then picking up her fork, deliberately sawing at a piece of sausage. Only up close can I see that her eyes are webbed with tears.

"Rose, I'm so sorry, I wasn't thinking." Tillie falls over herself in apology. "It was just a figure of speech—half a brain, you know—and a clumsy, insensitive one."

"It's all right," Rose says quietly, still sawing her food into ever-tinier pieces.

"It's not, though. It was—"

Rose finally stops slicing the food on her plate and sets her fork down on the side of her plate. She looks up.

"I just wish you could have known him. Everybody always wanted Carlos around. He livened up any party. That's how I met him, at a party, and I was too shy to talk to anyone but he came over to the punch bowl and made sure I was introduced to everyone, and by the end of the night..." She trails off and shrugs, helplessly. "For the rest of my life, nobody I meet will ever know what Carlos was like before, and I just wish they could have known him. And it makes me frustrated that everyone here thinks the boys coming home are just brave heroes. I wish someone would tell the truth about what happened to them over there. Every family I know wishes that."

She goes back to her plate now, not eating but pushing bits of food around, having said all she plans to say. Helen and Tillie also make an effort at returning to their meals, forcing down unconvincing mouthfuls of food and making strained conversation about a book the two of them have read.

I can't bring myself to join in. I keep replaying Rose's words: *I wish someone would tell the truth about what happened to them.*

You have to tell the truth.

That's what the caller on the line had said. I knew it was a warning, but I hadn't thought it was also a clue, something revealing the identity of the speaker. But now, listening to Rose, I wonder if it was exactly that.

I feel around in my pocket for my coin purse and my fingers land on the creased, careworn paper that is always tucked inside, frayed around the edges so that it already looks decades old instead of weeks. The paper I guard with my life, the paper I did not want Theo to see.

I unfold it again and look at the text already burned into my memory:

Thirty-four members of the Forty-Eighth Regiment perished yesterday. Their names were as follows:

I carry these names with me. To work. Back home. Always tucked in the breast pocket of my ratty coat, close to my chest.

"Do you really believe that's true?" I ask Rose suddenly, again halting the conversation that had only just begun to pick up again. "That every family wants the world to know the truth about what happened to their sons or fiancés?"

Helen and Tillie exchange glances, wondering why I'm kicking up this tender topic again. But Rose is already nodding, even while her eyes brim over with emotion.

"It's the only thing we want," she says with surprising strength. "It's the only thing we can ask for."

The families.

The word that I cut off—the word that started with an *F-A*.

The families.

I don't know why I didn't think of this possibility before with my mysterious caller. The most likely person to want to remind me of that day wouldn't be a fellow operator, or even the commanding officer whose orders I flubbed. It would be the families of the boys I betrayed. The boys who were lost. The boys who were dead. The families would want me to tell the truth, somehow, about what had happened to their sons and how it was my fault that it happened.

They would want the world to hear the truth about their sons.

And these families wouldn't have to call from France. Baltimore is only forty miles away. Not a local call, but if someone wanted to reach me at Central, it wouldn't be impossible for them to come and call from Washington.

Tell the truth before it's too late, the voice said, and then the war ended, and now everyone is coming home.

Was there a threat implied? If I don't tell, does it mean that the voice will tell for me? That I'll be punished, or worse? *What could be worse?*

But I know the answer to that. What would be worse than to be punished is to be exposed. For someone to tell the world about what I did that night and to assume that I did it because I was evil, or because I didn't care, instead of just that I was—

"I—I have to go," I say, fishing some money out of my coin purse, more than I owe, and tossing it on the table.

"Where?" Helen asks.

"Don't let me chase you away," Rose says.

"You aren't. I have to go."

"At seven thirty in the morning, *where?*" Helen repeats.

"I need to find a Polk's."

8

ERROL FIGUIERA

In the brass public telephone vestibule just outside, I drop a coin in the slot and sigh with relief when the operator is able to connect me to Aunt Tess.

"Could you meet me at Union Station?" I ask without preamble. "And bring the coffee canister from under my bed—the one where I keep my money?"

"Now?" she asks dubiously.

"I wouldn't ask if it weren't important. I need it to buy a ticket for the eight thirty train. I can't get back in time to pick up the money myself."

Instead of an answer to my question, I hear paper rustling in the background. Aunt Tess must be sitting down in the parlor with the morning news. Now she changes the subject entirely. "Why didn't you tell me about your colleague at Central?" she asks. "Is that why you were so out of sorts last night?"

"My colleague at Central?" I repeat, distracted, looking at the small handful of coins in my palm, calculating how many minutes of conversation I can buy.

"Your colleague. Louisa Safechuck."

"Aunt Tess, can you bring the coffee canister or not? I need to get to the station and I swear I have no ungodly idea what you're talking about. Who is Louisa Safechuck?"

Only saying the name out loud prompts the vaguest memory. Louisa. The operator whose elopement caused Miss Genovese to be absent.

"We weren't colleagues," I say. "We didn't work the same shift. If I ever met her I don't remember." This entire conversation is baffling to me. "Why would I tell you about her? Do you know her?"

"It's a senseless tragedy. She's not the first operator to die this way. Normally the Equal Justice League's attention is on women in lower-class professions, washerwomen or factory workers, but—"

"She *died*?" I stop rolling the coins in my palm, jarred by the revelation. "I thought she got married. That's what the gossip was at work, that she ran off and—"

Aunt Tess's voice softens a measure. "I thought for sure you would have been told. Haven't you seen the paper this morning?"

I'm about to respond that of course I haven't seen it, I've been at work since last night, but then I see a fresh copy of the morning edition sitting in the telephone vestibule, left there by a previous occupant, and I flip past pages of armistice coverage to the death notices.

"Louisa Safechuck, 20, a telephone operator with the Bell System, was found dead in her apartment on Monday of an apparent self-inflicted—"

"She took her own life," Aunt Tess says, now unnecessarily but no less horrible.

I've never met Louisa but I can picture her because I can picture all my colleagues: plain black skirt, white blouse, tidy hair. Or would it have been untidy? If she were like me, disturbed and struggling, would her hair have been untidy?

Not like you, I tell myself. *Nothing like you.*

"It's not natural, what they ask of you," Aunt Tess continues. "To be unallowed to even whisper to one another, much less talk or laugh. To lose your position if you go on a date with a boy."

I had no idea my aunt was even aware of the particulars of my job, much less that she had an opinion on them.

"As I said, we normally focus more on the working conditions of lower-class women in factory settings, where their daily duties put them at risk of considerable harm," Tess continues. "But the Equal Justice League is interested in Louisa's case because it might represent a pattern. An operator in San Francisco took her own life last month. She hadn't passed the most recent weight examinations and she was told she'd be terminated if she didn't pass the next one. Are you sure you didn't know Louisa?" Aunt Tess asks again.

"You just said. We're not allowed to talk or whisper." My voice sounds testy. "How would I know her?"

I can hear Aunt Tess nodding on the phone. I've sufficiently convinced her that I have nothing more to contribute to this conversation.

"And you would tell me, wouldn't you?" she says. "If they were asking too much of you there? I know you're stronger than the other girls—you've been to war; you're prepared to hold up under more strain." She says this last part with a twinge of pride in her voice. Her niece, gone to war. I know the suffragettes have made use of the Hello Girls' service for their own cause. *If you can trust a woman in war, you should be able to trust her in the ballot box.*

"But I wanted to check anyhow. You would tell me if the job was too taxing?"

Aunt Tess had sat in my family's parlor in Baltimore, had told me that my French could be put to better use overseas than working as a fancy governess. Aunt Tess had said I needed to do something with my life, that a girl shouldn't rely on her parents for the first half of her life and a husband for the rest.

"You would tell me," Aunt Tess says again, but this time she doesn't say it as a question, she says it as an affirmation that she already knows the answer to.

"Please just bring me the canister."

. . .

"Coffee delivery, at your service."

In the grand concourse of Union Station, I slowly turn toward the voice approaching behind me. I've been waiting longer than I'd anticipated and I have only a few minutes before the train departs. My makeshift piggy bank has arrived in the nick of time. But the voice delivering it is…not the one I was expecting. Theo finishes crossing the tan marble floors and holds up the tin jar labeled Monogram, presenting it as if he were a fancy butler.

"What are you doing here?" I ask, confused. "Aunt Tess was supposed to meet me."

"I'm meeting you."

"When I telephoned I asked Tess, specifically, if she could bring my bank here. I wouldn't have asked you to go out of your way for me."

I'm not being considerate of his time—I'm feeling tremendously awkward about facing Theo, in person, after everything I told him through the door last night. I'd hoped, somehow, that I could avoid him for days. That he'd still be in bed, sleeping off his own hangover.

"I'll take the canister," I say, but as I move to grab it from Theo he holds it just out of my reach and raises an eyebrow.

"*You're welcome, Theo,*" he says pointedly. "It was awfully kind of you to rearrange your schedule to help me, Theo, when my aunt realized she couldn't bring it herself, Theo, even though it would mean you canceling other plans."

His tone of voice is exactly how we would normally talk with each other. This should make me relieved, but I somehow find it irritating in an entirely different way. *Does he not remember what happened? Is he trying to make me feel as though I imagined it?* Either way, his presence here is something I didn't expect and am not prepared to handle.

"Thank you for bringing this," I say stiffly. "I don't want to make you any later for your plans, so I'll let you go now."

"Where are you going? I assume it's somewhere on a train, but—"

"I have a personal errand to run. And I really should be hurrying."

I look over my shoulder to the clock in the middle of the station. I can hear the rumbling of the train. I'd planned to buy my ticket at the window, but there isn't time; I'll have to buy it on the train and pay the surcharge.

"Wait." He starts after me, stiff-legged because of his hip but still keeping up as we race through the station. "Last night I came by your door again and knocked, but you didn't answer. I wanted to—"

"I was at work. I didn't answer because I was at work."

The arrival of the train saves me from having to respond further. It's pulling into the station now, a cloud of steam and dust and screeching noise as I skid down the final steps. "None of this has to be your concern," I call over my shoulder. "I meant for Aunt Tess to meet me, and we can both pretend that's what happened."

The porter steps onto the station platform. *"All aboard. The train is now boarding."*

Aboard the train, to my left is entry to the first-class car, where I can glimpse businessmen in leather seats. I make a right turn instead, where the seats are more modest and crowded more tightly, searching for an empty row so I won't need to sit with a stranger.

Once I've found one, and settled in next to the window, the porter approaches and extends his white-gloved hand. "Two tickets?" he inquires.

"One," I say. "To Baltimore."

"Two is correct," says a voice approaching from the opposite direction—the second time I've been surprised to hear his voice this morning. Theo has followed me onto the train.

"What are you *doing*?"

Instead of answering he extends his own hand to the porter, producing enough money for two tickets. Without questioning Theo's authority or checking in again with me, the porter dispenses two tickets, handing Theo the printed billets and moving on to the next passengers.

"So we're going to Baltimore."

"We're not going anywhere," I sputter. "I am going to Baltimore. You are getting off at the next stop." The fluster that I felt back in the station has developed into irritation here on the train, now that I can't so easily walk away. "You had no right," I begin, getting more worked up as the train rumbles away from the tracks. "To show up to the train station unannounced, and—"

"How was I supposed to announce it?" Theo asks, throwing his hands up in the air. "Send a carrier pigeon to the train station first?"

"*To show up unannounced*, and then follow me onto the train, and, and—"

"Edda, I didn't wake up this morning and randomly decide to come to Union Station, propelled by a mysterious force," he says as if this should all be self-explanatory. "You called your aunt on the telephone and asked her to bring you something; she had something come up at the last minute, so she asked me to do it instead. And the reason I agreed is because last night you seemed genuinely distressed."

He means to be comforting, I think, but the reference to how I'd come undone in front of him is more than I can take.

"Last night *was a mistake*." My voice has risen above a hiss, coming out as a mix of embarrassment and anger and defensiveness. A woman reading a newspaper two seats over looks up and raises a reproachful finger to her lips. "After three glasses of champagne I told you something *once*, and now I have asked you to leave it alone, but here you are *on this train*."

I wait for his next rejoinder, his next extravagant eye roll. Instead, what happens is genuinely surprising: Theo neatly folds his hands in his own lap. "You're right. Of course you're right. I'll get off at the next stop and leave you, then."

He stands and backs into the aisle, giving an awkward little bow at the waist.

"You—really?"

"Edda." His eyes look pained. "Despite whatever deserved reputation Georgetown boys might have, the halfway decent ones aren't interested in forcing their company on those who don't want it. And I am, I'd like to think, at least forty-nine percent decent. I shouldn't have pressed the issue; you made your feelings perfectly clear. I'll find someplace else to sit and then I'll get off at the next stop."

"I—well—thank you," I stammer. "I appreciate it."

He nods again, the stiff little bow he'd done before, and then moves along into the next car. I feel a pang of guilt watching him go, wondering if I should have relented. He did come all this way.

Because he decided to, I remind myself. He decided to come, of his own accord. I don't owe him anything. And yet, pushing at the corner of my mind: Theo was supposed to be earning extra credit this week. That's what he'd said yesterday, that he sorely needed it. The plans he rearranged to come here weren't just sleeping late or breakfasting with friends.

I close my eyes and press my forehead against the glass of the train window. It's Tuesday. Barely thirty hours have passed since

I received the strange call, and now I'm on a train to the city I left because I didn't want to run into families of the Forty-Eighth Regiment, and I am returning there specifically with the intention of seeing them. My stomach is in knots.

"Ahem." I look up to see Theo standing awkwardly at my seat again. "Well, this is embarrassing."

"Yes?"

"There are no more seats available in second-class, and when I tried to just stand in the aisle, the porter said I couldn't loiter and I needed to return to the seat I paid for. I really did try. You can ask him yourself." Theo turns and flags down the conductor, who sees him and makes a sharp jab with his index finger, a gesture telling Theo to sit down. Theo raises an eyebrow.

"Go ahead," I relent.

When he sits again, he assiduously avoids eye contact. He pats down his breast pockets, presumably looking for something to read or otherwise occupy his time, but, finding nothing, he instead folds his hands in his lap and looks studiously down at his thumbs. He keeps his knees squeezed together, making sure they don't cross over onto my half of the train seat.

I sigh.

"I'm going to get a Polk's directory," I tell him.

"Are you talking to me?"

"That's why I'm going to Baltimore. I need a city directory with Baltimore listings." Theo looks at me with confusion and I continue. "The families. We didn't know who would want to reach out to me, but isn't it obvious? The families of the boys who died. It makes sense, doesn't it?" I prod him. "*F-A. Families.* That's what the voice on the phone was trying to say before I interrupted. The families."

"I—I don't know," he admits. "Logically, none of it makes sense."

"But emotionally?"

"Well, then yes. I hadn't thought about it, but it's hard to think of someone going through the trouble of tracking you down and wanting you to confess if it wasn't someone with a deep emotional connection to one of the boys. But I still don't understand..." He trails off and presses his lips together as if he's unsure whether he should continue.

"What don't you understand?"

"I'm just trying to figure out the goal. Why you need to do this at all. What you think will happen if you don't."

I struggle to explain myself, because explaining myself requires me to think about what happened, more than I want to, more than I ever have.

"I don't know. It's that—for two months I've been back and I've been doing nothing but trying to ignore everything that happened over there," I say finally. "I thought, if I could leave France it would go away. And then I thought, if I didn't go back to Baltimore it would go away. And then I thought—if I just went to work and nowhere else, if I just slept enough, it would all go away. But it kept not going away. And then yesterday morning—"

"Yesterday morning you got the telephone call," Theo says.

"But it was more than a telephone call. It was the past coming after me. The past won't end because the past isn't finished."

"But what kind of endings do you think you can give?" Theo asks. His voice doesn't sound wheedling, it sounds genuinely curious. "You can't rewrite what happened, no matter what you do. None of us can. Whatever happened is what happened," he finishes.

I shake my head, no, I refuse to believe that. "There has to be something. There has to be some kind of finality. Some kind of way of making peace. It can't be the case that something horrible happens and you just have to live, forever, with this feeling of— of—" My voice is rising in pitch, as I talk faster and faster. "This feeling of—"

"Edda," Theo interjects carefully. "Are you trying to find an ending for yourself or for the boys of the Forty-Eighth?"

His words stop me cold; I don't know how to answer them. I don't even know how to understand them. I cannot separate out what happened to the boys that night from what has become of me.

Theo doesn't press the issue. He doesn't say anything for a long time, in fact, while the train makes a stop in a town called Carrollton, and passengers disembark and new passengers board, squeezing past us with their traveling bags, going about their lives that seem so easy and uncomplicated.

Only when the train is moving again does Theo speak.

"I know how you feel," he says quietly. "I do, I know something about guilt."

"Am I about to receive an apology for all the food and cigarettes you've borrowed from me?"

"I know something about guilt," he repeats steadily. And when he holds my gaze, the eyes that meet mine aren't the ones full of mirth that I'm accustomed to seeing. They're the eyes I saw yesterday when Theo didn't know I was looking at him in the hallway, deep and serious. "I'm home right now and not in France at all. I didn't do what the boys of the Forty-Eighth did, risk their own lives."

"But that's not your fault," I tell him. "You would have done what the boys of the Forty-Eighth did, if you were asked to. It's what all the boys over there did. It's completely different."

"Was it?" he asks. He stares down at his leg.

"Do you mind if I ask what happened? Is it something you were born with, or—" I continue and then stop myself.

"You want to know why I limp."

"Yes, unless—is it rude or am I permitted to ask?"

Theo hesitates a split second while considering my question, before his face arranges itself back into his familiar grin. "It's rude, of course, but you're permitted to ask. I wasn't born with it. Hunting accident. Just before I was scheduled to leave for the front."

"What kind of hunting accident?" I lean back into my seat and he leans back, too, setting in to tell me a story.

"I was going to be the first man in my family to go to war. My grandfather in the Civil War—he had paid a replacement to go in his stead, and my father avoided the Spanish-American War. I was going to be the hero. So the week before I was supposed to ship out to Northern Africa, my father decided we should have a send-off. Three generations of my family on my grandfather's estate, hunting pheasants. Up before dawn, racing around in tweed."

I can picture all of this: three generations of laughing Theos, downing mugs of coffee and biscuits, storming out garrulously into the dawn, wearing wool hunting hats and surrounded by baleful golden retrievers.

"Which one of them accidentally shot you?" I ask.

"I don't know. Nasty little pheasants all look alike to me."

I punch him in the arm. "Which one of your relatives accidentally shot you?"

"Myself. Myself shot myself."

"*What?*"

"I sat on it. I sat on my ass, which sat on the rifle, which had belonged to my grandfather during the Civil War that he did not fight in."

"You shot yourself in your own rear end."

Improbably, for the first time this week and maybe for the first time since I've been home from France, a giggle tugs at my lips. Not a polite, genteel smile but an actual unexpected giggle.

"It wasn't just my buttocks. It went through to my leg," he

explains. "Enough buckshot to damage nerve endings, which is what kept me home. But yes. The majority was buttock. Which is why instead of serving in North Africa, I spend my days loitering outside your room bumming cigarettes and inviting myself along on your train trips."

Now I'm actually laughing on the train car, laughing out loud over the disapproving glance of the elderly woman across the aisle, and Theo is pretending to look wounded but glancing at me slyly enough that I can tell he's not actually bothered.

"I want to help you," he says, more seriously now. "I owe it to you to help you. You didn't get an ending and I didn't even get a beginning."

"You don't *owe* me," I start to say.

But I've already done the hardest part of accepting Theo's help— I've told him the story of why I need help to begin with. And I can't deny that talking to him has been helpful. Without his questions I might not have realized that the call must have been local.

Meanwhile, the train is slowing to a stop; Baltimore's Penn Station—less grand than Union Station but still stately and cavernous—has come into view. We'll be there in a few minutes.

"So, is your plan to look for a public telephone at the train station and see if they have a Polk's there?" Theo asks. "Or a library might have a copy."

"I don't want to go someplace to borrow a directory, I want to go someplace we can take one. We're going to my house."

9

ZACHARIAH FLEMING

"You're rich."

Theo's mouth has fallen open, staring up at the gabled, columned, gated home in Roland Park where my parents live. "Your aunt owns the boardinghouse but I always assumed, with you up in your weird little bird's nest—"

"Pheasant nest," I correct him.

"Your weird little rat's nest—I always assumed that Tess must be taking pity on a poor relation. But you're rich, richer even than my family."

"My grandparents were rich," I say reflexively. "The rest of us are just lucky."

But I know he's right. When I applied to the American Expeditionary Forces I was asked how it was that I came to speak French. Some girls had learned out of necessity—a French parent—and some had learned via classes in high school. I had learned via private tutors, because learning French is what was done, because my parents speak it, because my father is an important historian at an important college that doesn't admit women but believes the future wives of its students should speak French or Italian.

They won't be home now; it's the reason I'd wanted to take the train we did. My father will be at his office, and Tuesday mornings are when my mother makes her weekly round of social calls.

The front door isn't locked; it never is. The foyer is dark and paneled, the public rooms of the house branching off to either side.

I gesture for Theo to wait in the guest parlor to the right, while I continue to my mother's private study, the place where she would plan the week's menus and write her correspondence.

On an end table next to her settee, a telephone. And in the end table's drawer, a fabric-bound book, inches thick. *Baltimore City Directory*, the cover reads. Just inside, a note identifying the publisher as R. L. Polk & Co, the name everyone uses when they talk about the compendium of businesses and people.

Every year when I was growing up, a new directory would be issued. My mother would throw out the previous year's and place the new version in its spot. We used it every day; it's how we would locate the address of a locksmith or florist or furniture upholsterer, or any number of the women who volunteered in my mother's benevolent societies.

I know even without consulting my creased newspaper clipping who I'm looking for. Not Davy Wagner, for example: There is a whole page worth of Wagners in the directory.

I'm looking for the Dannemans, a name that sounds wholesome like a pastry. I'm looking for the family of August Danneman. August, who I imagine went by "Augie," who I imagine was born not in August but in June.

The August Danneman in my mind was more comfortable around animals than people, carrying a pocketful of birdseed that trailed from the holes in his pocket. Dogs loved him, and on long walks he would stop to throw them sticks.

Three Dannemans in the directory. But I'm not familiar with the addresses, and there is no clue as to which one might be August's family. Still, one of them must, and my breath catches at this evidence that the boy existed in reality. He did not merely die in France, he lived in Baltimore.

My mother's creamy embossed stationery sits next to the telephone. I pick up her fountain pen and just as I've circled the listings to mark the Danneman addresses, I hear the front door swing open. I freeze, hoping my ears were mistaken, but no: the sound of a bag being dropped, of a soft hat landing on the rack. My mother shouldn't be home yet. She's never home at this time; her social calls should keep her away until after lunch.

"Hello?" a familiar voice calls.

Oh God. Of the two options, this is the one I would have least preferred—not my mother, my father.

"Hello?" he says again, heels clicking on the parquet floor. "Edda?" he continues. Somehow he's both home and he knows I'm here.

Theo. Theo is still in the guest parlor, about to be discovered.

"Father, I'm coming!" I slam the directory closed and, nearly tripping over myself, race through the parlor and present myself in the foyer. "What are you doing home?"

He raises a single eyebrow. "Am I supposed to ask permission to be in my own home now?" He is elegant as always, broad shoulders, gray silk suit. He never had patience for rumpled academics; he likes things to be in their places. "Tess telephoned this morning and said you planned to visit. I cut my work short and came home," he explains. My father looks at his watch, though I can't imagine he doesn't already know the precise time. This show of timekeeping is for my benefit, not his. "I thought I could spare thirty minutes for my only child. Let's sit."

When I telephoned my aunt and asked her to bring my piggy bank to the train station, I knew that mentioning the time of my train would tip her off that I planned to go to Baltimore—but I thought that information would work in my favor, in persuading her to meet me at Union Station. *I've missed two weeks of letters. It's not fair to my parents. I should go visit them in person.* I never dreamed that she'd telephone them to announce my arrival.

When I haven't followed my father's suggestion to sit down, he sighs and looks at me shrewdly. "Edda, if I didn't know better, I'd almost wager that you didn't expect your mother and me to be home."

"I just thought that I would surprise you," I stammer. "My plan was to get here first when I knew you'd still be out so that I'd have time to—to—" I search for an explanation that will appease him.

"To politely attend to me." Both of our heads swivel around to where Theo stands in the parlor, an apologetic look on his face. "It's my fault that Edda didn't give any advance notice," he continues. "I'd asked her to take me to Baltimore to show me some gardens for an architecture project I've been assigned at Georgetown. Naturally she didn't know how long that would take, and she didn't want to keep you waiting while I dillydallied around."

Theo's lie is smooth and charming. Not only is it plausible, but it also kindly removes the blame from me. One look at my father's face, though, and I can tell he hasn't bought it.

"How considerate," my father says to me dryly. "You didn't tell us you were coming, but on the other hand when you showed up unannounced you also showed up with company." He now turns to Theo. "And you are?"

"Theo Graybill." Theo gives a formal bow at the neck, which he must intuit would appeal to my father's sense of respect and decorum. "Your daughter's neighbor."

"And here I thought Tess rented only to feminists and Bolsheviks."

"Miss St. James's funding the works of feminists and Bolsheviks requires capitalists paying their rent on time, sir," Theo replies, so earnestly that it's hard for even my father to find fault with the cheek of the statement.

The three of us sit in the parlor. My father takes a cigar for himself but doesn't offer one to Theo, and of course not to me. If my mother were here, she would think to offer cake and coffee. No matter what she thinks of anyone, or what her mental state is, she always thinks to offer cake and coffee.

"Is Mother on her way home as well?"

My father blows out a puff of smoke. "It was my office that Tess telephoned. By the time I heard from Tess I couldn't reach your mother; she was already out on her calls. And if Tess was wrong, and you didn't turn up, I wouldn't have wanted to get her hopes up." He raises an eyebrow. "So why don't we not mention this visit to her, in the letters you're not writing us anyhow."

I wince, but it's hard for me to defend myself against his accurate accusation.

"That telephone company must still have you on the night shift"—he carries on, saying this phrase like it tastes bad: *night shift*—"if you managed to take a train in the middle of the day."

"Yes. I still work the night shift."

"And you're well? You're healthy? You don't need any money?" he continues. "I presume you're not spending much, with your room and board taken care of."

"I don't need money. I don't go many places."

"We gave you the names of those friends of ours in Washington. They said they'd be happy to have you over for a game of cribbage. If you're not going to call on them, you should have said something earlier." His tone is somewhere between rebuking and resigned, as if he's disappointed in me but didn't expect to be otherwise.

"I'll call on them this week."

As I say this, I really mean it, or I think I do—I really do think I'll go play cribbage with his friends. I should bring them a nice hostess gift; I should behave so charmingly that they later compliment me to my parents. Because this is what talking with my father does to me. The rebukes I can handle. But the resignation—part of me always thinks there's a way I could overcome that. Surprise him. Delight him. Go to France and return smart and sharp, watch him swell with pride when I returned home.

"They told your mother they wanted to hear about France over tea," my father says. "I said to them, good luck, since you never wanted to tell us anything." I can feel the wheels about to come off the conversation, the rising annoyance in his voice as he sets down his cigar. He turns to Theo. "Did she tell you about France?"

It takes Theo a moment to realize that my father is speaking to him now. He has been dragged into the conversation, which he had been observing with the affectation of someone hoping to recede into the wallpaper.

"Did she tell me about what?" he asks blandly.

"Did Edda tell you how she ran off to France? She was never exactly a paragon of responsibility, but we were working to make a plan for after graduation. And then Edda just ran off! Like she was going ice-skating or out for an egg cream, after seeing an advertisement in the *Suffragette Daily*. We had to cancel her graduation party."

"It was the *Baltimore Sun*," I whisper. "There is no such paper as the *Suffragette Dai*—"

"War is not a place for flighty girls." My father's mustache quivers as he bangs his hand on the end table. "It is a place for serious young men, not for eighteen-year-old girls to flit about and see the world, getting in the way of things. Warfare is a man's story about men's business and men's strife. Did I try to tell her this? Of course I did."

"I didn't—" Theo begins, but it's clear my father doesn't mean to allow him to get a word in edgewise.

"And then she comes home from France. Like nothing has happened. A telegram arrives, informing us that she'll be returning and she arrives like a ghost, telling us nothing is wrong, but of course something is wrong. Her room is a pigsty. She has to be dragged into the bath. Her mother throws her a welcome back party, hoping to cheer her up—one thing Edda always liked was a party—and she spends twenty minutes with her guests. Then the chancellor's son, my boss's son, takes her hand for a dance and she behaves as though he has leprosy, running back up to her room. Her mother was *sick with worry*, and Edda's solution was to leave again, to go to Washington."

I'm biting back tears at this description, at these memories. I don't like to think about those early days home from France, before I learned I could sleep away some of my pain. I don't like to think about how crowds would startle me and quiet would startle me, and being left alone would startle me, because I was never really alone, I was always with my thoughts.

I had tried to dance with the chancellor's son, I had tried. But even making my feet move felt repellent, and halfway into the song, he mentioned that he had a cousin named August who was over in France. *A cousin named August, or second cousin, actually, on my mother's side. Whatever happened to good old August anyway, let me call over my mother and ask her.*

And all I could think was *August Danneman. His name is August Danneman.* Or maybe it wasn't. But it was only a matter of time before it was. Before I went to a Ladies' Aid luncheon and ran into the mother or aunt or friend of one of those boys. All I could do was wonder whether I'd known one of those boys myself, in a previous life. How many times had I gone to a party and accepted a dance with a boy whose name I never caught? How did I know such a dance hadn't happened with one of the boys whose life I would later end?

I needed to get out of Baltimore.

My parents acted furious when I said I wanted to move in with Aunt Tess but I can't help but imagine that part of them was relieved. They didn't know what to do with me by that point. I didn't know what to do with myself, and mostly, I didn't care.

Theo is witnessing this. I try, out of the corner of my bleary eye, to discern what he might be thinking, but his face is impassive.

And then before he's forced to comment either way, the grand-father clock in the hallway begins to strike. It's noon. Thirty minutes haven't passed yet but my father nonetheless rises abruptly. "I can't stay away from the office forever. Your mother will be sad that she missed you."

"I'll write this week," I promise. "I'll write twice."

He nods to Theo—"Mr. Graybill"—and then unceremoniously leaves the room, gone by the time the clock finishes striking, and Theo and I are left alone with just the sound of the quiet tick, and I think that I should stand up, but feel glued to my seat, stuck and weighted down.

"I put them through hell when I came back," I tell Theo quietly. "And then again when I left."

"It sounds as though you were very—"

"I don't want to talk about it."

"Are you sure you—"

"I don't want to *talk* about it."

I'm embarrassed that Theo has just seen a private family exchange, and I'm even more embarrassed that he has heard a description of who I was before the war. The flitting. The buoyancy. My father wasn't wrong about that. I had treated going to war like it was a solution to my own personal questions about my future. I had thought—naively it turns out—that the endeavor, the focus, the plan, might actually make my father proud.

Finally, Theo speaks. "I could be wrong," he says dryly. "I could be completely mistaken. But I can't help but get the oddest sense that your father didn't believe it was a good idea for you to go to France."

"Oh, he wanted me to go," I say bitterly. "He's a military historian at the United States Naval Academy; of course he wanted me to go. He just wanted me to go as a boy. Why do you think I was named Edda?" I don't wait for Theo to answer. "Because he was so sure I would be a son named Edward that there wasn't another name picked out."

Theo doesn't know what to say to that, then. I've unleashed too much bitterness; the conversation is impossible to save with jokes now.

"Let's go back to the train station," Theo says quietly. "Just take the directory with you."

I look down to where it's open in my lap. Open to the page with the Dannemans.

That's when I realize his isn't the only name on this page. There's another boy from the Forty-Eighth here, too, a few lines away.

Charles Dannenberg.

I'd assumed all the boys would have lived with their parents and all the listings would have been under their fathers' names. Charles must have been a junior, then. He must have had a father with the same name, whose name I am now staring at in this directory.

The Dannenbergs' listing doesn't have a telephone number affiliated with it. It does have an address, though, and I immediately recognize the name of the road. Reisterstown is long and winding and cuts through the whole city, weaving in and out of genteel neighborhoods and slums. We could intersect with it in a thirty-minute walk.

"Edda?" Theo waves to get my attention. "Back to the train station?"

"No." I lift the directory and point to the listing. "We came all the way here to look up these addresses. Let's go to Reisterstown Road."

10

Robert Gilman

I had never worked so hard. In my entire life I had never worked so hard as I was working in Paris. My regular shifts were ten hours long, longer if it was busy, and at the end of my shift Luc would present me with study guides that he had handwritten himself and I would pore over in my room at the hostel for another hour or more, even later into the night. Then every morning Luc would quiz me in person before my shift began, correcting my pronunciation, having me repeat the terms until they rolled off my tongue smooth as marbles. This is how I learned that I didn't need to say "le lieutenant," that French military slang shortened it to "le lieut'" just as it shortened "colonel" to "colo'" and called junior officers not "aspiring officers" but rather "l'aspi'."

This is how I learned that policemen were not "les gendarmes," as I had been taught, but "le flic," that short trenches were "sausages" and long ones were "beans" and that soldiers didn't malinger but instead were said to have "nickel feet." Every type of artillery had a nickname— toad, monkey, bee—as did every piece of equipment and every type of transportation, and sometimes the French slang terms were different entirely from the English ones.

"I almost feel as though I didn't know any French at all before I came here," I said to Luc at the end of one session, my brain feeling swollen and heavy.

"I know these sessions are taxing," he told me. "But I can see you are improving. And I think that with more practice, more concentration, you really can catch up with everyone else here."

"I'll practice harder."

I wanted to be one of the best. Even if I had to work ten or twelve or fourteen hours a day in order to do it. Even if I had to work so hard to be the best that I was too exhausted to ever actually be my best. It felt good to feel as though I might be good at something, to feel my brain exhaust itself in ways it had never been asked to by me or anyone else.

"Good," Luc said. "I was hoping you would say that. Because if you continue to improve, I think there will be opportunities for you."

I thrilled at the thought of this and wanted to ask him for more details, to know exactly how far he thought I could go. But it was already nearing the start of my shift. I turned for the door but paused once I got there.

"I wanted to thank you," I told him. "For how—"

"I am only doing what I would want someone to do for Grace," he insisted, cutting me off before I had to find the right words. "I tell her of your progress in my letters; you have quite a fan in her."

"I do?"

We talked about Grace sometimes, the way she was fiery and romantic and how she wished she could do what I was doing, how the Hello Girls were inspiring girls all over the world. We talked about my father sometimes, the way he didn't think I belonged here, and Luc said that my father had no idea what women were capable of.

"So you see, you must continue or my little sister would never forgive me. And I think—" Then there was a knock at the door, so I didn't get to hear what Luc thought. He waved me along, gesturing that I could leave. "Now go. Time for your shift."

. . .

That day my job was accommodations. Bigwigs in the American and French armies were coming to Paris for an important meeting. Every call I sat in required me to translate the logistics of lodging and how to get there, how many tables would be needed and where people would sit. This was a typical day's work. It often wasn't exciting work but it was important work, I reminded myself. It was the kind of work necessary for an incremental war effort.

As the end of my shift approached, I heard the sound of a throat clearing behind me. I looked up to see a creased wool pantleg, and then, higher, the face of the commanding officer, an older man with a not-unkind face.

"Come and see me, Miss St. James, as soon as you finish your shift."

"Is something wrong?" I asked the CO.

"Straightaway," he said. "My office."

This was the first time he had spoken directly to me, and as he walked away my initial reaction was to be scared, to wonder whether I'd done something wrong, to wonder whether Luc's lessons hadn't caught me up enough after all and I was about to be sent home.

And then, a voice behind me:

"You left your hat on the bed."

The voice over my shoulder belonged to Mae, and when I pivoted she was holding out my wide-brimmed army-issued hat.

"What are you doing here already?" I asked.

We didn't usually overlap shifts like this; I was used to coming home just as she got up to splash water on her face. I would study her as she got ready in the hostel sometimes, just like I'd watch her finish out her work shift if I arrived for duty early. The way she could juggle three or four calls at once without ever getting mixed up, the way she kept a wry look on her face even when talking to superiors. Everyone there was so very good at their jobs. All the Hello Girls, competent and unflappable. But Mae was the one I could observe every day, sitting in the window-sill studiously reading the foreign pages of the newspaper. Holding a cup of tea that she'd brewed with a modern tea bag instead of the loose-leaves way my mother had at home, looking out the window like a page from a magazine.

"Commanding officer told me to come in early," she said now. "He

103

said he wanted to meet before my shift." She looked distracted, only half engaged in our conversation.

"I'm supposed to see him, too," I said. "You don't know what it's about, either?"

"Is that coffee?" she asked instead of answering my question, pointing at a pot on the small table next to me.

"From hours ago, I think it's cold now."

She reached for the pot anyway, but the mug that accompanied it was cracked; lukewarm coffee started seeping onto her fingers.

"Shit."

"The word you are looking for is merde," I told her, trying for a joke.

"What?" she asked, sounding distracted and annoyed.

"The word you're looking for is merde. Like you told me the first night?"

"You shouldn't leave without your hat again," Mae said. "In your hat, you're almost a soldier. Without it you're just a girl."

. . .

Mae was already in the commanding officer's office when I arrived a few minutes later after freshening up. I took my place next to her, the two of us standing with our hands neatly clasped behind our backs.

The commanding officer was there, too, and Luc, which reassured me—of course I should have known that the commanding officer wouldn't issue me any instructions without Luc's knowing. Arms folded, he leaned against the desk but he didn't speak and I couldn't catch his eye for a hint at what Mae and I might have been brought in to do.

"You've been recruited for a special assignment," the CO said to Mae and me, skipping any pleasantries or welcomes. He reminded me of my father a bit, in the tight-jawed way he spoke. "Be prepared to ship out by tomorrow morning, oh-five-hundred hours."

"Assignment?" I blurted out, at the same time Mae said, "Very good, sir."

I couldn't tell if that meant she'd already known, that Luc had managed to give her a preview, or if it meant that she was just better than I at accepting professional news.

"You'll be heading to Souilly," he continued. "It's in northeastern France."

"Near les bouches?" Mae asked, more sharply than I would have dared. "Where they are so short on pig snouts and coffee grinders and there are all the reports of Harries winning the wooden cross?"

I knew that "pig snout" was slang for gas masks, and "coffee grinders" were machine guns—but half of Mae's question was still completely foreign to me, and all of it revealed that her understanding of where we would be going was miles beyond my own.

"What is our assignment?" she continued.

"You'll learn when you get there. When Captain L'Enfant requested you, he assured me you wouldn't let us down."

My head jerked up. Requested. Luc requested me, in particular, and I felt a swell of pride before it was replaced by doubt. Mae made *sense—everyone knew she was the best operator. But I was just working to not be the worst. To get up to par with the other girls. To prove that I could work hard enough to belong here. I couldn't help wondering if it was a mistake somehow, if Luc had misspoken.*

The commanding officer dismissed us and I lingered outside of his door longer than I needed to, straightening and fiddling with my uniform.

"Miss St. James." Luc appeared at last.

"Is this the opportunity you mentioned?" I asked him. "I know you said something might come up if I kept working, but I didn't expect something so soon."

"Nor did I. But then I was asked to recommend two girls. Do you not think you are ready for it?"

"I'm still not as good as Mae is."

"Mae wasn't as good as Mae is," Luc said. "Not until she asked for the opportunities and pushed to be better."

"Can you tell me anything more about what our assignment will be? If you know, that is—I just want to do well," I added hastily.

He appraised me. I could see him weighing whether to tell me, and for a moment I regretted asking, wondering if I'd pushed things too far, taken too much advantage of the dedication Luc had shown to my success. "Can you keep a secret?" He'd lowered his voice enough that I had to lean in to hear him, enough to make it obvious that this was an important secret. "Can you promise not to share with anyone else in the operating pool?"

"I promise."

"We think that our lines might be compromised," he told me.

"Compromised?"

"The ultimate goal of going to Souilly: The Germans have been aware of our movements more times than just luck would have it. We need to make sure we aren't being spied on, and to do that we need one trustworthy operator."

My heart skipped a beat.

Spying via telephone was such a modern concept I could barely even imagine such a thing, nor could I begin to think of what I could do in order to investigate.

To go from table arrangements to catching spies—it felt as though I had leapfrogged over weeks or months of training.

But this is what I had come for, I reminded myself. I had come to prove myself. I had come to test my own capabilities. I was getting better every day and Luc knew it.

One.

Suddenly my mind bumped against how Luc had described the assignment. One trustworthy operator. And yet he had requested both Mae and me. One of us must be a backup. One of us is coming in case the other can't do the work. And by "one of us," I surely meant me. Mae wouldn't be the backup; she was too good. But I decided then that it didn't matter. Whether I was the first or second choice I was still going.

"I can do whatever is asked of me," I told him, injecting confidence into my voice. "Whatever I'm told."

Luc nodded. This was the right answer, the only answer that a top-flight Hello Girl could have possibly given.

"I can tell you two more words," he said finally.

"Two more words about the assignment?"

He lowered his voice even further, waiting for me to lean even farther to him before speaking again.

"Firing lines," he said.

And so we were off to Souilly.

11

Marcus Herrington

The address is farther than I thought it would be, nearly too far to walk, but we've already begun and I'm afraid if we return to the train station for a taxicab I'll never make myself start out again. Up Reisterstown the houses grow closer and closer together until they transition from freestanding homes to row houses, and then from row houses three windows wide to just two.

"This one is it," Theo says, referring to the Polk's directory in his hands. The house in front of us is cheerful and well-kept: painted brick, with garden boxes of poppies in the window.

I have stories about all the boys who died. After my father's boss's son mentioned his cousin August I started creating stories in my head, about each of them.

Mickey Shea, for example, I picture as the class clown. He would have orchestrated the class prank at the end of each school year.

Jonathan Pierce would have been serious-minded, a bit of a loner, head often in a book.

The Charles Dannenberg in my mind was the middle son of a large Catholic family. Sisters on either side, living in the hand-me-down boots and jackets of his older brothers, a stairstep in the parade of Dannenbergs tripping off to church on Sunday mornings in height-descending order.

"This isn't—" I start to say, and Theo looks at me quizzically because he thinks I mean we have the wrong address, but really I mean that this isn't how I pictured it. This neighborhood is too far into the city; I pictured Charles living in the country. This house is too squat; I pictured Charles living in a ramshackle place a hundred years old, the type of location where knobs are always coming off bannisters in people's hands. "This isn't—" I try again, because it's beginning to occur to me that if I got the house wrong, then maybe I haven't thought through any of this well enough; maybe we need to stop and make a plan; maybe—

The front door opens. And in it stands a tiny woman, narrow shoulders, sallow cheeks, an apron tied loosely around her waist.

"You might as well come in," she calls out. "I assume you're here about Charley."

·   ·   ·

Is this the voice? Is this the voice from the telephone?

Mrs. Dannenberg spoke so unexpectedly that I can't really tell. And the difference in intensity between her voice and the telephone caller makes it nearly impossible—Mrs. Dannenberg has her voice raised, calling out to us from her stoop. But the Brightwood caller spoke barely above a whisper.

I need her to say something again, in a lower register, so I can listen more carefully. But Mrs. Dannenberg doesn't speak again. She doesn't even pause to wait for us. Instead she leaves the door open as she turns back into the house, clearly expecting Theo and me to follow.

Theo and I exchange a glance and then I make a decision, motioning for him to open the front gate as we hurry after Mrs. Dannenberg up the steps, into the dim foyer. Only when she's shown us to the kitchen table and placed two teacups in front of us does she speak again, in a flat, businesslike tone of voice.

"We don't have the body."

"The body?" I repeat weakly.

"We don't have it."

Back in the foyer the door has clicked shut, but I'm wishing it hadn't.

"In our correspondence," she continues, "you asked about a burial plot. I won't need a burial because there is nothing to bury. I don't have a body."

"Mrs. Dannenberg—"

"But I would like a headstone. He has one in Arlington, but I would like one in our neighborhood cemetery. I know you said that people in our *financial situation* sometimes just use a placard, but we would like a headstone. My husband says he'll work extra hours if that's necessary. And I don't care what it costs by the letter; my husband and I want a headstone with Charley's full name and a quote from William Butler Yeats."

The puzzle pieces fall into place and I know I must correct her, as gently as I can. "Mrs. Dannenberg, I'm afraid there's been a misunderstanding. We're not with the cemetery."

She shakes her head. "What do you mean? I was supposed to meet with the burial representatives Wednesday at one p.m."

Now it's Theo's turn to break in. "Mrs. Dannenberg, it's Tuesday."

And then her face falls in on itself. The flat stoicism of her earlier utterances disappears and Mrs. Dannenberg grounds her forehead into the palm of her hand.

"I knew that," she says quietly. "I really did know that; I woke up this morning knowing it was Tuesday. But when I saw you coming up the walk in your official clothes"—she gestures to my black skirt and cardigan, which do look funereal—"I just lost myself for a moment."

"Nothing to apologize for," Theo assures her.

"But—" Realization dawns on her. "If you're not with the cemetery, but you said—you're here about Charley?"

Theo is silent now, waiting for me to take over the conversation. To bring up the telephone calls, to bring up France, to bring up my errors, to bring up the entire reason we are here. But there is a frog in my throat. I can't do it.

"School," I choke out. "We knew him from school. This is Theo, and I'm Edda St. James."

I don't know why I give my real name. Out of the corner of my eye I see Theo glance at me but then quickly rearrange his face.

"Friends, then?" Mrs. Dannenberg's face softens, losing the grim determination of a business dealing that she had when she believed we were from the cemetery. "You were Charley's friends?"

"Yes," I say, and then backpedal, realizing that I've left us open to possible exposure. "Of course, I didn't know him as well as I would have liked."

She nods; what I've just said, for whatever reason, comports with what she knows of her son. "He never had time for much socializing; he was so busy helping my husband, earning extra money. He was on a scholarship, of course, and I know that most of you—" Her face colors and she cuts off without completing the sentence. Charley, a scholarship student at a fancy school, and she assumes she's talking to his rich classmates.

"I think everyone felt as we do," I tell her. "Wishing they'd known Charles better."

She smiles a little. "Is that what he went by at school, then? So formal."

Too late I realize my mistake: In the newspaper where his death was announced, Mrs. Dannenberg's son was listed by his given name, Charles. But his mother has now called him Charley several times. He must've gone by a nickname.

"I think it's what the teachers called him," I stammer. "It's what you would hear called out during attendance."

"I didn't want to name him Charles, you know. I wanted to name him after my father. But my husband was so excited to have a boy. So he said to me, 'You can name the next one, you can name the next five of them—just let this one be Charles.' And I agreed."

A clock ticks somewhere that I can't see, nearly ten seconds passing before Mrs. Dannenberg speaks again.

"Of course there wasn't another boy to name after my father. There wasn't another anybody to name after anybody. If I'd have known that was going to be the case, then maybe I would have, but—no, I still wouldn't have insisted we name him after Dad. He was Charley from the moment he came out, even I could see it."

Theo is looking at me, he's raising his eyebrows, silently asking what I want to do now.

What am I doing here? What am I doing here? What am I doing here?

"Mrs. Dannenberg, do you—if it's not too painful, do you know how your son died?"

She looks at me with faint surprise. "In combat. But we don't know anything more than that. He wasn't—he wasn't—the bayonets, you know? I hope it wasn't a bayonet. If it were I don't think I could—"

A sob rips through her body; her thin shoulders shake.

"We'd like to pay for Charley's headstone," Theo says suddenly, gaze focused intently on Mrs. Dannenberg while he ignores my questioning eyes. "The entire class does."

"You—what?" Mrs. Dannenberg asks.

"That's why we came here. We want to take up a collection and pay for his headstone, with whatever quote you would like on it."

I don't know why I didn't think to offer something like that myself. I glance at Theo, trying to convey my silent thanks.

"The engravers charge by the letter. Are you sure?"

I clear my throat, finding the voice to reenter the conversation. "We don't have the money now," I admit, glancing quickly at Theo to make sure I'm speaking correctly—I can't imagine he would carry this kind of money on his person. "But we can bring it back for you, if you write down the amount for the headstone. It's just—it's the least we can do."

. . .

"Edda," Theo starts as soon as we're outside and Mrs. Dannenberg has retreated inside.

"No," I tell him.

"Edda." He reaches for my arm as I stalk down the path, frantically jimmying the stubborn gate until at once it bursts open.

"I can't, Theo. I can't." I finally make it through the gate, bursting through to the other side and gulping air.

Theo scans the street, to make sure nobody is watching my breakdown, I assume. "There has to be a cafeteria nearby. A diner, anything. Let's find some place to sit down."

"I don't want to sit down, I just want to—"

"What are you doing here?"

We both pivot at the sound of the gruff voice. A man is exiting the Dannenberg residence—Charley's father, I presume. He still has his hat on, and work boots, as if he's just arrived home.

"You heard me," he says again. "I asked what you're doing here."

Theo takes the lead, as I'm clearly in no state. "Pardon us, sir, we were only—"

"I came in the back door only to find my wife in tears about Charley."

"We had no intention of upsetting your wife," Theo starts, as Mr. Dannenberg shakes his head. "Perhaps we should have called first."

"Don't have a telephone," Mr. Dannenberg interrupts him shortly. "Don't need one of those instruments. You couldn't pay me enough to have a telephone. Though it sounds like that's what you tried to do. Pay us off."

"Nothing could be further from the truth," Theo assures the man. "We don't want to pay you off, we came to offer to pay for your son's gravestone."

"We don't need that," Mr. Dannenberg says again, looking disgusted by the offer.

"Whether you need it or not, we made the offer to your wife and she accepted, and we plan to pay."

"I think you should plan to leave, and not come back," Mr. Dannenberg says. "You've found the gate; I don't think I need to show you out."

Theo opens his mouth again but I put my hand on his arm.

"We're very sorry for disturbing you," I tell him, pulling Theo back in the direction from which we came, the little house with the tidy garden boxes receding behind us on the street. Mr. Dannenberg watches us until we round the corner.

"It was horrible, Theo," I say when we're fully out of earshot. "I knew it would be horrible but it was—did you hear when she said she never got to name a child after her father? In my mind Charles had all these siblings, and that was terrible in its own way, to think of how many people would be grieving him. But this is a different kind of loss, it's so lonely, it's so *lonely*."

"Edda, I know that was hard, and awful," Theo says. "But I think there's one thing that came out of it."

"Nothing good came out of it."

"I didn't say it was something good, just that it was *something*."

"What? What can possibly have come out of it?"

"Mrs. Dannenberg didn't bat an eye when she heard your name," he explains. "And she didn't strike me as the kind of person who would be in a position to lie easily. She didn't seem to have a lot of details about how her son died—you would think if she blamed someone for her son's death it would have come up. And Mr. Dannenberg didn't seem to have any interest in ever having or using a telephone.

"So however awful that was," he continues, "I think we can eliminate them from the list of possible callers."

12

PETER HORNADAY

Aunt Tess is standing in the doorway holding my rain slicker.

"I have a meeting tonight and I thought you might like to come along," she says to me. "It looks like rain—here, you can switch into this coat." Before I can answer, she turns to Theo. "Mr. Graybill: Mrs. Pettibone needs help moving the settee in her room and has nominated you for the job."

Theo gives me a look, one that communicates neither one of us can save the other from my aunt's assigned tasks, before obediently stepping inside.

"What kind of meeting?" I ask once he's gone. At this point all I can imagine doing is falling into my bed for thirty minutes before my shift begins. "Is it one of your protests?"

"It's not a protest. It's a rally. To talk about the rights of women, especially working women. I thought it would be good for you to have something to do with your time."

She sets her mouth in a line of determination, and in that moment she looks like my father—the same creased brow and twitching jaw muscle.

Something to do with your time.

In all those before conversations, the before-I-went-to-France conversations about *what we were going to do with Edda,* that seemed to be everyone's concern. That Edda should have something worthwhile to do with her time. My aunt's ideas of how I should behave and what I should do had been different than my father's, but they were no less strong.

"You didn't need to tell my father I was coming to Baltimore," I accuse her now.

"Was it a secret? I assumed he already knew."

"If you assumed he knew, then why would you have to tell him? Were you just trying to get back in his good graces so he was only mad at one of us?"

"You're being silly, Edda." She brushes me off. "If you were going anyway, what does it matter when your father learned you were coming? I told him because I wanted to make sure your parents were home when you arrived. I didn't want you to travel all that way only to find them out of the house." She shakes my coat at me. "Now let's go. One of the speakers is going to talk about the switchboard operator, your friend who died."

"I told you, I didn't know her."

"You didn't have to know her in order to *know* her," Aunt Tess insists. "She was your sister in arms. You shared the same job."

"We weren't sisters *in arms*," I snap. "We don't bear any weapons at Central Dispatch. There is nothing about being an operator for Bell that is like being at war."

"It was just an expression."

But all I can think about is the events of the day swirling around in my head. Mrs. Dannenberg at her kitchen table, and my father chastising me for running to France. Charley.

"Do you know how many boys died on the western front?" I demand, suddenly furious. "Thousands. Tens of thousands, probably hundreds of thousands. And those are the ones who died, not the ones who lost arms or legs or suffered head wounds or who are being fitted for prosthetic jaws. They *died*. And there is nothing about working at a switchboard that is like going to war, whether it's a switchboard here or a switchboard in France. There is nothing that a girl like Louisa had to complain about."

My aunt looks shocked. "Edda, I am baffled by what I'm hearing you say. I would be from anyone, but from *you*, especially. You went to France. You put yourself in danger, just like men did. And I know that you must be traumatized by what you saw, or what happened to you, but—"

"Nothing *happened to me*. My job was to place calls on a switchboard, not to fight on a battlefield. I stared at plugs and wires, not bloody stumps and bloated corpses."

"That doesn't mean that you didn't—"

"It does," I tell her resolutely, exhausted. "It does mean that. Can we leave it alone now?"

Aunt Tess looks like she wants to say something more to me, but I can't stand the idea of lectures, or of someone else telling me how I should or shouldn't feel about France.

I brush past her into the house before she has the chance.

"I have to go and get ready for work," I tell her. "I'm late for my big, important shift."

. . .

But I'm not late. I'm incredibly early, for once. I have time to put on one of my new, clean shirts, and I have time to go to the bank and withdraw enough money to pay for Charley Dannenberg's headstone—money I promise myself I'll bring his parents as soon as I'm able. I arrive at Central just as the sky opens in downpour, early enough that instead of scrambling into the line of other girls just as the shift changes, I'm able to line up with everyone in the retiring room. Buttons neat. Hem straight. Bleary with exhaustion; aside from a short nap on the train back from Baltimore I haven't slept since my last shift; I've been awake for nearly twenty-four hours.

Forty hours since the call.

Helen slides into place next to me and glances over nervously a few times, finally gently clearing her throat, until at last I return her gaze. "Edda, I wanted to say that I'm sorry if things became uncomfortable this morning." She rushes through, placing her hand sincerely over her heart. "You left so quickly."

This morning feels like a hundred years ago; it takes me a moment to even realize what she must be talking about, the awkward breakfast.

I can tell she wants to say more, and I am relieved that ahead of us the line has started to move. I don't want to have this caring, concerned friendship; I don't want her to suggest another breakfast, another diner. "There is nothing to apologize for," I tell her out of the corner of my mouth. In front of us, skirts rustle and the row of operators from the day shift prepare to slide out of their chairs. I reach for the headset in front of me, glad for a reason to stop the conversation.

Almost as soon as the headset is firmly on my head, a bulb lights up in front of me, my first call of the shift.

"Number, please," I say, as Helen turns reluctantly back to her own switchboard and picks up her own headset.

"*You're the only one who can help them,*" the voice says. "Time is running out. *Brightwood.*"

13

LEMUEL HUBBARD

"*Who is this?*" I scream into my headset. "Tell me who you are!"

Immediately, I feel Helen's hand on my arm, alarmed, trying to still me. Immediately, I sense the hush around the room as other operators try to see what's going on.

"*Tell me who this—*"

But it's too late. The line is dead. Of course it is. I couldn't possibly have expected the caller would stay on the telephone. The line is dead and I am clinging to my headpiece like a madwoman, feeling everyone's eyes on me.

The first call wasn't a coincidence. I knew it wasn't—*I knew it wasn't*—but this second call solidifies that. It wasn't a word that I misheard or a misunderstanding. It was somebody who knew what

I did, who knew where I was, who knew how to reach me. I'm not crazy—I never was.

"Let's go to the retiring room," Helen says, quickly ushering me out of my seat. "Let's get you a drink of water."

I don't want to follow her, I want to stay at my switchboard. As if the person who is telephoning me is *there*, instead of being miles away where I can't see them.

But Helen puts a steadying arm around my back, and she's stronger than I thought she would be. She half lifts me from my seat, waiting until I can bear my own weight on the floor below. Stumbling, I follow her, but I can't stop looking back at my switchboard.

"You'll come back to work soon," Helen soothes me. "For now you just need a little rest."

The retiring room is empty; we only ever use it at lunch or the beginning of shift. Helen tries to maneuver me onto the sofa but I can't stay sitting; my body wants to pace.

"Should I telephone someone for you?" Helen asks, watching me circle the perimeter of the retiring room again. "You live with your aunt?"

"No," I tell her. "Don't telephone anyone. You can go back to your switchboard."

"No, I'll stay with you."

She perches on the sofa herself, but after fifteen minutes I can see her eyes travel back and forth between me and the clock on the wall, torn between wanting to be helpful and wanting to avoid her own demerit: She's already used the duration of an entire restroom break to get me here, and we're allowed only two per shift.

"I'll be fine," I tell her in a voice that barely convinces me, let alone Helen. "You should leave."

"If you're not—I don't want to—"

She twists her hands, but her decision is made for her when the door opens and Miss Genovese walks in. She's followed closely by Mr. Andrews, her own supervisor, whom I've seen but never spoken to. He's not usually here more than once a week.

"I'll take it from here, Miss Gibson," Miss Genovese tells Helen.

As soon as Helen leaves, I move to my own locker along the wall and begin to open it.

"What are you doing?" Miss Genovese asks.

"Getting my belongings. I assume that I'm fired."

I want out of this building. I want away from my switchboard and my headset and the telephone lines that feel like they connect all the way to France.

"Why would you think that?" Miss Genovese asks, nervously chuckling, and only then do I realize her own voice has a weird quality to it, strained and overly cheerful. "One of our star employees, whom Mr. Andrews has just this moment dropped by specifically to see. We're lucky to find you here."

Mr. Andrews appears, extending a fleshy hand for me to shake. While I do so, Miss Genovese's eyes flash behind him.

I cannot begin to imagine what this man wants from me, but apparently my job is saved by his surprise appearance in my workspace. If Miss Genovese disciplines me in front of him, she will lose the impression that she has total control over all the operators under her purview.

"Edda, is it?" He leans in and cups his hand to his ear. "Is that short for anything?" He gestures to the velvet sofa Helen had tried to make me sit on earlier. "Won't you have a seat?"

He himself sits in one of the two armchairs facing the sofa and Miss Genovese sits in the other, still eyeing me, a bit queerly, as if to make sure I'm of stable enough mind so as not to embarrass her.

"Miss St. James, I'll get straight to the point," Mr. Andrews says. "Grace Banker is getting a Distinguished Service Medal."

When I stare blankly, he continues. "Grace Banker is—"

"I know who Grace Banker is," I cut in. She was the first Hello Girl commissioned by the US Army, and the most famous. I wasn't stationed where she was, but we'd all heard of her. She was held up for all of us as a model for what we could or should be doing. "President Wilson is giving her a medal?" I ask, confused. "How can he—she wouldn't even be back in the United States yet."

Mr. Andrews taps the side of his head with his index finger. "Ah! Smart girl!" He applauds me. "Miss Banker will be receiving the Distinguished Service Medal at a later date. The promise has been made but the ceremony has not been scheduled. But to your broader point: Miss Banker is indeed still abroad. Most of the Hello

Girls are. They're not here to witness the nation's appreciation for their hard work and contributions to the war effort. But when the Bell System learned that we had one of our very own Hello Girls working so tirelessly at our switchboards—"

"They want to use you," Miss Genovese translates. "As far as we can tell, you are the only Hello Girl back in the United States."

"Use me?" I repeat. "Use me, how?"

"We don't want to *use* you," Mr. Andrews says smoothly. "We want to honor you."

How disappointed Miss Genovese must be in me. I remember when I first met with her after I applied for my job. She had taken particular interest when she learned I had been a Hello Girl. She'd asked where I'd served, who I'd served under, what I'd done. Through our entire conversation I had been listless and monosyllabic, half praying that I wouldn't get the job, that I would never have to look at a switchboard again. But Miss Genovese had hired me anyway. She had said it was her duty to look out for the girls who had been stationed in France; I'm sure she thought she would be gaining disciplined employees who knew how to do things like show up on time in freshly ironed clothes. Instead she got me.

"Miss St. James?" Mr. Andrews asks. I have been lost in thought for longer than I meant to be. "What do you think?"

I look at Miss Genovese to see what *she* thinks. Surely she must realize now that I am not an ideal advertising campaign, but when I look over to her she isn't returning my gaze; she is examining her fingernails.

"What would I have to do?"

"A parade, maybe?" Mr. Andrews muses. "We could have you on a float. On a throne, maybe, the Queen of the Telephone."

As he sees the look of horror that this suggestion prompts, he quickly backtracks. "Or perhaps not a parade. Perhaps we could just use your likeness on some promotional materials. Show the greater Washington area what a patriotic girl we have on our staff."

This is the opposite of what I want. The opposite of the anonymity that I came to this job seeking. My fear is exposure, and that's exactly what I'm being threatened with now, a threat disguised as a reward. I cannot possibly imagine accepting.

If I don't accept, what will happen to me? Will I be fired? It's what I thought I wanted ten minutes ago, and at first I thrill at this thought, that I could walk out of this building and never again have to return. Never again have to pick up my headset and hear an ominous voice on the other end.

But losing this job wouldn't mean protecting myself from exposure—if the voice can find me here, it can find me anywhere. I think of the kicked rock, the figure I thought I saw in the shadows of the doorway, the sense that someone had followed me to work the night before.

Losing this job would only mean having to move back to my parents' house in Baltimore.

"Am I being assigned to do this?" I ask, wondering if their invitation is really an order. "Is this compulsory?"

"No, I wouldn't say it's compulsory," Mr. Andrews says lightly. "But in looking over your employee records, I couldn't help but notice that you have had a few little infractions here and there, and I am sure you are looking for ways to prove you are a dedicated employee."

He trails off and says absolutely nothing more, but the meaning is clear enough. Compulsory, then.

14

CLAUDE JANNEY

Theo's door is ajar when I come home after my shift.

Wednesday morning now. *Fifty hours after the first call. Ten hours after the second.*

When I peer into the room it's empty, no sign of Theo, but the unlocked door makes me think he can't have gone far.

I've never been in here before. The room has the dimensions of my own, the sloping ceilings of my own, the same warped floorboards.

But that's where the similarities end, because of something I never expected: Theo's room is *beautiful*. Every wall is covered with drawings, in charcoal and colored pencil, of buildings, trees, plants, people. The White House at dusk, the length of the National Mall at midday.

Next to the bed, a penciled sketch of Theo, a middle-aged man, and an old one. His father and grandfather, I assume, each with a hand on one of Theo's shoulders, each in nubby sweaters, pushing him forward a little, presenting him. They look so—*robust* is the word I'm looking for. Strong and capable down to the steady grips in their penciled hands, down to the way they puff out their wide chests. Their eyes have something of Theo in them, but Theo's eyes have something else, too. *Apprehension?* A rifle leans against his grandfather's leg and I wonder if this drawing was made of the hunting party, of the day Theo was to have gone off to war.

In the next picture the oak tree outside my aunt's boardinghouse is captured, in grease pencil, at change of season, the leaves all reds and golds. Behind the tree stands the boardinghouse itself, as accurate as a photograph but different from one, too. My bedroom window is blacked out with a curtain as it is in real life. But in the drawing there's a glow coming through the cracks, a yellow warmth, a ray of light. And I can't believe that something like that would emanate from my room in real life. In my actual bedroom the curtains are drawn too tight; there is no room for shimmer.

Each drawing is meticulous in detail, but also *alive*. I must've known on some level that anyone studying landscape architecture, as Theo is, would have to be competent at technical drawing. But I wouldn't have guessed the work would look so much like art.

I wouldn't have guessed any of this. When it came to Theo, I simply wouldn't have *guessed*. It never occurred to me to spend much time thinking about his interior life, or even that he had one at all. But now in his drawings I'm looking at the way he looks at the world. The knowledge that he would knock on my door and steal a cookie and then sit down and create this entire universe on paper—it feels as though I've walked in on a secret, and—

"Good *lord*, Edda, you scared the absolute daylights out of me."

I yelp at the noise. Theo, at the door, carrying a cup of coffee in his hand. Rolled-up sleeves and charcoal smudges on his nose and elbow, hair wild and raked through. He doesn't seem upset that I'm in his room, but having seen what I've seen I feel intrusive nonetheless.

"I'm sorry. Your door was open, but I didn't mean to—I should have—I didn't know this is what you were doing in here all the time," I finally blurt out, gesturing to his walls. "All of this."

He looks pleased but also embarrassed, trying for a dismissive shrug as he takes a sip of his coffee. "Well. I needed to cover the ugly wallpaper with something."

"But these are beautiful, Theo. They could hang in a museum, except that—" And then I don't know how to finish the sentence. What I want to say is that these drawings seem too personal for a museum, something I could understand if he didn't want the world to see. But then I would be acknowledging that *I* had seen them, without permission. "Did you study to do this? How did you learn?"

"I—no. I didn't study." He looks taken aback by the question, as if it's not something he's accustomed to talking about. "But when I was little, I would always save my allowance for charcoals, and I'd make a picture about the day. 'Draw about the day,' that's how I thought about it—was the day rainy or busy or sad. I didn't really show anyone in my family. I burned most of them in the fireplace. I don't know why."

He takes another sip of coffee, I think mostly to hide his face.

"And studying landscape architecture is—"

"Is a profession I can do with shrapnel in my rear."

He says this with humor but also with finality; I can feel him trying to end this line of discussion. I search for a way to pull back and be less probing.

"What's this?" I ask, pointing to the drafting table. On it sits is a drawing that feels less intimate, purely technical in nature. A large piece of graphed paper containing a design for an outdoor space: a fountain in the middle and pebble pathways spoking out from it.

"Assignment. Updating one of Washington's infernal traffic circles. We're supposed to consider the modern era: noise from automobiles more than the odor of horse manure, et cetera, et cetera. The end result will look like this," he says, pulling out another map, which I recognize as Iowa Circle.

"It sounds interesting."

"It's not. It is, however, due next week, so I've been locked up here since the moment we got home last night."

His face dawns in realization. "Good heavens, it must be morning now if you're home. Do you want some coffee? I started some in the kitchen downstairs."

His mentioning of my return home pulls me away from the fantasy world of Theo's art, reminding me of where I've come from and what happened there. "I don't want any coffee. I—Theo, they called again."

Theo stops, cup midway to his mouth, and then lowers it at half-speed.

"They—Brightwood?"

I nod.

"Jesus."

Without another word Theo springs to action, hastily depositing the coffee mug on the drafting table, shoving aside a wet pair of tennis shoes, an umbrella still damp from last night's rain, to offer me a place to sit on his bed.

"Sorry, sorry," he mutters. "Do you mind that the bed is damp?" Then he backs toward his drafting table, sweeping away his half-finished school project to reveal a blank page and picking up a pencil. "We should make notes now. Before we do anything else we should make notes on the call while it's still fresh in your brain. Do you still remember what they said? Was it just 'Brightwood'?"

"No, it was more, and it was different than last time. They said I was the only one who could help," I tell him, remembering as best I could exactly what the wording was. "And that time is running out."

"Time is running out?" He lifts an eyebrow, alarmed, I can tell, but he doesn't comment on this part of the message yet. Instead he makes me repeat the phrase a few times as he writes it down, frowning as he looks at the finished product.

"*The only one who could help them*," he says, reading it out loud, slowly. "And the voice—did you take better note of the voice this time?"

"It happened before I could think to take better note," I explain. "Last time, the call was my final one of the night. This was the first call of the night. When I connected the line my brain was ready to hear just a regular caller placing a regular call."

"But surely *something* registered. It registered enough that you were able to ascertain that it was the same caller from before, and not a different caller." He holds up his pencil expectantly again. "Man? Woman?"

"Fuzzy."

"Fuzzy?"

"Yes," I say, struck by something. "But not staticky. Normally if a caller's voice is distorted it's because they're calling from a great distance or we have a bad connection. But this sounded distorted in another way. Like perhaps there was a handkerchief over the receiver."

"Like the caller was sick?" Theo suggests. "Nasally, with influenza or a bad cold?"

"No, but…"

"But what?"

I'm trying to think back to the first call I received fifty hours ago. I replay it in my head now, slower and with new clarity now that I have something to compare it to.

"It sounded as though the caller had been crying. The first time, the call sounded insistent. But this time it was more…emotional. And maybe that's why I couldn't tell whether it was a man or a woman. Tears would make a man's voice more high-pitched. And the fuzziness."

Theo picks up his pen and writes that down: *Fuzziness*, circling it three times. But then neither he nor I know what to do with it, so he just adds a question mark and leaves it.

"Help *them*," Theo says. "It was *them*, you're sure of it?"

"Yes. Why?"

"It's just interesting—the caller could have said 'him,' and in a way that would have been more likely if it were a family member. Don't you think? Concerned for justice or retaliation for a son or husband, rather than a whole battalion of sons or husbands?"

"I don't know," I admit. "I'm not sure what a family member would have said."

"And 'help them.' What do you think that means—how are you supposed to help them?"

"By turning myself in?" I guess out loud. "By making a public announcement saying what I did?"

He looks down at the scrawling he's made on the paper, synthesizing everything he's written, as if expecting new information to leap out at him.

"*Time is running out*," he repeats. "Did they give a—a deadline or anything?"

"They just said that time is running out."

He drums his pencil onto the paper now, thinking. "I don't like this," he says finally. "It sounds—retributive. Like they expect that you should be punished."

"I *should* be punished," I say bitingly.

"That's not what I mean. It sounds like they expect that they should be the one to punish you. I don't like that."

He shakes his head and bites his bottom lip, rereading his notes on the drafting paper for the dozenth time, not realizing I'm still looking at him.

He is taking this seriously. He is taking me seriously. As outlandish as this all seems, he has never once been patronizing.

"Theo—" I open my mouth to start to thank him, but at the same time he says, "Edda."

"What?" I ask.

He taps the butt of his pencil hard on the drafting table.

"I think we need to be more methodical about this," he says.

"How do you mean?"

"Going to the Dannenbergs'—there was no rhyme or reason to it, was there? They just happened to be the first name you found."

"That's right," I acknowledge. I'd wanted to visit the Dannemans. The Dannenbergs rose to the top of the list by sheer proximity to the Dannemans in the telephone directory. "I found the name, and I knew roughly where their address was."

"We shouldn't keep doing that," Theo continues. "You said there are thirty-four names. Running around Baltimore trying to track down thirty-four families... it's scattershot. And it would take forever."

"What do you propose?"

"You have all the names written down somewhere?"

I do. My newspaper clipping. But I've never shown it to anyone. It feels furtive, secret, a relic I use to remember and to punish myself. But I take it out now; I lay it on Theo's desk.

Davy Wagner: A boy with a stutter, I've always imagined. A boy eager for the approval of his father, who keeps a sketch pad in his rucksack and draws plants and landscapes by starlight.

Timothy Speck: A rough boy. A boy who lacked discipline, whose family was relieved when he was called to France, hoping that maybe the rigors of the army would smooth out his jagged edges, help him grow up.

August Danneman, whose address I had narrowed down to

three possibilities yesterday when we visited the Dannenbergs, but whose house we hadn't gone to. The last boy who died. An outdoorsy boy. A boy who loved the company of animals more than people, who carried seeds in his pocket to feed squirrels, who made friends with every dog he met. A boy whose cousin I danced with, maybe? A boy whose life crossed paths with my own?

Theo finishes copying down the list, and I see he's writing them in alphabetical order. Next to Charley Dannenberg he puts a check mark. The others all remain blank.

"Now what?"

"Now we'll write down the addresses and try to figure out who lives near whom," he says. "We have the directory from Baltimore, but the families might not all live in Baltimore still. I was thinking that we should look through the telephone directory for Washington, too. If the family lived in one of the towns between, they could show up in either directory."

"That's not a bad idea," I admit. "I'll go get Aunt Tess's Boyd's directory from the parlor."

Ten minutes later we are staring at a list of twenty-three names with addresses, seventeen in Baltimore and six in Washington. The others either didn't appear in either directory or they appeared too many times to be able to narrow down with anything remotely resembling certainty.

"I know where most of these neighborhoods are," I say hesitantly.

"So I know which two or three could be visited in the same afternoon. But there are still a lot of names."

"I think we should focus on the people who have telephone numbers," Theo decides. "We partly eliminated the Dannenbergs because they didn't have a telephone and I think that's a sound principle: for someone to track you down as they did—we still don't even know how it happened, but it seems to me like it's much more likely for a person to figure out how to do that if they're familiar with the technology. Don't you think? I mean, *you* don't even know how it's done and you work as an operator. So for someone who doesn't ever use a telephone, or who only just got one to be able to make that call—"

"It seems unlikely."

Theo crosses off the names with no telephone numbers and then chews his pencil. "This is a little more speculative, but can we tell anything about the caller from the times they telephoned? Once close to five a.m. and then again just after nine o'clock at night?"

"I don't think so," I say slowly. "If they'd telephoned twice at the same time, maybe we could assume something about their work schedule. When the times are so different, it doesn't seem to mean anything. But there is something else."

I'm gazing at all the addresses Theo has written down.

3002 Columbia Road, Apt. #1203

1901 Thirteenth Street, Apt. #591

"What's the something else?" Theo asks.

"We should focus on houses. We can eliminate anyone who lives in apartment buildings," I say.

Theo tilts his head. "You think the caller was wealthy?"

"It's not a matter of wealth," I explain. "What I said Saturday, about how this was a local call because it came directly from the caller instead of an operator?"

"Yes?"

"Big apartment buildings have their own operators," I explain. "So do hotels and large office buildings. If someone had called from one of those places, it would have been placed through an operator. So we should at least eliminate the addresses with large apartment numbers—the ones with many stories."

Theo stares at me. "That's a huge and useful piece of information. And you didn't think to mention it before?"

"I hadn't thought about it until we looked at these addresses."

"Cities like Washington and Baltimore, a lot of people live in apartments. It's major that we can eliminate them from consideration."

We go through the list again, and sure enough, eleven of the addresses we were able to find appear to be apartments.

"Does that feel more manageable?" Theo asks, as we stare at the remaining names.

"It makes things more manageable, but I'm not sure that it makes things any more *reasonable*," I admit. "You said that thirty-four names was too many, that it was scattershot. But we still haven't been exactly scientific."

"We haven't. But—" He looks uncomfortable; I can tell he doesn't want to continue. "But Edda, the caller said time is running out. What else are we going to do?"

We.

Theo is handsome.

The realization hits me softly. Theo has full lips and when he bites the bottom one, the muscles in his jaw clench. I haven't noticed anyone was handsome in a long time; I'm not sure I expected to ever again.

I'm struck with a thought I should have had earlier, back when Theo came with me to the Dannenbergs, or back when he got on the train with me to Baltimore, or even back when he leaned against my closed door and asked me to tell him what happened.

"Theo, why are you helping me?"

He blinks and then looks away before deflecting my question. "You know I'd do almost anything to avoid doing my actual work?"

"Theo."

"You know I'm a naturally kind and giving person," he tries again. He rubs his hand across his neck and he won't look me in the eye.

"*Theo.*"

"You cry in your sleep," he says suddenly.

"I—what?"

His face colors and he bows his head. "I would be home in between classes, and you would be sleeping all day, and the walls up here are so thin," he says. "I wasn't trying to spy on you, but it was hard not to overhear. You would cry out. In your sleep. Sometimes a yell, and sometimes it was more like—" He swallows his words; he truly doesn't want to say them out loud. "Sometimes it was more like sobbing."

I'm mortified by this, mortified that Theo could hear me and mortified even more by the idea that he could hear me doing something I wasn't even aware I was doing. My body has betrayed me.

"Is that why you started stopping by?" I ask. "Because you heard me crying?"

I thought that Theo was coming to my room because he never had his own cigarettes. Really he was coming to my room because he heard me fall apart?

"I didn't say anything, to Tess or anyone else," Theo promises quickly. "I just—I could hear you. I suppose I could tell that something was wrong even before you told me something was wrong.

"Edda," he continues hesitantly. "Who is Luc?"

The air around me is very still.

"How did you hear that name?"

"I—I couldn't often make out what you were saying. And sometimes it was in French. But sometimes—sometimes I could hear you calling out for someone named Luc. And I wondered—"

"I'm sorry," I tell him, burning with embarrassment over the man who wasn't part of the Forty-Eighth, who was nonetheless a name burned onto my soul, whom I couldn't leave behind in France, whom I had to leave home in France. "You must have heard wrong."

15

CALEB KERR

Souilly.

A tiny town in northeastern France.

Paris had had all the markers of sophistication; even in wartime the city was like a beautiful woman merely wearing drab clothes. Souilly was barely a hamlet surrounded by farmland, a cluster of small cottages spoking out like a wheel from a modest stone town hall. There were no streetlights to dim in Souilly to protect the town from bombs; many of the residences appeared to have no electricity at all.

We rode there on a Liberty Truck, jostling in the back under a canopy of canvas. Mae and I in the back with rucksacks and supplies, Luc riding up front with the driver. When we arrived in Souilly, the bumps of a dirt road became bumps of a cobblestone road. I looked out the tiny window in the back of the truck and saw the building we'd stopped in front of: gray stone and three stories tall, grander than anything I'd expected to see in the middle of the countryside.

"Is this our hotel, do you think?" I wondered out loud, to myself more than to Mae.

"A hotel out here in the dead center of nowhere? This is probably where the muckety-mucks work while we sleep in a puddle."

"No, we wash in the puddle," I corrected her. "We sleep in the mud."

Mae snorted. I'd made her laugh, the first time I could remember doing so. I wasn't usually droll enough, snide enough, quick enough, and I swelled with pride at the achievement.

The canvas flaps in the back of the truck opened to reveal Luc.

"Welcome to the headquarters of the American Expeditionary Forces," Luc said. "The front is barely thirty kilometers that way." He gestured to the east. "At night you may hear firing."

"Oh," I replied, catching on. "The firing lines. Just as you'd said."

So that's what Luc meant earlier. When he'd said "lines," my vocabulary was still in the mindset of being a telephone operator. I had been thinking of lines like telephone cable. But really he was referring to the lines of soldiers, the trenches tracing along the front.

He checked his wristwatch. "The truck will take you to your barracks next, and then you have fifteen minutes to unpack your things before meeting back here to learn of your new assignment." He nodded to us before disappearing into the stone building. After a minute the engine revved again and the Liberty Truck bumped along its way. I could feel Mae looking at me.

"You already knew," she said.

"What do you mean?"

"When you said 'the firing lines' earlier. Luc already talked with you about Souilly?"

She seemed bothered by my possession of the information, and I couldn't blame her. This was a dangerous assignment, and anything we knew about our environment was important.

"I should have told you in the truck," I said apologetically. "Luc did tell me about the firing lines—but only because he's been trying to help bring me up to par," I explained. "So that I have the right vocabulary, so that I can keep up. He said I remind him of Grace—his sister."

"His sister Grace," Mae repeated coolly. Then she turned away and didn't say anything more.

. . .

Our barracks weren't in the mud, but there was plenty of access for the mud to be in our barracks. I had thought that the Hotel Piedmont was basic, but the barracks were barely a step above camping. They were little more than planks of unfinished lumber, with cots jammed into each corner and trunks at the end of them. We dug out our spare uniforms and our personal effects, hung our belongings on nails from the wall to keep them off the damp floor.

No sooner had we finished than Luc arrived again, carrying pieces of paper that he passed out to Mae and me. I sneaked a glimpse, thinking they might be instructions for our new assignment, but the rows and columns didn't make any sense to me.

"In Paris, the work you were doing was vital for the war effort," Luc said. "I don't want you to think it wasn't. Logistics of meetings and supplies—these are the things that can win a war, even if they are not so glamorous. We are indebted to your service."

He paused and looked at each one of us in turn.

"Here, you will take control not of logistical lines but of actual tactical support."

He waited for the information to sink in. I began to have a sense of the magnitude of what we were here to do.

"Tactical support is more than scheduling and supplies," he continued. "It is the war itself. The communication between troops engaged in battle—active battle. The telephone calls will be going literally into the trenches. The information will be sensitive and often classified. It will move quickly and require sharp thinking through your entire shifts."

"Who is doing the work now?" Mae asked.

"So far we have had only men perform this work. Trained soldiers. But many of them do not speak both English and French, and in the time of translation we are losing precious minutes in circumstances in which seconds can be life or death." He paused meaningfully. "Because that is what we are asking of you now, what these communications mean. These communications are life and death."

"The soldiers aren't leaving, are they?" I asked. Souilly was a smaller region than Paris, but it still would have been difficult to imagine Mae and I responsible for covering all the shifts ourselves.

"The soldiers will still be working," Luc said. "But you two here are a test, to see whether the work can be given over entirely to Hello Girls."

"Are the exchanges the same, at least?"

Luc shook his head. "The exchanges are the same. But now they will be in code."

"To make sure I understand the assignment," Mae said. "We will be connecting telephone calls between trenches as they are under attack, whilst simultaneously translating between French and English spoken by men who are terrified for their lives."

She sucked in a deep breath. "I'm going to get a cigarette and a shot of whiskey. Are you coming?" She turned to me.

"I don't drink whiskey." I told her. She hesitated a minute before leaving and I sensed I'd disappointed her. Back in the truck it seemed like she might warm to me, and now I was turning down her social invitation. I wanted to explain that I wasn't a prude, I just didn't like the taste of liquor. It always burned, and after an evening spent vomiting in the bushes the year before, I'd never been able to stomach it again.

When she left, Luc and I were alone in the barracks.

"Do you have any questions?" Luc asked me, but I was so overwhelmed I could think of only one.

"Why didn't you tell Mae about the compromised lines? The spies you think may be listening in?"

Luc raked his hand through his thick hair. "Are the two of you close?" he asked. "Never mind, it doesn't matter either way. I am your superior; I can't burden you with such things."

"No, you can," I insisted. "I can keep a secret. I already told you I could keep a secret."

"I know you can," he said. "You have been proving yourself ever since you arrived. But it's my job to protect you."

I thought I could see a tortured look in his eyes, a weighing of whether or not he should say something to me.

"It's my job to do my job," I told him. "And to do it well I need all the information."

Luc was a man of serious matters, a man who thought me capable of serious matters.

"So you can tell me," I insisted again. "I can keep a secret."

Finally, he relented.

"The compromised line. The leak in communications. We do not know where the leak is coming from, precisely," he said. He looked so relieved to be unburdening himself. "It's a mess, Edda. We do not know the origin of the leak and so we must all be on the highest possible alert, from all possible angles. The investigation into the leak—it cannot be revealed to everyone. Do you understand why absolutely all our inter-actions must be kept private? There are some people we do not want to know about the investigation."

He pleaded at me with his eyes. He put his hand over my hand, and the placement of his hand spoke a whole sentence, a whole paragraph. Then he removed it, hastily, and quickly shook his head.

"I should not have said anything to you. Please try to forget this. Your job is to do your job, to help us win the war. That should be your only focus."

"Of course," I promised, while my mind whirred.

It wasn't that they needed two operators, one to carry out a mission and one to be a backup. It was that I had been brought to Souilly because I could be trusted. Mae had been brought to Souilly because it was possible she was the spy.

16

REUBEN MONTGOMERY

Here is what I imagined about Barry Wyndham. That he was handsome and strong but painfully shy. That he was quietly in love with the girl next door but she didn't know it yet. That he had gone to France thinking that he would grow in estimation in her eyes. That when he came home he planned to propose and she would tell him how funny life was, that he'd had to travel halfway around the world before she realized her dearest love had been just down the street all along. That he was the eighth to die on that boat. That if anyone could have survived what happened on the boat it would have been Barry Wyndham: desperately in love, with every reason to make it home.

I had never pictured Barry Wyndham's house, but just a few

hours after Theo and I finished composing our list, here I am standing in front of it—an old Tudor, needing a new coat of paint.

Here I am knocking on the door, watching a figure approach through the glass: a maid in a crisp white hat.

She opens the door but guards the entryway with her body, a posture of suspicion. "May I help you?"

"Is Mrs. Wyndham at home?" I ask. "Or Mr. Wyndham."

"We don't want any solicitors."

"I'm not selling anything," I assure her. "May I please just speak to the master of the house? I've come to pay my condolences about Barry."

I'd practiced. After visiting the Dannenbergs, fumbling around without a story, I'd thought about what I was going to say at this house. The one thing I cannot do is upset them further. I am looking for one person who has telephoned me with alarming calls, but that means thirty-three have not. Thirty-three are simply grieving families, who deserve whatever peace they can find.

A few moments after the maid leaves a new figure is approaching through the glass door—a boy several years younger than I am, thirteen or fourteen, pale and sallow-cheeked.

"Yes?" he asks, and I silently curse the surly maid for making me go through this again after I explicitly said I wanted to speak to the master of the house.

"Are your parents at home?" I ask. "I'm here to pay my

condolences about your brother; I wanted to speak to the master of the house."

Down by the boy's waist, a pair of chubby hands appears, followed by the moon face of a smaller boy, a toddler who can't be older than three. "It's all right; go back to the playroom," the older boy whispers. When he turns back to me it's with a look of confusion. "*That* was my brother," he says. "And I am the master of the house."

"You are the—"

"Yes," he says. "I am the master of the house now."

Now.

I step backward on the stoop, hand involuntarily moving to my heart.

In my mind, the dead boys were all boys, recent high school graduates, barely shaving and wet behind the ears. In my mind, the families I would be meeting would be grieving parents. But I'd misjudged.

"Not your brother," I apologize, cheeks stinging from my mistake. "I came to offer my condolences about your father."

"Thank you," he says, sounding somewhat rehearsed. "Our family appreciates your kind words."

"Is your mother at home?"

"She's visiting family in Aberdeen today. Would you like to come in? I'm Joey, by the way. I mean, Joseph."

In what I recognize as a guest parlor, Joseph gestures to a visitors' book lying open on an end table. "You may sign in to the book," he says. "And then Sally will bring out tea and shortbread while we talk. Or if it's after one o'clock she can bring out cucumber sandwiches. Is it after one?"

Once inside I look around the parlor, the gold-and-green wallpaper, the matching velvet sofas. Above the fireplace is a family portrait: Joseph, his younger brother, and a pretty blond woman who must be his mother. And, with a clefted chin and strong cheekbones—with strawberry hair and his right hand on Mrs. Wyndham's shoulder—Barry Wyndham.

It's the first time that I've seen a face of one of the boys—*men*—of the Forty-Eighth. Tie neatly knotted, hair neatly combed. All around the parlor is more evidence of this man and his life. A pipe holder for what I imagine was an evening smoke. Empty of the pipe, though, he must have taken it to France. On the wall, a family crest. The bookshelves of the parlor are filled with books in various degrees of tattered, in the way of a collector who is interested in being a well-read person rather than just keeping up the appearance of being one.

"Sally should be in soon," Joseph says from his seat on the settee across from me, hands laid formally across his lap.

"Your father looks like he was very handsome." I nod to the portrait and realize my mistake just as I'm doing so.

"Didn't you know him?" he asks, furrowing his eyebrows together.

Damn.

"I—"

"I assumed you were one of his typists. He owned a business placing secretaries?"

"I'm—I'm more a friend of your mother's," I stammer.

Sally comes in with the tray, the lemonade and the promised sandwiches.

"I'm sorry to have missed her," I continue. "I can come back another time when she's home."

"She's away until tomorrow. I'm in charge of receiving everyone. We haven't had anyone in a while, though. Most everyone came to pay their respects last month. Right after."

I force the sandwich to my lips and it crumbles, dry toast smeared with butter, in my mouth. I thought I had a plan, I thought I'd say I was with one of my mother's charitable organizations, that I had been sent to call on grieving families, to see what they needed and how they were going. Her organizations do this sort of thing; they arrange meal deliveries and provide sympathetic ears. But sitting across from a grieving child, I can't bring myself to carry through with the plan, or to even be in the house at all. "Joseph, you've been so hospitable. But I really do think I should come back one day when your mother is home."

"Would you like to sign the guest book before you leave?" He walks it over, handing me a heavy fountain pen. I scrawl something unintelligible in the book and then set my plate awkwardly on the end table next to the sofa, ready to leave less than five minutes after I arrived.

"I'll see you to the door," Joseph offers, but then he doesn't make a move. Instead he purses his lips together. "You said you're my mother's friend?" he asks. "You didn't know my father?"

"I'm afraid not."

"It's all right. I was just wondering if—I was just looking for someone who could—"

I notice that the collar of his shirt is much too big, gapping out nearly an inch from his neck, and I wonder whether his mother purchased it too big for him to grow into, or whether, perhaps, the shirt belonged to his father.

"What is it?" I ask him. "I'll help if I can."

He looks up. "I don't suppose you know where he was sleeping, before he went over to France?" Joseph says. "How he was doing? He sent postcards sometimes, but otherwise it was hard to tell if—he did say he missed us."

He looks terribly embarrassed now—hopeful and needy and then embarrassed for being hopeful and needy. The little boy in him is bleeding around the edges of adulthood.

"Your father hadn't been living here since before he went to France?" I surmise.

Joey shakes his head slowly. "Not for a couple of months."

"I don't know where he was staying. I wish that I did, but truly I never met your father at all."

Joseph digs his toe into the carpet. "That's all right. Mother said that he was going to France because it was easier than fixing things at home. You probably know that already, though, if you're her friend."

"Joseph," I begin, foundering well beyond my depth. "Grown-up relationships can be very complicated. Not even adults understand them sometimes."

At that point Sally the maid returns to the room, noisily clearing my barely touched plate and making a show of checking our teacups to see if they need refills. I can't imagine there's a single word of our conversation she didn't overhear from the kitchen, ear pressed to the door.

"Will there be anything else?" she asks, words that are technically directed to the master of the house but which I can tell are actually meant for me.

"I was just leaving," I tell her, and receive a small nod of approval in return. She already has my coat and hat for me, helping me into them even before we reach the door.

• • •

The Dannemans. August Danneman, now.

The Polk's directory had contained three different Dannemans, but when Theo and I looked closely at the addresses with a

159

Baltimore map in hand, they were all located within a small radius of one another, just a few blocks apart. I wonder if it's a family compound of sorts. Sure enough, when I knock on the door of the first address, the man who answers the door tells me that it was his nephew who died in the war: His sister's house is the one I want to visit.

But when I reach that house, a tidy little bungalow with a cat preening in the window, nobody answers the door. Nobody is in the back, either, where undershirts flap on a clothing line and a garden bed, dirt and weeds in November, sits waiting to be readied for spring. I've come all this way and hate to turn back, but my return ticket is scheduled for a few hours from now and I have to get back to Washington.

I take a piece of stationery from my purse and write a hesitant note to the Danneman family, leaving it folded in the letter box by the front door.

As I walk back to the train station I wonder what kind of afternoon Theo had. After we finished making our list he started off with his own two names—families who live near Georgetown, whom he planned to visit after his classes ended for the day. He might have visited them already, in fact, but I won't have a way of checking in with him before my evening shift begins.

Maybe he solved it. It's a crazy hope, but I can't help but fantasize that while I've been out alone this afternoon, Theo has somehow found the right family, received a confession, explained that I am sorry, arranged for the phone calls to stop.

And if he hasn't...then what? Then I am heading back to my job now.

And the caller might telephone again. *The caller might telephone again.* The thought repeats itself in my brain, gets stuck in a loop, all through the train ride back to Washington.

By the time I get to Union Station it has grown from an intrusive thought to a tightness in my chest, a dull ache, and then grows heavier with each passing step as I near Central Dispatch, until it feels as though a fist is grasping my heart and I stop to lean against a lamppost.

The caller might telephone again.

There, in my chair, at my switchboard, at any moment I could hear the voice in my headpiece.

It's just a telephone call, I try to tell myself. *It can't hurt you if you listen to it. You can always disconnect the call. You are not helpless.*

But I am, I feel helpless.

Two of the past three shifts at work have contained a call. Something I had no control over. Something I had no way to predict. Something I had no choice but to answer. When I sit down at my switchboard I must remain sitting there for eight hours. Not allowed to stand except with express permission. Not allowed to decline a call. Not allowed to refuse.

It won't happen again, I tell myself because I need to tell myself this. *It won't happen tonight. You will get through your entire shift without another telephone call; it won't happen again.*

It's not helping that I'm exhausted, that in the span of less than seventy-two hours I've gone from sleeping all day to sleeping barely at all.

I enter the building. I walk into the retiring room. I remove my coat and place it in my cubby. I line up to start my shift. I tell myself, *It won't happen tonight.*

But it doesn't work, it doesn't calm me. I'm standing in line with all the other operators, all of us dressed in our white blouses and navy skirts, but instead of focusing on the shift ahead of me, my palms are shaking and then my whole body.

"Switch places with me," I hiss into Helen's ear.

"What?" she mutters. The doors have opened; we're walking now.

"Switch places with me; let me sit at your switchboard tonight."

"Edda, we—"

"Please," I beg. "I'll buy you a coffee, I'll take the blame—anything, just switch places with me for today's shift. Please."

I don't know whether it's just because decent Helen can't help but do the kind thing, but after my last *please*, she nods her head, almost imperceptibly, and then steps out of line just long enough for me to slide in front of her.

The setup of Helen's switchboard is identical to mine; I am not more than eighteen inches away from where I usually sit. But those eighteen inches might as well be a mile, a buffer of safety.

"Number, please?" I ask the first caller, and then my chest loosens a notch when it's a woman asking to be connected to a courier service, and then it loosens another notch when the next caller asks for a French restaurant.

Helen glances at me a few times, and it's odd to see her out of my left eye rather than my right, but after the first half hour she stops checking in on me. Eventually she becomes at ease, convinced, at least enough, that me sitting in her seat hasn't caused me to behave in any abnormal or dangerous ways, and that I don't plan to ransack her workstation.

After the first hour I myself manage to relax, comforted by the routine numbness of my job, the way it allows your mind to go blank as your fingers do all the work. When I took the test to become a Hello Girl I thought I might love the work. It sounded so chic and cosmopolitan.

"Number, please?" I say at a little after two o'clock in the morning.

A little static, someone fumbling with the receiver.

"Number, please?" I ask again.

A pause.

"Edda?"

17

RUDOLPH PALMETTO

"Edda?" the voice asks again, followed almost immediately by, "Don't disconnect—it's me, it's me."

My heart has already started to race, my mind has already started to go blank, and I have to work to bring myself back to my body.

"Edda?" the voice asks for a third time as I finally begin to settle enough to process what is happening.

"Theo?"

"My god, I can't believe it actually worked."

"Theo, what are you—how did you?"

Next to me Helen has noticed that something has happened but then her switchboard lights up and she can't focus on me.

I lower my voice and tuck my head toward my chin to be as

unobtrusive as possible. "How did you reach me? Or are you—" A different idea occurs to me. "Are you actually trying to place a call?"

"I've been trying for four and a half hours to place a call."

"I don't understand."

"Can you talk?" he asks.

I glance around as Miss Genovese turns onto my row. "Keystone 8240, please hold," I say in a raised voice and then, lower, "A little."

"I've been trying for four and a half hours to place a call to you because that's how long it takes," Theo continues. "Or rather, that's how long it took me. I supposed I could have gotten lucky and reached you in hour one or two, back when I still had a concept of linear time, but four and a half hours is how long it actually took."

"Theo." I keep my voice low. "Take a deep breath and explain how you are on the telephone with me right now."

I can picture his hair wild and sticking up, the way I've seen it after a long night of studying, fingers run through it again and again.

"All right," he says after another deep breath. "We agreed that it would be impossible for someone to reach you on purpose. Correct?"

"Yes," I agree.

"But the more I thought about it, the more I realized that if a caller has no control over which operator they get, there's no reason why they *wouldn't* reach you, eventually. It doesn't require a miracle, it just requires patience and a lot of time."

"Right," I say slowly.

"Right, so, I wondered how much patience and how much time. So at nine p.m., right when I knew you would be starting your shift, I picked up the telephone and waited for the operator. And when it wasn't you, I hung up. Approximately three hundred attempts later, here I am."

"Theo, that's—I don't think there's a word for it."

"*Impoverishing* is the word for it. And possibly *homeless*, because I can only imagine how many of the other residents complained that I was monopolizing the telephone; Mrs. Pettibone is definitely going to murder me in my sleep. But Edda—" he rushes on. "It's *possible*. That's the main point. If you're determined to reach a particular operator, it's *possible*."

"And that would explain why I got a call at the beginning of one shift and the end of another," I agree. "And why one shift I didn't get a call at all."

"Yes. Because it was entirely random. The caller might get lucky and reach you immediately, or it might take them all night or it might never happen."

My mind turns over this concept, picturing a caller doing what Theo did, sitting by the telephone, picking up and replacing a receiver over and over again, all through the night.

"Edda? Are you still there?"

"I'm here. It's just—what you're saying solves a mystery, but I'm not sure that it makes me feel any better. The idea that someone would be willing to put that many hours into reaching me, listening for my voice. It feels—"

"I know," Theo breaks in. "I do know."

But then neither of us knows what to say next, and after a minute I can't stand to let my mind linger in that place.

"Did you go to the Palmettos' house?" I change the subject.

"Yes, and the Saprezzas', and then I had extra time so I went to the Steins', too. But none of the visits were fruitful."

"How do you mean?"

Rudolph Palmetto: I pictured him with a shock of red hair and a piercing whistle.

Antonio Saprezza: I pictured him with neatly manicured nails and skin so smooth he barely ever needed to shave.

Buddy Stein: I pictured him telling scandalous jokes, cracking his knuckles when he got to the punch line.

"The Saprezzas are an immigrant family. Italian," Theo says. "They don't speak a word of English. Even for as little as you were able to tell about the voice on the other end of the line, I think you'd be able to tell if they were speaking in a different language. The Steins moved to Seattle two months ago, a neighbor said. So it would have been a long-distance call for them to call you and we're already certain this wasn't."

"And the Palmettos?"

"It wasn't the Palmettos, either."

"Why not?" He doesn't answer so I repeat myself. "Theo, why not?"

"The Palmettos were really just Rudolph and Javier," he says finally in a small voice. "A father and son. And the father apparently died the day after he learned his son had passed."

Of a broken heart. He died of a broken heart.

"What about the families you visited?" Theo asks. I hear a rustle of paper in the background and realize he's checking the notes we made; he won't have the names committed to memory the way I do. "The Wyndhams and the Dannemans."

Miss Genovese is rows and rows away, so I speak low and quickly. "The Dannemans weren't home. And as for the Wyndhams—I don't think so. Things weren't going well in that marriage; he'd moved out of the family house before he went to France. I didn't get to speak with his wife, but the impression I got from her son is that she was glad for her husband to be gone. It seems as though if you felt that way, you wouldn't want to taunt the person you believed was responsible for his death."

"Instead you'd be thanking them?" Theo asks wryly.

"It's just—the emotions in that house all felt...complicated. And the person who called me, the emotion was...*pure.* I can't think of how else to describe it."

Again I hear the rustling of paper as Theo goes through our notes. "That's four more names that we've eliminated, then. And I wanted to ask you about something else. The United States Pension Bureau."

"What about it?"

"The Saprezza family thought that's where I was from—a neighbor translated for me. It's the building where the widows and orphans of veterans go to collect the money they're owed from the war. I thought we should go there."

"Why?" I ask. Miss Genovese has rounded the corner, I know I have only a short time before she's close enough to tell I'm not doing my work; I'm amazed that I've managed to talk this long without being reprimanded.

"Because they must keep personnel files on all the soldiers whose families are receiving pensions, and if we can look at the files, we might learn something that points us in the direction of a particular family," he says. "And because the voice told you time is running out and I don't think there is any more time to lose."

18

NICK PAPADOPOULOS

Did I believe, at first, that Mae could have been a spy?

Who knew what to believe?

What I believed, at first, was that there were things about this war that I did not understand, that were above my station and pay grade. What I believed is that she was the best operator I'd ever seen, that I wanted her to like me, that there was a sharpness to her. I wondered whether I had been an idiot, confusing sophistication for secretiveness, but then again Luc hadn't said anything was certain. He didn't know anything for sure, I didn't know anything for sure, none of us knew anything for sure. War was violence in the trenches, but in the switchboard room it was only confusion, only knowing pieces of the puzzle.

The only way I knew how to contribute then was to tell myself that my job was to do my job.

What would have happened if I had asked her outright whether she was a spy? I asked myself that question a lot later—whether I could have changed the course of action if I had confronted Mae. But even later I wasn't sure what I would have said.

A week after our arrival in Souilly, I walked into the switchboard room and there she was, Mae, not finishing her work as she should have been, but still firmly planted in her chair. It took me only a moment to realize she hadn't ended her shift because her shift wouldn't let her. She was the only operator in the room and her hands were flying, connecting one call after another with no pause in between. She barely had time to register my presence in the room; I could see sweat pooling around her temples. I had been following radio dispatches. I knew that the front had moved even closer to us.

"He didn't show up," she barked at me between calls. "The soldier who was supposed to start with me a few hours ago, he never—Number, please?"

Before I had time to respond to that or think about anything else, my own switchboard flared up. Not just one bulb but many simultaneously, a deluge like I'd never seen.

"Number, please?" I barked into the headset even before it was fully on my head.

For the next hour it was like that. The calls kept coming, unrelenting, my hands flying faster than they'd ever been asked to before. Out of the corner of my eye I could see the same was true for Mae; her hands were a blur and her lips never stopped moving.

"Number—" I asked the next caller, but a young-sounding voice interrupted before I could even finish the greeting.

"I need to reach Nemo," he yelled into my ear in French. "Immédiatement."

Nemo. My brain raced to remember the codes I had memorized the night before. Nemo was the Fourth US Army Corps, stationed in Saint-Mihiel, leading French and American troops in an attempt to capture the city of Metz.

"Did you hear?" the voice pleaded into my ear. "Nemo! This is Fresno calling for Nemo."

I was already connecting him, my hands in motion even while my brain was catching up.

"Oui, immédiatement."

On the other end of the line a voice—a young man, they were all young men—picked up the line, in his own trench, in his own command post.

"Hello?" he said in English, with an American accent.

"Nemo, this is a call from Fresno," I said to the second man. And then, to the first: "You have Nemo."

The first man immediately began speaking in rapid-fire French.

"Are we advancing?" he asked. "We thought the Germans had retreated but we are running low on artillery. Are we still advancing?"

"*The Germans have retreated—*" the American began, as I translated.

"*No, we only* thought *they had retreated,*" the Frenchman corrected him, overlapping my translation. "*But they have refortified, they are attacking again, and we don't have enough supplies left to make it to Metz.*"

"*They've—*"

"*Are we trying to take Metz or not?!*"

While translating one sentence I was listening for the next, trying to keep up with the conversation and translate everything perfectly while I could barely hear either of their voices over the sounds of the bombs and explosions.

"*I will ask Major General Dickson,*" the American promised. "*Only he can make the call.*"

And then the American voice was gone, his line was just static as he left to go find his superior officer. I pictured what it would mean for him to ask Major General Dickson. He would be running through trenches, hundreds of yards long, packed with sweating, scared soldiers and seeping with mud. Dickson could be anywhere. There was no way to know how long it could take to find him.

"*Is he there?*" the Frenchman asked me. "*Is he still there, I can't hear him.*"

"*He's getting an order.*"

"*Can you tell him to hurry?*" On his end of the line I heard rumblings, bombs, explosions.

The quaking from the Frenchman's trenches got louder. It thrummed in my eardrums, I could feel the vibrations in my own body.

All of a sudden I became aware of shouting in the dispatch room where Mae and I sat. The commanding officer's secretary, a red-cheeked man with a duck-like walk, burst in the door.

"There are bombs," the secretary shouted to the operators, his voice high and urgent.

I ignored him, I closed my eyes, trying to block out all the din around me and focusing only on the voices in my headset, where the Frenchman was keeping his agonized wait.

"Do you have an answer?" the Frenchman begged into my ear. "Please, can they hurry, it's bad—" He cut off and I heard him yelling rapidly at someone next to him. I heard not only the sound of explosions in the background but also the sound of screams of pain. When he came back on the line he was panting. "It's bad here. We need an answer."

"I'm trying," I told him, working to keep the panic out of my own voice. "Any second now, I'm sure. I'll have an answer for you any sec—"

And then my headpiece was ripped from my head. The secretary again, grabbing at me, a dazzlingly impertinent offense while I was trying to do my job. "A bomb," he said again.

"I know they're under fire," I hissed back, trying to snatch away my headpiece.

He wouldn't let loose, though. "No," he said, ever more frantic. "There are bombs.*"*

Finally, I looked up.

The wall was gone. The whole western wall of the building where I was working had become just a gaping hole. Destroyed by something dropped by a German plane. And the hole was surrounded by flames.

"We have to go," the secretary shouted. "The barracks will burn down."

In a split-second I tried to take in the whole picture. The flames licked the edges of the bombed-out hole. It was wet outside. It had been raining, and that would help a little. But the interior of the barracks were those rough, dry wooden planks. It would take only one spark, one ember, to make a leap into the barracks and then I would be trapped, up in flames in a matter of minutes.

Out of the corner of my eye, I saw Mae. Her eyes met mine, and in them was something steely and impenetrable and daring. She had seen the fire, too, and she had been waiting to see how I would react. And I was doing the same to her. I was staring at her, thinking that if she wasn't leaving, there was no way I would leave.

Was this how a spy would behave? Was this the deepest possible cover, to outwardly throw yourself so into your work that nobody would think to question whether you were working for the right side?

I made a decision.

"I have to finish this call."

The secretary reeled back, stunned. "You—"

"If I don't finish this call, the Forty-Second won't know whether to fall back or attack," I yelled over the licking flames. "I have to finish this call."

I didn't give myself another minute to question this decision, or a minute to acknowledge the sweat pouring from the palms of my hands. I snatched my headpiece from the secretary, jamming it back on my head.

Mae turned back to her own switchboard but I felt as though I could still feel her looking at me.

"Number, please?" she shouted into it. "I'm connecting you to Wabash right now."

"Allo?" the boy in the earpiece asked me desperately.

"Je suis ici," I told him, reassuring him that I wasn't going anywhere even while the flames at the end of the barracks kept growing.

Come back, come back, I silently begged the American who had gone to fetch his superior. Come back, come back, every second is life or death.

The smoke was getting thick, burning my lungs every time I inhaled. I pulled a handkerchief from my pocket to breathe into; it barely worked.

A crackling on the line: The American was back, panting, out of breath. He may have been gone only minutes, but it felt like hours of my life had passed.

"What did you learn?" I demanded, my voice breaking as smoke seared my lungs.

"Fall back," he gasped out. "Tell Fresno not to charge."

"Avez-vous entendu?" I asked the French soldier, continuing in French, "Did you hear that? He says you are not to charge."

But then there was nothing on the other end. Just after I delivered my message the line disappeared—cut by Germans or German bombs.

I'd made it, though. Adrenaline coursed through my veins. Just under the wire I'd made it, I'd done it, I'd prevented the charge.

"Edda, come on."

It was Mae now. She was up from her switchboard; she'd finished her own call and was beckoning me toward the door. I could barely see her; the air around us was acrid and thick.

We burst out of the barracks, into the gray sky, and for a moment I was the heroine of the war.

19

WILLARD PIEDMONT

The headquarters of the United States Pension Office is a redbrick building with massive marble columns marching abreast a soaring atrium in the middle. Filling the atrium: soldiers. Soldiers in uniform, soldiers in street clothes, soldiers with empty sleeves neatly pinned up to their shoulders where arms used to be.

"Over here, I think," Theo says, pulling me in the direction of a hanging sign reading VETERAN RECORDS. It's Thursday now, a little after eleven o'clock in the morning. I slept for only a few hours after my shift ended to give us more time at the pension office.

Beneath the sign, a pinched-looking woman sits with her hands folded behind a counter, peering observantly over her glasses.

"She's not going to just let us in to pick through the files," I mutter to Theo.

I don't know why, but when Theo had described the pension office to me I'd pictured it like a library, a place we could walk around and peruse books and papers. That doesn't make any sense, of course—these are private files of pensioners; two strangers would never be allowed to thumb through them without permission.

"I'll do it," Theo says resolutely. "And then I'll come and find you in there."

"You'll do what, exactly? What are you going to tell her?"

But Theo is already removing his hat and charging over to the woman behind the counter. "Good morning!" he says brightly. "I was hoping you could help me with something."

"Yes?"

"It's a rather complicated question, though, so would you mind if we sit down back in the lobby?" He taps at his hip and winces theatrically. "You understand. It's bothered me ever since the war."

The clerk's face is overcome by a look of concern and she immediately raises the swinging counter to join Theo. He doesn't look at me as they pass, but behind his back he waves me along. Before I can question myself, I slide under the counter myself and into the records room.

It's vast. What we'd been able to see from the other side is only a small fraction of the archives this room must maintain: rows and rows of shelves. It *is* like a library, except instead of books there are files. Thousands of them, each one representing a deceased veteran whose family is now due his pension. And arranged alphabetically, rather than by regiment. If my goal is to pull the files for the remaining boys whose families we haven't visited there's no way for me to do so en masse. I'll have to race around the entire archives grabbing them one by one.

Some of the files are new and crisp, envelopes of the recent dead. And some of them are old and crumbling, back all the way to the Civil War, pensions for the last remaining widows on the Union side.

My own list emblazoned in my brain, I manage to find a dozen files for the deceased members of the Forty-Eighth in about twenty minutes, all with no sign of the archivist returning. I can't imagine what convoluted story Theo has come up with to tell her, but whatever it is must be a prizeworthy performance.

Files in hand, I crouch down low next to one of the shelves, positioning myself so I can't be seen by anyone standing near the desk, and then spread the files out in front of me. Each one has the name of the soldier written on the front. Next to the name, a paper-clipped photograph, taken upon enlistment, I presume, when the boys and men were freshly shaven and their eyes were not yet tired.

What I'm looking for in these files, Theo and I decided, is something that stands out in the soldiers' personal histories. A family member who was an inventor, maybe, who might have a deep understanding of telephone technology. A father who was a general, who would have special ways to find out what happened in France.

I try to page through the files quickly, machinelike.

Horace Whitley: fair-haired, I hadn't expected that. Father was a chemist.

Willard Piedmont: ears that his face still hasn't grown into, and might never. I hadn't expected that, either. Lived on a farm.

August Danneman: The final boy. The boy whose door I knocked on just yesterday. It's too soon to expect a response, even if his family saw my letter and immediately wrote back to me, but I am thinking of him nonetheless.

Silas DuBois.

I look at the photograph for Silas DuBois in confusion. And then I look back through all the other files that I've already marked as read. Something is very odd.

20

JONATHAN PIERCE

Silas DuBois and Mickey Shea have the same face. The same long nose. The same prominent Adam's apple. *The same face.*

But how can this be? I'd already looked through each boy's file with nothing unusual standing out—one boy lived at home with his mother and father in the Canton neighborhood of Baltimore; one lived with his parents in the suburb of Timonium. Now I read through them again, more carefully.

I scan back and forth between the two files, making sure my eyes are seeing what I think they're seeing, and just as I've decided I'm not mistaken, I'm seeing *exactly* what I think I'm seeing, a pair of trousers appears in front of me—Theo.

"What have you found?" he asks, squatting down on the floor next to me.

My eyes dart to the entrance of the archives, looking for the erstwhile clerk, but Theo shakes his head that I have no need to worry.

"I think we still have a few minutes. I asked her for some obscure paperwork that I'm fairly sure doesn't exist, because I made it up, so it will take a while for her to find it."

I nod, relieved but distracted, looking back at the file in my hands.

"Did you find anything?" Theo asks again.

"I don't know. But look at these two boys."

He takes the files from me and reads the names out loud: "Silas DuBois, Mickey Shea."

"No, *look* at them," I suggest, and he now does as I ask and peers closely at the photographs.

"Is this an error?" he asks. "Did they accidentally double up the photographs? This looks like the same person."

"I don't think it's an error, and they're not the same person—see? Silas DuBois has a mole on his left cheek and Mickey Shea doesn't. They're not the same person. But look at the names written for each of them inside the box reading 'father.' "

Theo finally reads what I had seen: Philip Arnold DuBois. Philip Arnold Shea.

"You think that Philip Arnold DuBois and Shea are the same person? This man has a secret family? He's a bigamist?"

"I realize how this sounds," I say apologetically. "But we did decide that I would try to flag anything that seemed out of the ordinary. And this seems like—"

"Two sons both serving in the Forty-Eighth is out of the ordinary," Theo catches on. "Meaning their father might be a man with particular grief. Even greater, maybe—"

Theo cuts off. His finger flies to his lips in a shushing motion even though he was the one talking, and then he nods toward the entrance where I can hear the unmistakable sound of the swinging counter creaking open.

On my hands and knees I peer around the wall of files and see the clerk returning, carrying a sheet of paper. Apparently the imaginary form Theo requested exists after all. She cranes her neck a few times looking for Theo, the person who sent her on this errand to begin with, before finally appearing to give up, settling back into her chair.

What should we do? I mouth silently to Theo, raising my eyebrows. He thinks for a moment and then points to a clock above the clerk's desk. He mimics eating. It's nearly noon; she'll have to go for lunch soon, he's saying, and when she does we'll have a chance to leave.

A few minutes pass as we sit smashed against the stacks, as silent as possible, but Theo was right: The clerk looks up at the clock just as it strikes noon, and then gathers her hat and pocketbook.

But my relief was preemptive. A jangling sound emerges from

the clerk's pocket. She produces a set of keys with her right hand and with her left grabs a folding gate—*how did I not notice there was a gate before*—and pulls it across the width of the entrance. She uses her key to secure it tightly before walking away.

We're now locked in the records wing.

"*Well, dammit,*" Theo says. His voice echoes absurdly off the tall stacks, and he ends up covering his mouth and lowering his voice. "*Well. Dammit.* I guess we have to wait until she comes back from lunch and come up with another story?"

But I can't mimic his cavalier tone. The sound of the locking gate keeps replaying in my mind, the definitive clank of it, metal on metal, leaving us imprisoned.

Boys in trenches, boys on a boat, a girl in a room.

"Edda?" Theo is tugging on my sleeve. I've risen to my feet without realizing it, making for the gate. "Edda, we can't get out, she took the keys."

"I'll call for help," I say quickly. "Maybe there are other patrons outside, maybe they can—"

"She took the *keys*," Theo repeats, and then, seeing the distress on my face, calms and softens his voice. "Edda, she'll be back soon. It can't take her long to eat a sandwich. But unless it's an emergency, like the building catches fire, I don't think we want to alert security guards that we're in here. Right?"

Eventually I reluctantly nod. "Right." But my eyes still keep traveling nervously toward the locked gate.

Searching for a way to distract me, Theo sits back down and points to the stack of files on the floor. "Are those the ones you haven't been through yet?" he asks. "If we're stuck in here now, we might as well use the time."

Without waiting for me to respond, he divides the pile in two and takes half for himself. "Reuben Montgomery's father is a naval engineer," Theo says, reading from the first file open in front of him. "Is that something worth flagging? Oh, but it seems like he died of influenza a few months ago; there's a note in the margins here that Reuben's mother will be the one collecting the pension. Here, you take this pile."

Slowly I slide back to my knees next to him and we begin to work side by side, quietly flipping the pages and jotting down anything that seems noteworthy. I'm jumpy at first, but then calmer. I know at some level that the act of poring over the files is unseemly. We're here without permission. But it also feels purposeful and even soothing somehow. To be learning about these boys rather than just imagining them, to be trying to solve the mystery of the call in an orderly way rather than merely by hopping on trains.

"Grover Cleveland had his inaugural ball in this building," Theo says after a few silent minutes of flipping through pages.

"What?" I ask, so deep in my work that for a moment I wonder whether Grover Cleveland is a name of one of the boys that I'd somehow forgotten.

"In 1885. President Grover Cleveland's inaugural ball. Did you know that?"

Now I look up. "Why would I know that?"

"The roof wasn't finished yet so a temporary wooden roof was placed over the top to keep all the guests protected from the winter." He notices my incredulous expression and explains, "We studied this building in class."

"Theo, are you missing a class now?" I ask, aware not for the first time of the effort that Theo has put into helping me this week.

"Am I *missing* class? I wouldn't say that I ever *miss* class when I'm not in it."

"That's not what I—"

"I wouldn't say the class is missing, either—I mean, I always know where to find it."

I raise an eyebrow, trying to keep a straight face. "Theo. Is there a class currently scheduled for this time, which you are not sitting in, but which you would normally be sitting in if you weren't here right now?"

"If you're asking *that*, then, well, yes. I am absent from a class. But it doesn't matter. Perhaps I can get my professor to credit today as a field trip." He cranes his neck to peer at the clock again. "I wonder whether Miss Godwin gets a full hour for lunch or only thirty minutes. Do you think *we* should get some food when we leave here? At a restaurant?"

"There is a box of raisins in my handbag," I tell him. I'm on my last file and realizing that I might have pulled the wrong one. Davy Wagner is a common name, and this Davy appears to have served in the Civil War, not the Great War. "You can eat those now if you're hungry."

Theo takes up my bag, but instead of opening it he fumbles with the handle. "Do you ever think about the fact that other people have dinners entirely outside of their boardinghouse rooms that aren't composed of foods that come in tins or boxes?"

"Do I spend a lot of time thinking about other people eating? Not really."

He blushes. "That's not what I'm saying."

"What are you saying?"

"Nothing, apparently. I'm quite terrible at this, aren't I?" he mutters.

"It depends on what you're trying to do."

"I'm trying to ask you to dinner, Edda!" He looks up at me and bites his lip. "I'm trying to ask you to dinner. With me."

"I don't...understand."

"Let me try this another way," Theo says. He sets the file in his hand down on the floor and places his palms on his knees, and when he looks up at me his eyes are the deepest gray. "Did you know that I don't smoke?"

"What are you talking about? You've borrowed at least forty cigarettes from me."

"And have you ever seen me smoke any of them?"

I'm about to say, *Of course I have, you smoke all the time*, but when I really think about it I realize that's not true. A dozen scenes flash in front of my eyes: Theo fiddling with a cigarette, pocketing a cigarette, saving one for later. None of the scenes I imagine involve Theo smoking a cigarette.

"Well?" he asks softly.

And I wasn't being honest a few moments ago. I *do* understand. I understand that the records room is quiet and still, and Theo and I are alone in here kneeling beside each other over our pile of folders, close enough, I'm now aware, that the folds of my skirt brush the folds of his pants, our clothes meeting even where our skin doesn't. And I understand the hopeful, liquid expression in his eyes, and the way he searches my face for a response. I understand that *"with me,"* those two syllables that he added on to the end of his invitation—*dinner, with me*—I understand that those two syllables somehow felt so vulnerable to him that they made him blush.

"I borrowed all those cigarettes because"—Theo swallows—"because I wanted there to be a reason for me to see you every day. Because I hated the days I didn't see you."

"But—why?" Even as I can see what Theo is feeling, it's hard to imagine why he would feel it for *me*, the nocturnal, feral creature I've become since living with Aunt Tess. "Why?" I ask again, and I move my skirt away from his pants, because that brushing of cloth feels too visceral now, because I don't yet know whether I want the tingle it left on my leg.

"I—God, Edda, can anyone ever answer that question?" He throws back his head, exasperated. "Because the days that I saw you were...better. Because I liked who you were. I liked that you *were* who you were—that was a terrible sentence, but I don't know how else to say it. I liked that you were who you were. The first time I knocked on your door, it was the middle of the day and you were sleeping. But you didn't apologize for sleeping in the middle of the day, you didn't even seem embarrassed by it. You sort of...politely tolerated my presence and then told me you wanted to go back to sleep. I'd never seen anything like that."

"Because I was a mess, Theo," I explain slowly. "Not because I was trying to be coy or unavailable. Because I was a mess. Am a mess."

"Yes, you were a mess. You weren't concerned about how you might look or what I might think. You weren't trying to hold yourself together because we were strangers or because you are a girl and I'm a boy. You were just—you were complicated. And people in my family don't do that. They don't let their masks slip. If they're suffering, we just—they just—we just carry on. We're never a mess on the outside."

"Are you saying you felt sorry for me?"

He's shaking his head vehemently before I even finish that sentence. "I'm saying I admired you. I was jealous of you and then I admired someone who didn't pretend they weren't in pain.

Watching you was a kind of reminder? That there was another way to be even if I couldn't be that way myself. It seemed...freeing."

"It's not freeing," I interrupt. It hasn't been freeing to live in my body. It hasn't been something to aspire to.

"Maybe it wasn't freeing," he acknowledges. "But it seemed honest. It seemed brave. It seemed—and I really was not planning on having this conversation with you today—from the outside it was a relief to see? You were proof, in a way, that life is hard. It's not wrong to be ground down by life when life is so actively grinding.

"Anyway that's how it started," Theo finishes, trying for a smile. "Liking you. That's how liking you started. Also your raisins. You always carry things like raisins."

I start to roll my eyes, because that's what I've done with Theo, a hundred times. Because being around him has always felt so uncomplicated. Because I never had to think about it. Because I never had to think about what it meant for us to share a wall, for him to appear in my doorway every day.

His expression has turned serious again, exploring, and then I can't make myself roll my eyes. I'm thinking about how we laughed on the train. The confident, unhurried way he addressed my father, the dozens of jokes he made about Miss Genovese. The shape of him in my doorway and how seeing him there, rumpled and angular, almost never seemed out of place; it seemed as though he had come with the room. I am wondering what charcoal pencils smell like, whether Theo's skin smells as smoky as I now am wondering if it smells, and I don't know whether I wanted to move my skirt away.

I never had to think too hard about being around Theo, and I'd written that off as superficial. I'd protected myself by saying our interactions were all shallow. That's the thing about uncomplication. It's so easy to overlook how rare it is.

"What came next?" I ask him, wanting to look at Theo and then finding it too much when I do. "After you realized that you—that you liked me?"

"All of it, Edda," he says simply. He moves, now, so that instead of sitting next to me he's facing me, so that I have to look at him. So that we are both kneeling on the floor, barely an inch between our knees. "All of it came next. I liked the way you would pull the door shut with your foot when you left for work in the evenings and your arms were all full of coats or handbags. I liked the way you roll your eyes at me. I liked hearing you come home from work and flop into your bed—this little noise you would make, this exhale, like you were just relieved to be done with the day. I liked your hair.

"There's this piece of it," Theo continues. "That emphatically does not do what it's supposed to do, ever. It's always marching in the opposite direction of the rest of your head."

"Theo," I begin without knowing how I plan to end the sentence. I know the piece of hair he is talking about. My mother was always trying to tame it when I was younger.

"This hair of yours is on some kind of protest mission," he

continues throatily. "Like it should be carrying a sign and circling in front of the White House."

His hand lifts up then, and it rests in the air between us, a few inches from my head. And I can feel it there, the heat coming off his hand, the static, like there's a kind of charge in the air. He swallows, hard, and when he speaks again his voice is barely above a whisper.

"This piece here," he whispers. "The one you always tuck behind your ear. May I?"

May he?

His fingertips are smudged with charcoal, as they always are, and I am thinking about what he uses them for, all the beautiful artwork in his room. I am thinking about the drawing of the boardinghouse, and of my window, and how there was light glowing from around the edges of my curtain. How Theo had seen things that I hadn't seen and been things that I hadn't expected.

How if I think too hard about that it will become complicated, and how right now I want the gift of uncomplication.

I nod, and with the tips of his fingers Theo takes that escaped lock of hair from where it's fallen and he tucks it where it belongs in a gesture so familiar it's almost as if I'm doing it myself. He lets his hand fall slowly, carefully, tracing my earlobe and then the line of my jaw before it drops to his lap.

He is looking at me, trapped as we are in the pension building, with an intensity I've never seen in his eyes before.

"Edda," he says, and my name breaks in his mouth; it comes out guttural and raw. And then—"You're crying," Theo says, horrified.

Only when he says that do I feel the tears pooling in my eyes and know there is no way I can explain them—how this is the first time someone has touched me since I came home from France. How this is the first time I haven't recoiled at the thought of being touched since the night I forgot the code. How I'd wondered if I'd ever feel like I deserved or wanted the feeling of someone else's skin again. How I'm not brave, I'm not even honest, but what I am is hungry. To be both of those things and to not have to think about being either of them.

"Did I do something wrong?" he asks.

"Do it again," I tell him, hastily brushing away my tears. "Exactly what you just did."

He lifts his hand again and this time moves even more slowly, his thumb falling from my temple all the way down my cheek, pausing at the corner of my mouth. I feel his thumb quivering as if he wants to brush it against my lips. But he doesn't. He bites his own bottom lip and continues on, doing exactly what I've asked him to do, no more and no less, and ending with his hand again in his lap.

"Now what?" he asks.

"Now..."

And then I reach up to his mouth and do what he wanted to but wouldn't do to me. I place my fingers on his lips, the fleshy pads of them against his soft mouth, and feel his sharp intake of breath, the sucking of air between my fingers.

"Now," I say again, letting the word roll deliciously on my tongue because it has been so long since I've thought of *now*, since I haven't been haunted by the past or dreading the future.

He lifts his hand up to meet mine, his fingers tracing my forearm to the inside of my wrist where I am sure he can feel my pulse, and wonder if he can tell that it's racing. "Is this all right?" he asks, breath again against my fingers.

"Don't move," I tell him, because it *does* feel right, and I want it to stay in this place of feeling right. Now I am the one moving, closing the distance between us, moving my fingers from Theo's mouth to his hair, which slips through my fingers like water and—

He reaches up and clasps his hand around my wrist.

"*Stop.*" My voice reacts a split second behind my body. My hands have already reached out to push him away, firm against his chest, my face has already twisted away.

Theo immediately unhands me, putting his palms in the air to show he has no intention of touching me again and looking worried and baffled at once.

"I'm sorry," he blurts out. "I'm sorry, I'm sorry, I shouldn't have—" He breaks off, trying to figure out what to apologize for. "I'm sorry, I don't know what I did."

I don't know how to tell him what he did, either. I only know that I need to get out of this records room, now. I need to not have to explain anything more to Theo. I need to—

"Is this about Luc?" he asks.

Luc.

And then all at once I have my chance to escape: From the front of the records room, the gate rattles. And then it pushes open. The clerk has returned; I can see her carrying in a shopping bag and placing it under her desk. We're freed.

Without saying anything else to Theo, without even thinking, I heave myself off the floor and run toward the exit, brushing past the stunned clerk and her half-eaten sandwich, not even worrying about what she'll think or if she'll try to stop me. The atrium is busy, lots of people arriving at their lunch hours to fill out forms and check on the status of their applications. I brush past all of them until I emerge into the pale sunlight, gasping for breath, angry with myself for what I did to Theo, knowing that I needed to do it for myself.

By the time Theo reaches me a few seconds later, I've composed my face.

"Edda, what was that?" Theo's face is a mixture of hurt and confusion. He lifts his hands, palms up, in a helpless gesture. "What... was that?"

"Nothing! I just figured that we had a chance to escape if we left right away, before Miss Clerk had settled back in."

He furrows his brow. "I'm not talking about you leaving. I'm talking about what happened before."

"*What* happened before?" I ask brightly, hoping he'll leave it alone, hoping we can both leave this behind.

"Edda."

"We don't have to talk about any of this," I reassure him. "I think we both agree I have bigger things on my mind right now?"

"Edda, please," he says plaintively, searching my face. "I just want to say that if there was someone else romantic in your life, I'd rather know than not. I don't want to be chasing someone who is already committed to someone else, even if that someone else is still back in France."

"He's not back in France," I say shortly. "He's not anything."

21

FRANK PYDNOWSKI

I arrived at the café, the only café in Souilly, still smelling of smoke from the fire in the dispatch room. I was too elated by what had happened earlier that day to notice how absolutely exhausted I was. The barracks didn't burn down and that was all that I knew—I had stayed at my post while a fire raged around us, and I had connected the telephone calls between the trenches as the French and Americans planned to take the city of Metz.

I had returned to my bed to find a note lying on the pillow, from Luc. It said I should go and splash water on my face and then I should meet him at the only café in Souilly so we could toast my heroic actions.

"Edda Grace!" he bellowed, ecstatic, as I walked through the door.

And then he pointed for me to sit at the table he'd already secured and at the drink he'd already ordered.

"A sidecar for you," he said, handing me the narrow-stemmed glass. "It's a new drink; it tastes like oranges."

"What have you heard?" I demanded. "Has there been any more news from the front? Did the Americans take Metz?"

"They haven't yet, but they are on their way."

My drink was tangerine-colored and fresh-looking, but when I took a sip it burned as it went down my throat—brandy, I thought, sweetened with something cloying.

"It is a bit strong?" Luc said.

"The last time I drank liquor I ended up sick in someone's gardenias and I haven't been able to stomach it since."

"How long ago was that?"

"Months. I was going to try it again at my graduation party, but..." I trailed off and shrugged.

"But?" He looked at me quizzically.

"There was no graduation party. I came here instead."

"Of course you did." He nodded, he'd forgotten. "Listen to me. I do not mean to diminish the importance of a graduation party in a girl's life—but I will say that what you came here to do is so much more important."

"I know that, of course. My mother didn't, though. She had already hired a band; she had a dance list."

She'd been so invested, my mother, in making sure I had the right kind of party. Elegant enough for her friends. Current enough for mine. Polished enough for my father's.

Luc slid the glass of alcohol away from me. "There will be a time when I will insist you have a proper, adult drink with alcohol, to rid you of this memory of vomiting in the flowers. But for now, I will get you a Coca-Cola?"

When he returned from the bar, fizzing bottle in hand, he sat down next to me, and I saw him glance about the room in a way that seemed casual but purposeful.

"I brought you here to celebrate," he said when his eyes had finished sweeping all the corners. "But I also brought you here because what you did today, it proves that you are ready."

"Ready for what?"

Ragtime music filled the air. People were dancing now in the café. I had to raise my voice to be heard over the music.

"Ready for what?" I repeated.

There were a pair of large menus on the table and Luc stood them on end, arranging them in front of us and making it so our conversation couldn't be observed, not even by someone who could read lips.

"It's about the compromised lines," he said. "The reason you were brought here."

Sucking in a breath, I resisted the urge to raise my head and look around the restaurant, something that would only look suspicious and increase our chances of detection.

"*Compromised lines?*" *I asked, speaking even below a whisper. "Is there a plan?*"

"*Our plan is to simulate a call between French and American offi-cers,*" *he said. "The information they pass will be decoy intelligence, but we want to see if there is German movement in reaction to the information.*"

"*Staged conversations.*"

I tried to keep my tone as calm as Luc was keeping his. I wanted to show that I understood the seriousness of the matter and appreciated that I was the one he'd chosen to confide in.

"*Staged conversations, precisely. And in such staged conversations it is imperative that translations be exact—do you understand? Not a word out of place. The messages have been crafted with input from as high up as General Pershing's office. This is why we needed to wait until we were sure you were ready—something that you more than proved today.*"

"*I think I've learned all the terminology,*" *I told him. "I'm dream-ing of mortar shells in my sleep.*"

He looked at me peculiarly, with an expression I didn't know how to read. "It's more than that," *he insisted. "I've been watching in the past few weeks. You're developing a quality that I wouldn't have been able to teach you, that nobody could teach you. It's a skill that operators either have, or they do not. Do you know what it is?*"

"*I don't.*"

He raised an eyebrow as if he couldn't believe I didn't know what he was about to say. "The best operators have a way of making a phone call feel like home."

"We are trained to be friendly," I acknowledged.

"It's not a matter of friendliness. It's a matter of... invitation. When I hear the voice of a good operator, it is conspiratorial. A secret. Do you understand? A good operator makes you feel as though you are the only person in the world and your call is the only important thing in her world."

I hadn't thought about it. I hadn't thought about anything remotely like this. In our training we were taught, of course, that some people had the voice for telephones and some did not, that there were ways to make your voice more pleasing. But I had never heard of the job described in the nuanced way that Luc was describing it.

"So you are the one I need," he said. "And if this mission is successful, then we can begin to plan the rest of your future. What do you want after the war, Edda? A house? A grand house with servants, and spots on all the prestigious social committees? What should we make happen for you?"

"I—I hadn't really thought about it," I admitted. "I know my parents would like those things for me."

"You could want this," he said, gesturing broadly around the room. "This?"

"After everything, maybe the army will open up to women. You could be the head operator in an overseas command post, traveling the world, seeing the pyramids or the Taj Mahal. Or maybe you don't want this—the wet feet and chilblains and infection and chaos. Perhaps you would prefer to be an operator for an important government agency, placing telephone calls for ambassadors and politicians like in Washington, DC. I could write you a letter of reference."

"You would?" I asked, fully aware of all the doors that such a letter would open for me. I could see it in my head, possibilities I never would have imagined for myself before coming to France. I had looked at the Hello Girls as an escape, something to briefly interrupt the life I had waiting for me back home. But what if it was a doorway? Something that I could walk through that would completely change the course of the rest of my life? I wouldn't have to be like my mother, arranging her tea fundraisers and her social calls. I wouldn't have to be like my aunt Tess, marching in front of the White House for the right to vote on political matters I'd never even cared much about. I could be connecting calls inside the White House.

"I want the letter of recommendation," I told Luc. "I want the options. I wouldn't have known I did when I first came here, but I didn't realize how much more I could do."

I trail off because I don't have the words.

"Are you saying you're ready?" he asked.

I'd come so far, and so much was riding on this assignment: My future, Luc's reputation. The fate of the soldiers in France.

"I'm ready."

22

SETH RABINOWITZ

Friday morning, the wee hours, almost through my shift and ninety-four hours after the first telephone call.

"Are you ready, Edda? It's nearly four a.m."

Miss Genovese taps her foot impatiently as I look up, confused. Nearly four a.m. means it's ninety-*five* hours since the first telephone call. And it means it's sixteen hours since I thought Theo was going to kiss me, and that is what I have been thinking about, in between each call I pick up. How he touched my hair, how I touched his mouth, how I ran out of the building, how all of those actions felt confusing, as if either action was a betrayal of the way some part of me felt.

"Edda?" Miss Genovese says again. "Are you ready?"

But if it's only four o'clock in the morning, I can't think of what I should be ready for. My shift doesn't end until five.

Miss Genovese nods behind her. Mr. Andrews stands with a man carrying a modern-looking camera and a younger woman holding other pieces of photography equipment.

The advertising campaign, the one to make me the face of Bell. I'd completely forgotten the photographs were today, if indeed I ever knew. I guess they want to strike quickly. I won't be the only Hello Girl in America for much longer, and when the others return my stock will plummet.

"They want to take some pictures while you work," Miss Genovese explains, and then she holds up a garment bag. "And they want you to wear this."

"What is it?

She unclasps the bag to show me: a belted dress in a dark shade of olive green. It's not a color I would normally be permitted to wear for my shift, and it's not a style any of us typically dress in, either. What it resembles isn't a Bell System dress but rather a Hello Girl uniform.

"The company is trying to reinforce the continuity between your military service and your service here," Miss Genovese explains.

"Now?" I ask, glancing back at my switchboard where lights are still continuing to flicker—calls I am missing, a job I am still supposed to be doing. "I should leave my switchboard and change now?"

"That's what they want."

I untangle the headpiece from my hair and leave my station, but in the retiring room, the dress stares at me and I stare at it and I don't want to wear this uniform again.

It's not your uniform, I try telling myself as I step into the garment. *You're no longer in France.* I will myself to think of it as a costume instead of a uniform. Not something connected to my past, but a fanciful dress-up game that means nothing.

The last time I was in a dress like this was—

"It fits?"

Miss Genovese has poked her head into the retiring room to monitor my progress. I'm just finishing the last of the buttons marching up my front.

"It fits well enough," I tell her.

"Edda," she begins. But then I don't know what would have come next because Mr. Andrews appears behind her in the doorway, knocking awkwardly, asking, "Is everybody decent in there?" even though it's not "everybody," it's only me.

He's holding a hat in his hand, the wide-brimmed-hat style we Hello Girls had used when traveling, which looks almost cowboyish in nature. The finishing touch to my costume.

"I thought you could wear this." He extends it toward me.

"We wouldn't—" I start. "This is a traveling hat. We wouldn't wear it while actually working."

"We just thought it could finish off your *ensemble*. Is that what women call it? It's what my wife calls it. Make you look more professional."

"My girls are always professional. Whether or not they are at war." Miss Genovese's smile doesn't reach her eyes; she seems offended by the notion that her own dress code could be improved upon, or that her operators would be less accomplished than the Hello Girls overseas.

"All the same." Mr. Andrews hands me the hat and mimics adjusting it on his head. "This is going to be wonderful for Bell System."

Left alone in the retiring room, Miss Genovese again starts to say something. "Edda—"

"Yes, Miss Genovese?" I ask. I hear the exhaustion in my voice. The lack of sleep catching up with me, the fear and tumult over the last week.

But before Miss Genovese can tell me whatever it is she wants me to know, another interruption: The photographer pokes his head into the retiring room.

"Her switchboard is the empty one on the end, yes?" He addresses Miss Genovese first, and then turns to me when her only answer is an irritated expression. "Miss St. James? We're ready for you now."

· · ·

The last hour of my shift is a farce. It's impossible for me to do my job and pose as the photographer would like me to. He keeps asking me to smile more, cheat away from the switchboard, use only my right hand so that my body is more visible to the camera or so the inaccurate wide-brimmed hat doesn't cover up my entire face. Every few minutes his assistant scurries forward to repowder my nose or fix a loose strand of hair, but it feels like she's trying to tend a garden while it's raining: The more anxious I get about the photographs the more bedraggled I know I look, until finally my shift mercifully ends. They take another series of photographs in the retiring room—me sitting at the piano, on the settee—and by the time those are finished I've nearly sweated through my pretend uniform.

"Is that everything you needed?" I ask weakly, once I'm finally relieved of duty, as his assistant shovels equipment back into a black leather bag.

"It will do," the photographer says brightly. "Now on to your house!"

"My—house?" I know that the conversation about this promotional campaign had been a blur, but I also know I never would have agreed to the photographer coming to my home.

"To capture the whole war hero, the whole girl. Here she is at work, connecting important calls of the country. Here she is at home, reading and doing her needlework, perhaps by the fireplace."

"No," I say simply.

He tilts his head, bemused. "No?"

"Surely what you have here is enough."

I want to be out of these clothes, I want to be away from this building. I cannot imagine strangers coming into my room.

Before I can protest further, the photographer flags down Mr. Andrews. "This is what you wanted, isn't it? This is what we agreed on?"

"The whole girl," Mr. Andrews says enthusiastically. "I'm sure it will take only a few minutes. Faster to get it done with than to stand here and debate it."

I see it in his eyes. This part of it is compulsory, too.

And so instead of walking home I find myself squashed into a taxicab with the photographer, who finally introduces himself to me with a name that I promptly forget, and his assistant, to whom I am not introduced at all.

"The stairs are narrow," I say when we arrive back at the boardinghouse. Less of an apology than a warning, something I hope will make them turn back rather than maneuver all their equipment to the fourth floor.

"That's quite all right," the photographer says, mistaking my tone. "Three flights of stairs is nothing. You've no idea the kinds of environments I've worked in. I was once hired by the sanitation commission to produce a pamphlet about safety protocols for sewage workers. Pitch-black down there, and I don't mind telling you—"

I've shoved open the door to my room and the photographer breaks off midsentence, closing his mouth as neatly as a purse. His assistant, too, is pressing her lips shut, as both of them take in my room.

When I first arrived at Aunt Tess's boardinghouse, this was a tidy little space, plain but clean, with homey touches like fringe on the curtains, the kind of space I am sure the photographer envisioned when he suggested this particular setting. Now I can see him take in the actuality: the piled boxes and rusty tins, the clothing in various states of rumpled. Nearly every horizontal surface in the room is coated with dust.

It's the assistant who speaks, ultimately, tasked with the job via unspoken prodding from her boss.

"Is there a bedroom with...better light?" she asks delicately. "This is rather dim."

I could offer to draw the curtains but I know she's speaking in euphemisms; no amount of drawn curtains could make my room presentable for the subscribers to Bell System.

"We could go back down to the parlor," I offer.

"My instructions were to photograph you in your bedroom," the photographer says. "As if you were getting ready in the morning for your workday."

"My workday begins at nine o'clock in the evening," I say. "I'm never getting ready in the morning for my workday."

"Of course. It's just—there was a certain concept that Bell System had in mind. A vision."

I hesitate before making my next suggestion. "I suppose we

could—what if we went to my neighbor Theo's room? He should have left for class by now. His room is next door and might have the lighting you're looking for."

The photographer visibly brightens at the suggestion. "Let's try it! We'll just take Miss St. James's hairbrush and a perfume bottle or two—something to gussy up Theo's room and make it look as though a young lady lives there."

My personal effects in tow, the three of us walk next door where Theo has, as I'd hoped and predicted, left his door unlocked. As it swings open the photographer holds his breath in anticipation.

"Yes," he says finally. "I think the lighting in here is much better."

Again in his element, he directs his assistant to remake the bed as he arranges my own belongings on Theo's bureau. "Would you straighten the desk?" he asks me. "We might want to photograph you sitting at it. Writing your letters to the soldiers back in France."

I pause before following his instructions, in a way I wouldn't have a few days ago, back when Theo's things were just *things* and Theo was just a person who lived down the hall. But now the act of touching where his hands have touched and sitting where his body has sat—it all feels so intimate I can barely stand it. As I sweep away his pencils I think about how I've seen him put the ends of them between his teeth, and I think about pressing one to my own lips, and I think, *Stop thinking. Stop thinking, you pushed him away.*

But I'm also thinking about what might have happened if I hadn't.

The pencils straightened, I turn my attention to the papers scattered across Theo's desk, trying to transfer them from drafting table to floor without upsetting too much of the order: notes from his classes, scribbles for his projects.

My fingers slide across an envelope and then stop because I am looking at my own face. My own face in graphite, sketched on the back of this envelope, half in profile as if the artist has just called my name. My expression is inscrutable but penetrating, hard but not brittle. In this picture, under Theo's hands, I look nothing like what I imagine myself looking, but somehow look exactly like myself.

Can I keep it?

This is my first thought, that I want to keep this drawing of me, I want it for my own room. Surely Theo won't notice, as cluttered as his desk was, and if he did notice it might take weeks. There's nothing special about the envelope that the drawing is on. It is one of many identical ones; a small stack of them sits in the middle of Theo's desk. Still, I flip this one over to make sure there's nothing important written on the other side.

In the left corner of the envelope, in the sender field:

AMERICAN EXPEDITIONARY FORCES
OVERSEAS SERVICE
PRIVATE THEODORE GRAYBILL

My brain reads the words over and over again. I grab another envelope. The same return address is in the left-hand corner of every envelope in the pile.

In the right corner of the envelopes, the stamps have been canceled. These letters have been through the postal system. They were sent from where they say they were sent from.

These letters were sent from the front.

Theo sent these letters from North Africa.

But how could that be possible? Theo was never at the front; Theo was never at war. Theo accidentally shot himself in the buttocks on a hunting trip with his father and he never even left the country.

Behind me, the photographer and his assistant are readying their staged version of what they think my life should look like. A golden necklace with a cross that does not belong to me has been artfully draped on the bureau next to a pair of demure white gloves and a jar of cold cream. It looks like a painting, a gauzy advertisement from a women's magazine.

Why would Theo have sent letters from the front?

Theo didn't go to war. Theo was never in North Africa. Why would there be letters postmarked from the front of a war Theo never fought in?

Myself, he had told me on the train while we both laughed. *Myself shot myself.*

I know I hadn't misheard it; that's what he said.

And then something happens that banishes even that mystery from my head.

The last layer on Theo's drafting table is another map, one that must have been here for days, buried under these other papers. It's not one I've seen Theo working on before; it's penciled in with rich greens and blues.

A word is typed in the corner. And the word that is typed in the corner, buried under these piles of papers, is one he must have typed before I ever told him about mysterious telephone calls and dead soldiers, before I ever confided in him about anything.

And the word that is typed in the corner is in all capital letters.

And the word that is typed in the corner is *BRIGHTWOOD*.

23

ANTONIO SAPREZZA

The room was lit, as always, by gas lamps, casting a glow over the switchboard. My chair was positioned, as always, squarely in front. The only difference between tonight and a regular assignment was that I would be alone. After I took over from the soldier on duty, no other personnel would enter. Luc had told me it was important we control all the variables: He posted a DO NOT ENTER sign on the door because he didn't want anyone else to overhear the conversation. We had to be this careful, in order to know where the leak was coming from.

On the table in front of the switchboard lay a single sheet of type-written paper. I scanned the first line. It was the codes, the daily codes, freshly written and there for me to memorize.

"You're the first to see them," Luc said, entering the room to find me already examining the codes. "The first person besides me, of course."

"Besides you? I didn't realize you wrote the codes," I said.

"Who did you think did?"

"I suppose I never really thought about it. How do you do it?"

"Cities, towns, state capitals. The trick is for the codes to be new but easy to remember. 'Springfield' would be a good code name; nearly every state has a Springfield. Or 'Chaplin,' everyone has heard of Charlie Chaplin. Things that are difficult to pronounce, or obscure terms that Americans aren't familiar with—those are bad code names."

His face turned serious, he tapped the paper gently with his forefinger. "Time to memorize. The staged call could come any time during your shift. You won't know which call it is, so it is important that you translate everything perfectly through your entire time on duty."

Quickly, I began to scan the paper in front of me. FRESNO. KEATON. SENECA. SIOUX.

"Are you sure you shouldn't just do it?" I asked him, suddenly feeling scared of this responsibility. "If you wrote the codes anyway, are you sure you shouldn't just be the operator for such an important call?"

"It should be you," he said firmly, encouraging. "You've worked hard for this. But I can sit near you through your shift so that you know you're not alone."

At this, he brought over a chair and set it up near my workstation, scooting it over so he was less than an arm's reach away.

And then we started at the switchboard, waiting, my hands clammy and shaking.

"We really won't know which is the call?" I asked desperately. "It could be any of them? Will there be any clues?"

"Nothing overt," Luc told me. "But perhaps small things. The message might be repeated a few times. That was part of the discussions: If the line truly has been compromised, we want the interloper to have every opportunity to hear the false message, so the information might be repeated multiple times."

"I understand," I said, though I didn't know how helpful this information was—it wasn't uncommon for messages to be repeated multiple times anyway, just because of static or bad connections.

"And remember, Edda Grace, it's important that you translate exactly what is being said."

"I always do."

"I know you do," he said, and I was thinking about how far I had come since our first introduction, when he deposited me, bedraggled, at the door of the hostel and I told him I'd never done any of this before. I knew what I was doing, now. I was good at what I did. "But in this case," he continued, "what's important isn't that the information is wrong, but the way it's wrong. The Germans need to think they are receiving correct information. The only way we can know whether they intercepted it is if they act on the incorrect information. And so you must sell it. You must make them believe that the information isn't incorrect at all."

"Anything else?" I asked.

But there was no time for there to be anything else. In front of me, a bulb had lit up. I reached my hand to the wire, but instead of picking it up immediately I looked one last time at Luc, waiting to see if he had any more instructions.

"Go," he said, and I picked up the line.

"Number, please?" I asked, and my voice was authoritative and strong.

"Bonsoir," the caller said. *"Get me Tennyson. I have important orders about Ipswich. Do you hear? Get me Tennyson. I have important orders about Ipswich."*

"Hold, please."

The dance had begun.

24

LLOYD SARASOTA

"Are we done?" I ask the photographer, from my perch at Theo's desk, the one that I am supposed to be pretending is my own desk as I write fictitious letters to the boys on the front.

"Almost," he says. "Can't you give me a little bit of a smile? The Bell System has happy girls."

My lips try to stretch over my mouth but my teeth are too dry, my mouth is too gummy.

As soon as the shutter clicks on the photographer's camera my pretend smile disappears. "Are we done?" I say again, rising from my chair, and this time it's clear that I'm not asking.

The photographer and his assistant begin to pack up their equipment and I stand paralyzed in the center of the room, a statue they must maneuver around. I am still standing there when they finally leave, thinking about what I'd just discovered on Theo's drafting table.

The blueprint. The letters.

Was Theo part of the Forty-Eighth Regiment? Is that the answer? Did he know what had happened because he survived the attack?

The morning I received the first call, it was at the end of my shift—I got the call and then I immediately ran home, and Theo appeared shortly after.

I remember something about that morning. When Theo came to my door, he was already dressed. But when had Theo ever been awake and dressed that early in the morning? *Never.* I even thought it at the time, that I'd never seen Theo awake so early. And with his coat on—why would he have his coat on just to stop at my door?

He had his coat on the first morning because he'd been outside already. He had it on because he'd just come from using a public telephone to harass me.

And then the morning after I received the second call, I came home and I went to Theo's room and Theo's shoes and clothes were wet. I had to move them. I had to move Theo's wet clothes from the bed so I could sit on it. But Theo said he hadn't been outside all night, not since we got home, and the rain didn't start until much later—it was only beginning to rain when I reached Central.

Theo had already proven he could reach me once: Perseverance, he said. *Three hundred calls.*

What if he'd done it again? Hiding in plain sight, all along? He told me that I cried out while I slept, he told me he could hear me through the walls. What if crying wasn't the only thing I did? What if I talked, too? *What if him trying to kiss me was just a way of trying to torment me?*

What if the story that was unfolding in front of me wasn't the story I'd thought I was reading? What if I'd gotten it wrong all along?

I need to confront him and it needs to be in public. I am not going to face off against Theo in this garret of a bedroom, no exits, slanted ceilings. I am not going to be trapped again.

Just as I've decided to run, Theo opens the door.

. . .

"Edda!" he says.

Our last interaction, at the pension bureau, had ended so awkwardly—I'd told him I didn't want to talk about Luc and then hurried off, inventing an errand before he could follow me. Now he sounds pleased to see me, pleased and surprised, until he notices the expression on my face, notices the way I am planted in the middle of the room as if I'm standing on a rocking ship and doing everything I can to keep my balance.

"Is it you?" I demand, keeping my eye on the door behind him, still ajar as he hasn't yet had the chance to close it. "Were you the one who telephoned?"

"The one who telephoned?" he repeats stupidly. Or is he actually being stupid? Is it a tremendously brilliant show of ignorance?

He takes a step forward. Or could it be he truly doesn't realize I've found him out?

"You know what I'm talking about."

He takes another step forward. "Edda, I swear I don't have—"

The blueprints are still in my hand, and I shake them in his face. "Brightwood!" I spit out. "Brightwood, on your map here. Why would you have that word on your desk if it wasn't you?" I jab at the map wildly. "And I know you were in the army. I know you were in France."

Now, at least there is an expression on his face beyond confusion. There's a crumbling, there's a panic, there's something else I can't identify. His eyes are wild as he takes yet a third step forward.

"Don't come any closer," I warn him. I could still make my way around him to the door, but only just barely, not if he comes any closer. My eyes scan the room looking for something I could use to defend myself, and I end up grabbing the only thing approximating a weapon within reach, the tiny knife that Theo uses to sharpen his charcoal pencils. It wouldn't cause a mortal wound, but it would scratch him, at least. I think. "Not a step," I emphasize. "Stay where you are."

He stops, still several feet away from me but now blocking the door. I couldn't get around him if I tried to escape. *But I could scream.* We can't be alone in the house right now; the cook should be preparing lunch downstairs.

He is making calming gestures, calming like I am a wild animal and he is a trainer, hands flattening the air.

"Edda—"

"*Don't.*"

"Edda, can I see?" He gestures toward the map. "I won't take a step closer, but can I see? Put it on the floor or something and slide it over."

"I will scream," I tell him. "If you move suddenly, or reach out to me, or—"

"I believe you," he says quickly. "I'm going to kneel to the floor now. I'm not going to put my hands anywhere but on the ground."

I use the toe of my shoe to shove the blueprint toward Theo, who crouches down to examine it while I clutch the knife.

After fifteen seconds he hasn't moved or spoken. I don't understand how he would need to examine the map for so long. Is he just buying time? Is he plotting something, waiting for me to let down my guard? Just as I've nearly decided to scream, Theo makes a subtle motion.

"Edda," he says, "I think I know what this means."

"It means you've been lying to me."

He looks up at me, raising both hands so I can see his empty palms, pleading. "I'm—just go and get the other map that I showed you a few days ago—the one of Iowa Circle."

The paper in question is still on Theo's bed where I'd piled the other papers earlier, right on top. I grab it quickly, trying to do so without turning my back to Theo.

"Now look in the corner," he instructs me.

I do what he says and immediately become disoriented. I know the map is of Iowa Circle, but the upper right corner says "Jamaica."

"The assignment," Theo continues to explain. "We're supposed to redesign one of Washington's circles? I pulled several old blueprints to help me. My professor had redesigned Iowa Circle himself, so I thought looking at his work might help me. That's when I learned that the neighborhood used to be called Jamaica."

The paper quivers in my hand. I look back and forth between the blueprint and Theo's face. "What are you saying?"

"I'm saying that maybe when this other blueprint was created, the neighborhood was called 'Brightwood.' But I never noticed it before, I swear, I never needed to look that closely."

Could it really be such a basic answer? *Brightwood.* It's not as though the name is completely unique. There are probably neighborhoods or streets called Brightwood all over the United States. *But the damp clothes. The envelopes. Private Theodore Graybill, Overseas Service.*

"Edda, if I was responsible for calling you and saying that word, why would I have typed it on that blueprint?" he continues from his position kneeling on the floor.

"Because you didn't want to forget it—you wanted to make sure you remembered it, to torment me with."

"But *typed* it? On a borrowed blueprint that I'll have to return? And then left it on my desk? Wouldn't I have just made a secret note and stuffed it in a pocket in my closet or something?"

"The letters." These, I grab now, fanning them out like a deck of cards, watching them flutter to the floor. "Why *the hell* do you have letters with yourself as the return address stationed in Northern Africa if you never went to war?"

"Because I—" he scrambles, looking for an excuse.

"Why would these letters be on your desk?"

"Because—"

"Why, Theo?"

"Because I went to war," he explodes.

My heart skips a beat, and then lands with a dull thud in my chest. And then there is quiet between us, quiet and the heavy weight of the truth.

"I went to North Africa," he says again. "And my family thinks I am still there."

Whatever I expected him to say, it wasn't that. I can barely make sense of what he's saying. "You said you shot yourself in a hunting accident," I sputter.

"It *happened* there," he explains. "I was already there. And, not hunting. A different kind of incident. And I didn't—I couldn't tell my family that I was being sent home. Not after I was supposed to be the first war hero of the family. So I asked a friend who worked for the Red Cross postal service: If I gave him empty envelopes with the address in my handwriting, could he mail them back to me postmarked from France?"

"And then you . . ." I trail off, trying to piece it together.

"And then I take them to my parents' house. Every couple of days. Or nights. I go in the middle of the night so they don't see me dropping the letters in their mailbox."

The wet shoes. The coat and outerwear at six o'clock in the morning. All because, as Theo would have me believe, he was stealing away to drop letters in a mailbox located blocks away because his parents think he is thousands of miles away.

"Theo, I don't understand."

"They live in Foggy Bottom. It takes me twenty or thirty minutes to walk there. The mail is usually delivered first thing in the morning, before either of my parents leave the house for the day, so as long as I take my letter in the middle of the night, it looks as though it's just arrived with that day's mail. Nobody in my parents' neighborhood works a night shift so nobody sees me."

He's saying all of this like it makes sense, like it's an explanation. But it's not an explanation, not really, because what he's describing isn't something a sane person would do.

"It's not the *mechanics* of your letter delivery that I don't understand, Theo. It's—any of it. You don't think your parents would be overjoyed that you're home?"

"That's not the point."

"You don't think that the point is that you are here in

Washington, blocks from your family, but you are letting them think you're still across an ocean?"

"That's also not the point."

A shortness has entered his voice. He won't meet my eyes.

"Then what is—"

"Can we just leave it, Edda?"

"No, because—"

"I didn't have an accident in Maryland, I had one overseas," he says testily. "I wasn't ready to explain it to my parents, so I let them believe something else. None of this is difficult to understand."

I've never heard his tone of voice like this before. In all the time I have spoken with Theo—every time he's been jocular, or dry, or self-deprecating, or sincere—he's never, ever had this kind of sharpness. It's becoming caustic and accusatory, and I don't understand how or why it's happening this way. *He* was the one lying to *me*, and now he's angry with me for pointing it out.

"Actually it *is* difficult to understand," I retort. "Because you told me quite cheerfully that you shot yourself in your own rear end and I find it hard to imagine there could be another accident that was more embarrassing than that—one that would actually prevent you from going home."

"I didn't say it was embarrassing, I said it was—"

"Different. Fine. It was a different kind of accident. That still doesn't make any sense."

He folds his arms across his chest. He's risen from his kneeling position; we're squaring off against each other in his small garret room. "I could be saying the same thing to you," he says.

"You could—what?"

"What happened at the pension bureau?" Theo throws these words like a dart and now taps his foot, elaborately, waiting for me to answer. "Hmm? What happened?"

My head reels from the abrupt subject change, and from the whiplash of this conversation, and from the way I don't want to answer Theo's question, the way it makes my throat close tight and makes me feel like a cornered animal.

"We were about to kiss," Theo continues. "*You* were about to kiss *me*. And then you ran away, out of the blue."

"And your ego couldn't handle that."

"Oh for God's sake, Edda, it wasn't about my ego."

"Then why are you bringing it up again? Why are you—"

"*Who is Luc?*"

He says this sentence with accusation in his eyes. Woundedness, fury, and it lands like a punch. I suck in a breath but suddenly there is not enough air in the room to suck in.

"When you cry out at night," Theo continues. "You say his name. And don't tell me that I'm mishearing, because I know what I've heard."

There's no use in denying what Theo knows he has heard, but I still can't believe he is asking me this, after I tried to put him off last time. After I've told him multiple times that I didn't want to talk about Luc.

"You—you have no right to ask me about that. No right to ask me about him."

"He wasn't one of the members of the Forty-Eighth. I've been through the list; there's nobody whose name is Luc, or who would even have Luc as a nickname. But there's something—"

"You've *been through the list*?" It's one thing for Theo to look at the names with me, plotting which families to visit next. It's another to think of him looking on his own, trying to investigate my past. "Do you have any idea how invasive that sounds?"

"Is it more invasive than inviting yourself to use my room for your photographs?" he spits back. "More invasive than pawing through my personal letters? I'm just saying, if you're in love with someone else, then—"

"My private life is none of your business."

"How is it none of my business when it's coming through my walls?!" He points at the wall we share, at my bedroom next door. "I think you owe it to me to—"

"*Owe* it to you?" I repeat.

"Yes," he says. Incredibly, he doesn't see what effect his words have had. "You don't think that after all I've tried to do for you, you don't—"

"I don't think we owe each other anything," I cut him off.

"I've put in hours of work this week to fix—"

"I am not something that needs to be fixed."

"Oh, you're fine, then?" he spits. "Your room, and your nightmares, and your clutter, and your secrets—all of it is fine?"

"I'm not saying I'm fine, just that you can't fix me."

He spits out a breath. "You can say that again."

The words hit me like a cruel punch.

Something in me has gone numb. Something in me has gone dead. And Theo can see it, can see that something in me has changed, that a light has gone off, that something in me has pulled away. And when he sees this, something inside him moves, too.

"Edda," he tries, extending a hand to reach out to me, but it's too late.

"Don't."

He tries again. His hand almost succeeds this time; it brushes my wrist. I leap back. I know my reaction is outsize. I don't care. I'm tired. I'm tired of holding it together.

"Edda," he says one more time, and this time the note in his voice is not an apology but something that sounds like fear. "Edda, you believe me, right? You know I didn't make that call."

And I don't know how to answer that, because now I *don't* think he made the call. But just a few minutes ago I was certain that he *had* been the one to torment me. And just a few minutes before that I was fantasizing about him touching me again, and just a day before that I'd pushed him away because he grabbed my hand.

All that I am learning is that I cannot trust myself when I feel certain of anything.

I was so sure. I don't know how to be sure. I don't know how to be with Theo. I don't know how to be.

"It doesn't matter," I mutter, moving quickly for the door. "It doesn't matter what I believe. It doesn't matter what you're hiding. Neither one of us needs to fix the other. Maybe we are too broken."

25

MICKEY SHEA

Sleep. This is my first thought. I want to sleep. I want to sleep like I used to, for hours on end, burrowed under quilts, sunken into the mattress, not because I'm seeking rejuvenation but because I'm seeking an escape from the rest of the world. I want to fall asleep and go to a place where Theo and I did not just have that fight. Where I did not just find a pile of letters on his drafting table.

I want to sleep so that maybe by the time I wake up, my body and heart and soul will have mended themselves without me even having had to do the work.

But I cannot sleep. Because it's Friday now; it's four days since the first telephone call arrived, and the caller said time was running out.

Running out until what? I still don't know what happens when my time is up. Does someone expose me? Does someone punish me?

I cannot sleep. I have to keep moving forward. I need to go somewhere, to do something.

Out of bed, I riffle through my handbag until I come up with my notes from the pension bureau, scanning over them, looking for something to quiet my brain.

Mr. Philip Arnold DuBois. Mr. Philip Arnold Shea.

I'd made that note before anything happened with Theo. The man who might have been a bigamist, who might have had two sons perish as part of the Forty-Eighth.

It had seemed, at the time, like a shocking coincidence. But now I can't tell if it means anything at all or if I'm just so desperate for meaning that I'm inventing it where there is none. I don't know if visiting Mr. DuBois/Shea makes sense anymore.

But what other choices do I have?

I'm not able to sleep, and the idea of doing nothing seems worse than the idea of *something*, no matter how far-fetched that something is.

I need peace, and I need an ending, and I need to make amends and have amends made to me. And I need to bring my soul back from France. I cannot keep living divided this way, I cannot keep feeling as though I am still in that switchboard room, still in that switchboard room with Luc.

· · ·

By the time the train reaches Baltimore it's late afternoon. Nearly twilight. Not so dark that the streetlamps have come on yet, but dark enough that I know I'll eventually wish for a lantern. The street I'm walking on hasn't been paved yet, it's cobblestone, and walking on it gives me a sense of déjà vu, as if I have been here before, seen this before, done this before.

France. It is like my first night in France, the click-clack of our steps on the cobblestones, the unlit streetlights, dark to protect the city from German bombs.

What if I had never gone down those streets? What if I had never boarded the ship that brought me to France? What if instead of coming in 201st in the telephone operator exam I had come in 202nd? Or 213th? What if I had believed my father when he told me women did not have the correct disposition for war, we were too tender, we were needed at home. What if I had never taken the exam at all?

Luc. Luc. Luc.

His name echoes in my heart every time my feet strike the cobblestones.

As I walk I realize that this street seems familiar not only because it reminds me of France but because I have been on it before, just a few days ago, with Theo.

Theo. Theo. Theo.

I'm just a few neighborhoods away from the Dannenbergs' residence. I still owe them the money we promised them for their son's headstone. I could walk there in fifteen minutes. I have the head-stone money in an envelope in my bag. I've been carrying it for three days now, ever since I went to the bank, meaning to bring it to the Dannenberg family. It's nearly five o'clock. Not quite dinner, but an hour in which Mrs. Dannenberg would likely have begun preparing for the evening meal. A good time to find her at home.

I shouldn't put her off, I admonish myself. The only thing the poor woman wants is a headstone, a place where she can remember her son. She should have that as soon as possible.

Darker than twilight by the time I reach the Dannenbergs' row house. I can make out the white house number, a little, but other-wise the dark makes the whole street unfamiliar. The tidy care of the neighborhood is invisible in the dark. The houses rise up on either side of the narrow street, each set of windows a pair of eyes.

The Dannenbergs aren't home. I knock twice. Still nobody comes to the door. I stand at the stoop, gravestone money in my hand, wondering what to do next. Leaving a sizable number of bills in the mailbox seems ill-advised, but I don't want to have to make a third trip to this house. I want it to be done. I want one thing to be done; I want one name to cross off my list.

"Mrs. Dannenberg is volunteering at the church bazaar."

I startle at the sound of a voice, and then squint into darkness to make out a neighbor leaning out her front door, drying her hands on a dish towel and smiling ruefully in apology. "Sorry. The walls are thin enough that you knock on one door, you're knocking on the whole block. Ruth Ann will be gone all evening," she apologizes. "But Charles should be back soon. He's usually home now but he got called out to repair some broken lines."

"Thank you," I say gratefully. "I have an envelope for them—would you mind if I left it with you?"

She extends a now-dried hand and I deposit the envelope into it, thinking that maybe this is for the best, to not have to see the Dannenbergs again, Mrs. Dannenberg's grief or her husband's anger, happy to be away from this house.

The neighbor turns back into her house and I'm nearly to the gate before stopping in my tracks.

"Lines?" I call back to her. "What did you mean, Mr. Dannenberg is repairing broken lines?"

"His job. He installs telephone lines for Bell. But today is usually his day off—as I said, he just got called out at the last minute. It's a local job, just a few blocks away."

"Mr. Dannenberg works for the telephone company?"

There is a whooshing in my ears. It must be the sound of my blood pulsing but it sounds like an airplane overhead, something I can't shake or run away from.

"They're having him work the oddest hours," the neighbor continues. "Out one day at eight o'clock in the evening; another day at three o'clock in the morning. Mrs. Dannenberg thinks he's having an affair."

"She does?" I whisper weakly, trying to hold myself together.

Three o'clock in the morning. Would leaving at three o'clock in the morning provide enough time to get to a public telephone and call me by shortly before five? "Why does she think that?"

"She found a train stub in his pocket. He told her it was for work, he was going to Washington for work, but the telephone company has its own truck, don't they? When is the last time you heard of a line repairman having to take the train?"

"Never," I manage. "I've never heard of something like that."

"Are you all right?" The gossipy neighbor cocks her head with genuine concern. "Would you like to come in for a glass of water?"

"No, no." I stumble backward toward the gate, and then think better of it. "You said that Mr. Dannenberg's work assignment was just few blocks away? Perhaps I'll take the envelope to him myself and have a chance to pay my respects. Do you know exactly where he is?"

"Suit yourself." She returns the envelope. "You shouldn't have any trouble finding him. He told me the downed line was in the train yard. Just follow the tracks."

I am doing something reckless, desperately reckless, and I know it and I'm going to do it anyway.

I don't have a telephone, Mr. Dannenberg had said the last time I was here, when Theo and I said we should have called first.

He'd implied that he didn't want anything to do with them. It sounded as though he barely understood how they worked. That's partly why Theo and I had ruled out the Dannenberg family.

But meanwhile he works for Bell, the same company that I do?

It could be a coincidence—it could be a wild coincidence just like the word *Brightwood* was a coincidence on Theo's blueprints. But the mysterious train ticket to Washington—would that be a coincidence, too? The late-night disappearances, which he claimed were part of his job, but which Mrs. Dannenberg found suspicious enough that she'd brought up her concerns with a neighbor?

I'm walking, faster and faster toward the train yard, where off-duty engines loom over rusty railroad ties. The chill is gone from my neck and replaced by something hotter and more desperate.

When Mr. Dannenberg came out of the house and saw Theo and me, the first thing he said was *What are you doing here?* It hadn't struck me as odd at the time, but if he didn't know who I was, then wouldn't he have said something more like *Who are you?*

I'm already more than halfway to my destination and now I can see where I'm headed: an empty lot, a telephone pole, a loose wire. Train cars scattered over hardscrabble ground. A man in work boots, up a ladder, completing the repair. As of yet he's just an outline, a silhouette against the moonlight. He begins to descend the ladder.

I pause. I hesitate. Do I have to do this now? Wouldn't it be smarter to wait until the morning, when it is bright outside, when it is public? When I could go to the Dannenbergs' row house where the walls are so thin that the neighbors can hear through them and would hear anything that went wrong? I wish Theo were with me, but it's too late for that.

And I don't actually wish he were here with me, not really. This has always been something I needed to do on my own.

The question isn't whether I should be doing this. The question is whether I can live with this being an unsolved mystery. Can I live with going to work every day and wondering whether this is a day when I'll connect a call, and that voice will be on the other end of the line? Can I live with going to bed and wondering what I'll dream, what I'll call out, what I'll scream? Can I live with so much unfinished business? For the rest of my life can I live in that kind of dread?

And then, in the distance, the figure in silhouette has descended the ladder and is packing up his toolbox. He's loading it into a truck, and he's about to get in the truck himself and drive off to I don't know where. The light in the sky is gone.

But I have to keep moving forward. Because I want this to end.

26

TIMOTHY SPECK

The dance had begun.

"I'll connect you right away," I said as Luc hovered expectantly over my shoulder.

"Very good. Central Dispatch?" a British voice asked.

"Yes, I'm here," I said.

"We have some important work to do."

"Right away."

I was mindful of what Luc had told me: that I needed to translate the conversation word for word, that ferreting out the leak was going to depend on exact translations and then on figuring out where the information from those translations reappeared. I knew we were all working off a script, and I knew it had never mattered more that my work was precise.

I closed my eyes and could feel my forehead knot.

But after a few seconds the translation became second nature to me.

Just as I'd been working so hard to do since arriving here, it only took a few seconds until I was immersed, completely, in the world of the telephone call. I connected the two lines and the caller immediately began making plans for the rendezvous of two regiments, a clandestine operation to outskirt the German units near the north of France. The details were so real: times, contingencies, strategies, and backup plans. If I didn't know the information had been planted, I never would have guessed that I wasn't translating a real conversation.

"At eighteen-hundred hours," I repeated clearly. "Oui, dix-huit."

Luc hovered nearby, as close as he could be without sitting in my lap. Occasionally he would seize the pencil and scrawl a word, underlining it, making sure I said it as I was supposed to.

All the while I was listening for clicks, listening to the sound we'd been told would signify a compromised line. Would I hear it? Was someone already listening in? Or were all of us engaged in this pantomime for nothing? Every time the line cut out I wondered if there was a German spy listening on the other end, and then I tried to make sure that my wondering didn't make me freeze, or think too hard about what I was saying instead of letting the words roll off my tongue.

Luc gestured for me to watch him, and once I did his eyes seemed *like a life raft; he nodded along with every word that came out of my mouth.*

Finally we reached the end of the conversation. I had no idea how long I'd been on the telephone; it seemed the longest conversation of my life.

I was euphoric. I was giddy with my own sense of accomplishment and possibility. Sweat poured from my brow and under my arms, but I was elated by what I had just done.

"Magnificent," Luc said, as I ripped my headset off and set it on the table. He took my hands in his and they were still shaking, residual shaking from the call I had just completed. "Magnificent."

I took my hands from his and pressed them to my cheeks, which were hot and damp. "Was that the call? Do you think that was the call?"

"I think that was the call."

"And I did all right? I translated everything as I was supposed to?"

"You didn't miss a word. Between this and your performance with the Metz incident, I wouldn't be surprised if you get a presidential commendation."

"It was all right?" I asked again. I still couldn't wrap my mind around the idea that it was over, it was over and I'd done it.

"Let's celebrate," Luc said.

From his satchel he produced a frosted glass bottle and two small glasses and began to pour. It smelled of peppermint and medicine, like aftershave or Christmas.

"You were so certain this would be a success?" I chided him. "Wait, is that liquor?"

"It's peppermint schnapps; I got it because it is the least alcohol-like alcohol. It tastes like candy."

"It won't to me." I laughed.

"Edda Grace," Luc said, pretending to pout. "I told you that one day you should celebrate like a grown woman, with an adult drink. If not now, when?"

"Oh, fine," I acquiesced. "I'll try it."

I took the glass and darted my tongue into it. He was right, it didn't burn as much as I thought it would, and the flavor was sharp and pleasant. He raised his own glass to mine and we clinked them together.

"It's not so bad, is it?" he asked. "Better than what made you sick last time?"

"It's not bad," I admitted. "But the taste reminds me a little of toothpaste." I took another sip, this one less tentative, and Luc raised his own glass.

"I promise it is not toothpaste," he said. And then, as if remembering something, he said: "What was the first dance?"

I cocked my head in confusion as he continued. "Before, you told me your mother had already planned the music for your graduation party. What was the first dance that she wanted?"

"Oh," I laughed. "The grizzly bear. She thought it would set a lively tone."

Luc set down his glass on the table with a smart little bang and then held out his hand. "Let's do it now. Celebrate your graduation."

"That's ridiculous," I said, but I was already standing and taking his hand; it sounded fun.

There was no music so we hummed, both of us, mostly tunelessly. It was odd to be alone in a room that was normally crackling with activity, but it was celebratory, too, I was enjoying myself.

When we reached the end of our sloppy, extemporaneous dance I started to perform a ridiculous curtsy that felt appropriate to the pantomime we'd been doing, but Luc held out his hand again. "Another?"

We danced again. We danced again, silly and staggering, and when we finished a second time Luc again reached out his hand. "One more!"

I was starting to feel tired—it was very late and this wasn't my usual shift—but I gamely put up my arms again like bear claws for a third round.

This time, instead of putting up his own hands, though, he reached for my wrists.

"That's not how this dance goes," I started to say, but Luc overlapped. "This is a different dance."

"What kind of—"

"You'll see."

Something fluttered unfamiliarly in my stomach, a little something, the kind of something that could have been something, or that could have simply been peppermint schnapps. Luc pulled me closer to him and I was still laughing, because this all still seemed like a joke, because what else could it be?

"I'm not sure we should be doing this right now," I started. "If someone walks in, they might think—"

"What might they think?" Luc interjected smoothly, beginning to hum again. "They might think that we were celebrating, deservedly? Don't you think I know what is allowed?"

He was right, of course he was, so I kept dancing as long as he kept humming.

"Have you thought more about your future?" he asked me as we swayed. "What you want to do next?"

"I think what I want to do next is go to bed."

"You don't want to celebrate more, for all the hard work we've done? You don't want to thank me for how hard I worked with you to make you ready?"

Confusion washed over me, and guilt, because he was right again. It's what I had thought a dozen times myself, that I was lucky he was championing my work and my learning, that without Luc I could not have succeeded here. I might have just been sent home.

But I wanted to stop dancing. At the moment my desires and my wishes and my plans truly were not any bigger than that: In that moment, my body was tired and it wanted to stop dancing.

"I want to thank you properly tomorrow," I started. "I want to take a minute and—and write a letter, and—"

But then he didn't let go.

I tried to shrug off his hands, but he didn't let go. They were tight on my wrists, and that's when something started to feel odd in my stomach. More than a flutter. A warning.

"You have done this dance before, yes?" Luc said.

"I can't move my wrists," I protested. "Luc—ouch. You're cutting off my circula—"

But he still didn't let go.

"You have done this dance before," he said again, but now it wasn't a question. "All American girls have."

He was still talking to me in a pleasant tone of voice, but my hands were pinned down by my sides. I was using half my strength to try to move them, but I wasn't using my full strength yet because—because I didn't know why. Because if I wasn't able to loose my hands using every bit of my strength, I didn't want to think about what that would mean for the position I was in.

Luc's body was pressed close to mine. I could feel a hardness down by my stomach, his belt buckle. When he leaned in, his breath hot on my ear, it smelled like peppermint schnapps and I realized that schnapps didn't smell or taste anything like toothpaste, not at all.

"Please, could you let go of my hands?"

And then I could feel a different kind of hardness, below his belt buckle, digging into my hip. I twisted my body to get away from that hardness, which I'd never felt before with a man, which made my face burn with humiliation.

"I haven't done—Luc, we should go," I said, and now my voice was

panicky, now it was the beginning of a beg. But I still thought that I could explain things to him. I still thought that I was at fault, I hadn't been clear enough, that he must not realize he was pressing into my hip bone.

"Go where?" he said. "Are you not having a good time?"

The door was closed, but it wasn't locked. My eyes darted to it. If I could just get across the room to—

"Don't worry," he said. "Nobody is coming in through that door."

Suddenly his knee was between my legs, I was being forced back against the table in the middle of the room, covered in maps and war secrets. My back hit it hard, the sharp corner digging into my spine, causing a shower of stars in my vision.

I cried out in pain, an involuntary guttural sound.

And Luc said nothing. I'd cried out in pain and he said nothing. But one of his hands loosed my wrist, and his hand was snaking down, snaking to my skirt. Trying to lift it, to pull it over my hips, and my face was pressed into his neck, the smoothness of it, but up close it wasn't completely smooth, there was sandpaper stubble.

And that is when I finally realized: He knew. He knew he was pressing against me, he knew I was hurt, he knew I didn't want to. He was going to do it anyway.

This wasn't a dance.

"Help!" I cried, but my voice was immediately swallowed by Luc's shoulder, my mouth full of cotton, gagging.

"Shhhhh," he said, as if he were soothing me. "We don't want any-one to hear us."

"Help," I tried again, throwing my head away from his uniform.

With my loose hand, I tried to push him off me and then, when I realized I couldn't, to claw at his face, and—

But he still thought we were having fun. Or he thought I was protesting because I thought I had to. I don't know what he thought. He caught my hand in his and tucked it underneath my own body, between my body and the table, and then he was unbuttoning my undergarments.

"Please don't."

My thighs were aching. My thighs were aching from where I was trying to keep them together while he methodically worked them apart with his hand and a knee.

"Just lie back," he told me, as his fingers found the place on my body that had never been explored by anyone but me, and as I wanted that place on my body to die. "Do you see? This could be nice for both of us."

I was crying by then. I think I was. Maybe I was crying only in my head. Everything was moving too fast and everything was going so slowly that I lived a whole lifetime in that moment. I know that I had stopped calling for help by then. I know that once his hands were on me where they were on me, I couldn't bring myself to call for help again. Because I shouldn't have put myself in this position, I should have known better, all along.

He was breathing heavily by then. Reaching for his own belt. As he undid it, I heard the metal scraping on leather.

As long as I live I will never forget the sound of that leather.

My thighs were aching, held open, holding Luc, and I just wanted it to be over, to end, to stop, to go back, to never have happened.

And then, a flashing bulb. I saw it, we both did.

A telephone call. The light burned white, a call begging to be answered, signifying a soldier asking for help. A call that must be answered.

All at once Luc let go of me. He let go of me as if we had only been play-wrestling. He made a chivalrous gesture toward the switchboard—and with an inhuman scream, the first sound I'd been able to make, I dove toward the switchboard and seized my headset. My entire body was gelatin, I was weeping in relief at this lifesaving miracle of a telephone call.

"Hello?"

It wasn't what I was supposed to say. I could barely remember what I was supposed to say, I was so glad to be talking to anyone at all. If Luc neared me again, I would do something. I would stab him with a pen, or something; surely there would be something I could stab him with.

"Hello?" I babbled again. I could hear my voice, how unprofessional it sounded. Because in that moment I did not feel like an operator, I felt like an eighteen-year-old girl.

A pause on the other end of the line. Barely a pause, but a pause nonetheless as the caller intuited that something wasn't right. I should have answered with Number, please, *and I didn't, so something must have been wrong.*

But they continued on because they had no choice, because I was the person who had answered the switchboard when they picked up the telephone.

"Brightwood," they barked. "Connect me to Brightwood. It's an emergency."

"Brightwood?" I repeated.

"Brightwood, do you hear me? My god, do you hear me? I need to tell the Forty-Eighth to fall back, immediately, or men are going to die."

"Brightwood," I said again.

The words were sluggish on my thick tongue and dull ears. I couldn't make sense of them. I couldn't make sense of anything. I was shivering even though I knew it wasn't cold.

"Brightwood," they shouted again.

Was Luc even still in the room?

The door opened and in walked Mae. I didn't know why. Had she forgotten something? Had she heard me call for help? I didn't care why, because as soon as she stepped in the room she knew something was wrong. I could see her take in my mussed hair, my white mouth. I could see her eyes move to my throat, and only then did I realize that a button was missing.

Mae took all of this in with her eyes in one second, and in the next second she realized I was on the line with a caller.

She walked over and firmly, decisively, removed my headset from my head.

"Number, please?" she said crisply, in exactly the voice we had been taught to use, in exactly the way we had been taught to use it.

And while she was saying that, I opened my mouth to say that I was sorry but all that came out were sobs.

Luc had left. I didn't know where he had gone, only that he had left, and I was in a place I didn't want to be.

War was no place for women.

Mae finished the call and then looked at me.

"He told me that he had a little sister, too," she said. "But he told me her name was Mae."

27

BUDDY STEIN

Mr. Dannenberg has recognized me. He has seen me coming; he takes his cap off his head, wipes the sweat from his brow, and then waits for me to cross the train yard, picking my way over the railroad ties.

Charles Dannenberg is a big man. He hadn't seemed that way to me when we first met, but when we met I didn't have a reason to take note of his size. But he's a big man, barrel-chested. Big hands, too, which now hold a rusted-looking wrench.

The wrench makes me stop, stare at it, wonder how heavy it is. Mr. Dannenberg follows the train of my eyes, sees me looking at the tool in his hand. But he doesn't put it down.

"Is that the blood money?" He's looking at something in my

own hand, the envelope, which I'd never bothered to place back in my bag since taking it back from the neighbor woman.

"It's the money for the gravestone."

He measures me for what feels like a long time. "I told you we don't want that. Don't want it and don't need it. You should go on home now."

It's delivered in a flat tone and I don't know how I could hear it as anything other than a warning. *I should go on home now.*

But I don't. I stand in the train yard, the ghostly, empty train yard, because it's now or never; I don't know that I'll get the chance to face this again.

"Mr. Dannenberg, do you know who I am?" I find my voice, sounding more confident than I feel.

He winces. "I'm not a damn fool. I've met you before."

"That's not what I mean. I mean—the last time I came to see you a few days ago, you were upset that I'd come. You told me I shouldn't have come. And I'm just wondering—do you know who I am?"

Mr. Dannenberg looks over to the truck, half-packed with the driver's door open. He seems to be pondering whether to answer me, or whether to just get in the truck and drive away.

"Please," I say.

"Do I know who you are?" he repeats, his face twisting. "You told my wife that you were a friend of my son's."

"I did tell her that."

"And she might have believed it."

"You didn't?"

"My wife didn't pay attention the way that I did. Children are cruel. They make fun, and keep tiny circles, and dream up little ways to keep the people out they want to keep out, especially when they have money and you don't. Even if your son is twice as smart and three times as hardworking.

"I'm not a damn fool," he says again, but this time there is less sarcasm in his voice than there was the first time he said it. Instead there's something darker. "I know you didn't come because you were a friend of my son's."

"You're right," I acknowledge because there's no point in pretending now. "You're right, I wasn't a friend of Charley's."

"You came for your own guilt. What you'd done. Why he's dead."

What you'd done.

"What I'd done?" I ask him. "What did I do?"

Say it, just say it, I will him. *Say what I caused to happen on that awful night.*

But Mr. Dannenberg doesn't say it. He trails off. He won't finish the sentence. His mouth opens and closes a few times and I think he's going to, I think he's going to say it, but then the moment passes, the spell breaks. He looks back to the truck and reaches into his pocket where I hear a jingle. The ignition key. He's going to leave if I don't do something to prevent it.

"Mr. Dannenberg, have you been contacting me?" I say suddenly.

The jingling sound in his pocket stops. "Contacting you?"

"I know you work at the telephone company. Your neighbor said you left sometimes in the middle of the night. Have you been leaving in the middle of the night to contact me?"

"My neighbor—Mrs. Lindy? She's a foolish woman. Nothing better to do than spy out her own window."

"She said you go to Washington," I press on. "In the middle of the night."

"What business is it of hers where I go?" he says angrily. "What business is it of yours?"

"So you don't deny it?" I press on. "You don't deny that you go to Washington in the middle of the night? Mr. Dannenberg, I think we both know that there are things in this conversation that we are not saying."

"I know that you showed up offering money we didn't ask for to pay for a son we can't get back."

"Can you just tell me why you go to Washington?" I say, half ordering and half pleading.

"Can you tell me why it's any of your business? Where did *you* go the last time you took a train? Where did *you*—"

"*Brightwood.*" The word explodes from my mouth; I issue it like a challenge.

"Where did *you*—"

"Brightwood," I say again, louder, and by the time I say it a third time I'm half-crazed, saying the name like I'm trying to erase it, deflate it, take away the hold it has over me. Mr. Dannenberg and I are overlapping each other, our voices rising there in the bones of the railway yard. "Brightwoo—"

"I go to visit his grave, all right?" The words rip from Mr. Dannenberg's barrel chest and come out as a roar. His eyes flash, defiant. "I go to Arlington and I sleep next to his gravestone, on nights when I cannot sleep. My son—he was claustrophobic. Hated small spaces. He never even wanted to play hide-and-seek as a child. And when I think about the trenches, the fact that he died in those trenches, knowing he was about to—knowing he couldn't—" He stops and furtively wipes away a tear with the back of his hand. "I go to his gravestone, all right? I go to his gravestone and I talk to him, and I tell him that I will make sure everybody knows the truth about what happened to him and why he died. That I will make sure the people at fault tell the truth, too."

The truth. Tell the truth.

I've caught him out. I've caught him out with this slip of the tongue, this phrase from the first telephone call.

He knows it. He knows that I know it, from the way that our eyes meet in that dark train yard.

"It's important to you," I say finally. "That people know the truth about your son. And how he died."

He juts his chin out. "*I* had to learn it. I had to investigate it. Letters. Telegrams. When you are a parent you want to know about every moment of your child's life, including the moment it ends. You want to know the truth. Can you imagine—" His voice cracks on this word, *imagine*. "Can you imagine what it's like trying to learn about the last breath your child ever took?"

"I can't," I tell him. "I can't. What did you learn? What is the truth?"

The pain emanating from this man—I want to apologize for ever turning up at this man's door, for ever coming to find him here and demanding he tell me about his schedule, for ever existing.

"The truth," he scoffs. "The truth is that boys like him are expendable. They fought in trenches but the decisions about their lives were made over the telephone by people who got to keep their hands clean. That boys like my son never belonged in France, and died there because of people like you. Because you were cruel and careless. My son paid with his life, and the people who drove him to enlist, and the people who should have looked after him once he got there—they didn't pay at all."

His eyes are defiant. He is not going to apologize for wanting this kind of retribution for his son. Even when he knows it is not dignified, not patriotic. But behind the defiance is a deep, primal woundedness. Not the open brokenheartedness I'd seen from his wife, but something darker and more secret, something I doubt he allows many people to see.

And I recognize that. I recognize pain stuffed down. I recognized buried hurt, untended grief. I know that pain intimately.

"Would it help—"

"Nothing would help," he interrupts.

I try again. "Would it help," I ask him and my throat catches with the emotion I usually manage to stuff down. "Would it help if you knew that I never stopped thinking about your son? Wishing every day I could go back in time to that day and do everything differently? Would knowing that I—would it help at all?"

My lips continue to move and I know where this apology is coming from. It's what I want to say to the families of all the boys of the Forty-Eighth, but it's also the apology I wish was given to me. It's the things I wish Luc had said. It's entirely insufficient, but all words are. Words are not equipped to be apologies but they are the only building blocks we have for them.

Mr. Dannenberg takes a step toward me. It's hard to see his exact motions in the dark. I think I can make out something in his hand. The wrench he was holding when I first arrived? Is he still holding the wrench in his tightened fist? He takes another step forward and my muscles harden and tense, ready to run if I have to. *This time I'll be able to run*, I tell myself, because I am always back in the switchboard room in France, the room it feels like I never left.

Luc telling me he had chosen me to come to Souilly, Luc congratulating me on becoming a Hello Girl. Luc escorting me to the Hotel Piedmont. The deeply, deeply unfinished business of Luc.

But I'm not running, I'm still not running. My eyes are squeezing tight, waiting for a blow, waiting for a grab. *Again, again, why am I not running?*

A second passes and nothing happens. Another second, a minute, a lifetime. I don't hear his footsteps on the gravel. Is he toying with me? Sneaking behind me?

I squeeze my eyes open. Mr. Dannenberg is no longer moving; he's standing right in front of me. And now he extends his hand. But it's not in a fist. It's flat, open-palmed, waiting.

I look at him, confused.

"The money," he says gruffly. "You said you brought the money for the headstone."

"You said you didn't want it."

"Just give it to me, all right? Before I change my mind about taking it."

Hastily I hold up the envelope of bills, and when I give it over my hand shakes only a little. It doesn't shake any more, at least, than Mr. Dannenberg's hand shakes as he receives the envelope. Folds it in half without looking at it. Tucks it in his pocket.

Then he turns back to his truck, grabbing the engine crank on the front to start the motor. I realize he means to leave without saying anything else to me at all.

"Wait?" I mean it to come out as a command but it comes out as a plea. He starts to turn the crank, efficient semicircular motions, jerking the crank upward and then releasing and repeating. "Is this the last—will I ever hear from you again?"

Will you telephone me in the middle of the night? Will you follow me in the dark?

The question even Mr. Dannenberg can't answer: *Will your son haunt my dreams for the rest of my life?*

He finishes preparing the engine and walks to the driver's seat of the car, repositions his toolbox, and climbs in. He sees me watching him but doesn't answer me until the door is already closed.

"You should leave now. Go back to your nice future, your wealthy neighborhoods, wherever you all live," he says. "We don't ever need to have another conversation again."

I think about that phrase. *Another conversation.* And I wonder what he counts as conversation. He and I have had two official conversations, this one today and the one when Theo and I came to his house four days ago. But to look at it another way, he and I have also had four conversations: two in person, and then the times that he telephoned and I was pinned at my switchboard, barely able to respond.

And to look at it yet another way, he and I have had infinite conversations, all in my brain, from the moment I forgot the code. Conversations where I imagined all the loved ones of the boys, berating myself and becoming paralyzed with guilt and confusion.

And then, without saying another word, Mr. Dannenberg drives away.

28

ALAIN TOUSSAINT

And then I am standing there alone in the train yard in a night that has gotten so black it is almost inky, watching the truck drive away until I cannot see it, only hear it, and then until I cannot hear it, either.

I wanted more than that. I wanted to know exactly how he found me. I wanted an explanation for how he learned about me. I'd wanted to ask him all of that—I needed to ask him all of that. But in the moment of the conversation my pointed questions had flown out of my head and they were replaced instead by grief and confusion.

I wanted resolution.

I wanted his forgiveness.

I wanted an ending.

But you can't have that, I tell myself.

Forgiveness can't be forced, and resolution can't be forced, and sometimes resolution doesn't come.

I do know that. I do know that sometimes resolution never, never comes.

I don't know what time it is, but it must be late. I can't remember when the last trains stop running and I don't want to be stranded in Baltimore. I start to walk, trying to breathe the night air into my lungs, to settle my body. To take whatever peace I can find from the conversation with Mr. Dannenberg.

To tell myself, again and again, that everything is over now.

From a distance Penn Station looks like a postcard, still and silent, the tall facade lit from below by the gas lamps lining the street. As I grow closer, signs of life become apparent: a mix of horse-drawn and horseless taxis out in the front, passengers rushing in or strolling out.

As I approach the station, I keep waiting to be afraid of the sound of a skittering rock, a shadow in the doorway, an unrecognizable voice. I keep waiting to be afraid but it never happens.

• • •

I am wrung out. I am wrung like laundry come from the washing—wilted, damp, waiting to be pinned up on the line.

But also there's this:

What if this is the peace? I left for Baltimore earlier this evening, back when I thought I'd be visiting a different family, because doing anything felt better than doing nothing. I'd wondered whether I could make peace if I never knew what had happened, if I never knew when another call would arrive, if I never had answers to what had happened and why.

But what if the half answers I have now are the only ones I'm going to get?

This is what I keep asking myself now, on the train home, and then in the taxi ride home, and then in the last few blocks after I ask the driver to let me off early so that I can keep walking.

What does life look like when you cannot have the ending you want, you only have the ending you get?

As I approach Aunt Tess's house I see a figure on the stoop, a slim-built young woman, my age or maybe a little older, about to knock at the door. I know I've never seen her before and wonder whether she's one of Aunt Tess's friends, or perhaps a new boarder, arrived late and unsure of whether she should ring the bell.

"Are you here to see Tess St. James?" I ask as I walk up the stoop. "I'm her niece, Edda."

"I'm here to see you, then," the young woman says, extending her hand. "I'm terribly sorry for the late hour, but your note did say to contact you at any time, and this was the only time I knew I could pass by your address."

She waits for recognition to dawn on my face and when it still doesn't she fills in:

"I'm Eliza Danneman. You left a note about my brother." She pauses. "August Danneman."

August Danneman. The last to die, in my imagination. The gentle boy, in my imagined version of him. The boy who would rescue baby squirrels and nurse them back to life with an eyedropper.

"I didn't mean that you needed to come out of your way to visit me," I apologize. "I left my address but I thought you might use it to write or telephone. I feel awful that you're here so late."

"It wasn't out of my way. I work in Washington; I'm a secretary for an insurance agent. Tonight he kept me late, working on a claim, or else I would have come earlier. I hope it's all right that I'm the one who's come," she continues. "The note was addressed to my mother but she wasn't up to talking to you herself. It's hard for her."

"Of course, I completely understand. It was good of you to come for her."

"Yes." Eliza shifts her weight on the stoop and looks back over her shoulder, as if she might have somewhere else to be.

"Would you like to come in?"

"Pardon me, it's just—I don't really know why I'm here. I mean, I'm here because you left a note at my parents' house, but I don't really know what you wanted. My fiancé is waiting in the car." She nods to where a neatly mustachioed man sits in the driver's seat of an automobile on the street. "Will this take long?"

August Danneman's sister is standing on my front stoop and now, after coming back from meeting with Mr. Dannenberg, I have no idea what to do with her.

"Truly, I feel terrible that you came all this way," I end up saying.

"I just—I wanted to express my condolences for your loss. He was taken before his time."

"He was," she agrees. "And I will pass your condolences along to my mother; she's always comforted to know when people remember him. I do try to remind her—he was taken before his time, but we still had him three months longer than we thought."

Her voice has a bravery to it, and she punctuates the sentence with a firm little nod.

"How do you mean?" I ask as delicately as I can think to. "How do you mean that you had him for three months longer than you thought?"

"Oh, the Forty-Eighth Regiment," she explains. "It wasn't his regiment. He was with them on a special detail, only we didn't know about it at the time. The boys he'd been sent over with— they'd died three months before. A flash flood in their trenches. We were notified of his death back then, because everyone assumed he was there. And then a month later, we received a letter from him, dated after his supposed death. We received three more letters from him before he actually died."

"I can't even imagine," I say, and I truly can't. To have someone taken away from you, and then returned only to be taken away again.

"You can't," Eliza says. "I can barely even imagine it, and I went through it. But I think, as awful as it was—I'll always be grateful for those letters. My parents, they had an idea of who August was, but it wasn't who August really was. They wanted him to become an attorney like my father. He didn't want that, he never had, but he didn't have the courage to tell them, and then he was called off to war. By the time he sent the letter he'd worked up the nerve. He told them he'd been accepted to a program in Boston to study veterinary sciences."

"He was going to be a veterinarian?" I interrupt. "Work with animals?"

She nods. "He loved them. All kinds. Especially the small ones. Kittens and chicks."

And squirrels, I think. *I bet he also loved squirrels.*

A bittersweet smile pulls across my face. To think that I finally pictured one of the boys of the Forty-Eighth right, that the vision I had of them in my head might have resembled, at least in some small way, the reality of who they actually were.

"Whenever I'm angry," Eliza continues, "whenever thinking about my brother becomes completely unbearable, I try to at least hold on to that small thing: that when he died he had the extra time to tell my parents who he really was."

"But you *do* still get angry," I clarify. "You had him back only to lose him again."

"I am furious all the time," she says. "All the time. But as soon as he left to go to France, there were no good outcomes. Not when you go to war. Even if he had come back, I knew he wasn't ever going to come *back*, do you know?"

I did. I knew that for myself. I knew that the people we were when we got on those boats were not the people we would become by the time we returned on them.

She sighs. A deep, heavy, world-weary sigh. "I don't think I'm making any sense right now. I'm sorry. It's very late and I worked a long shift today. I think what I'm trying to say is that, if I could have chosen, he wouldn't have died. If I could have chosen, he wouldn't have gone at all. But I didn't have that choice, either. I didn't have any of the choices that would have made it better. The choice that I have now, the only choice in front of me, is to be grateful that while August was over there, he saw his own mortality, and he wrote my parents a letter, and he got up the nerve to tell them how he would be living his life. So I'm making that choice. I'm making the only choice I can make." She looks back again, to the man waiting in the car. I can make out barely a silhouette, but the man in the driving seat raises a hand off the steering wheel in greeting and Eliza waves back affectionately in return. "In a way, it saved my life, too. My parents' plans for me involved me getting married, but not to Franklin. After August died, I got up my own nerve to tell them that. And life gets bigger. You know? You expect that as time passes grief will get smaller, but grief doesn't get smaller. It's just that life gets bigger."

"I'm glad for you," I tell her, my voice full of emotion.

And I am. I'm glad for this girl I don't know, and for whatever amount of solace she managed to find after a terrible situation. "I'm glad for you and I'm really glad, also, that you stopped by."

Eliza is still looking back to her fiancé in the car. It's clear that's where her attention is, that she wants to be getting home and not continuing to stand here on the porch with me.

"Anyway. I should be going," she says finally. "I'll tell my mother that you were just a friend who wanted to pass on condolences. That's right, isn't it? I'm sorry—did you say you were a friend?"

Not for the first time in the past five days, I find myself searching for a plausible story. But this time I find no plausible stories.

"I actually—I didn't know him at all," I say, "but I've spent a lot of time thinking about him. About all the boys who died when he did. I was there. I was with American Expeditionary Forces, and I was in France. The deaths of the boys from the Forty-Eighth feel very personal to me."

She nods. If my explanation seems strange to her, she doesn't say it. Maybe it doesn't seem strange to her. Or maybe she just wants to move on.

"We got three months more than we thought we would" is what Eliza Danneman says finally, softly. "We did get that."

Life doesn't make sense sometimes and we never get the choices we want, only the choices we have.

I watch Eliza Danneman drive away with her fiancé.

Is it possible that I did the best I could, with the choices I had?

Is it possible that what happened to the boys from the Forty-Eighth was because of something I did, but not my fault? Is it possible that I am to blame, but not to punish?

For the weeks and months that I've been back from France, I don't think I would have believed there was a distinction. And maybe there's only a sliver of one. But a sliver is enough to let the light in. A sliver can be enough.

Is it possible that I have already punished myself?

29

ARTHUR VALDOSTA

Inside, the house is dark and muffled, silent but for the tick of the grandfather clock in the parlor, the cough of a boarder on the second floor. I tiptoe up the stairwells, trying not to make a sound as I pass the other bedrooms. I'm never here at night like this; at this time I'm usually hours into my shift. The housekeeper must have come this afternoon, polished the wooden furniture with lemon, and wiped the windows with vinegar.

Clean. Everything smells clean.

It's nearly midnight when I finally stand in the doorway of my room. My bed awaits, the nest that it always is, but instead of throwing myself onto it, I find myself examining it. When was the last time I straightened the sheets, pulled the quilt up snug around the headboard? How many water glasses have collected underneath, or crumpled pairs of stockings?

I finally enter my room. I take off my coat. And then I silently begin to excavate the mess in front of me.

I sweep the empty cookie tins from under my bed, arrange my dirty blouses into a pile. I pull the hairs out from my comb and lay it next to my washbasin. I wipe away the sticky circled residue left by half-drunk glasses, and I close the books splayed open with broken spines and tuck them back on the shelf. I make my bed. While shaking out the quilt, a little piece of cardstock falls out. *Welcome, Edda!* Left by my aunt on the first night I arrived.

So there is the answer to the last time I made my bed. I've never made it, not since I moved in.

Cleaning up takes hours. By the time I'm finished it's after five o'clock in the morning and it must be starting to get the smallest bit light outside.

I pull open the curtain by the head of my bed, and the yellow glow from the streetlamp outside reveals that the room, despite my hours of labor, still isn't as tidy as I'd believed it to be. Dust still covers my night table. The rug is caked through with crumbs, there are water stains on the bureau, there are smudges on the windowpanes. I thought I had fixed it but now I can tell I've only started it. There will be so many more days of trying to fix it, assuming it can be fixed at all.

Through the wall I hear something, the faintest of scratching noises.

Theo.

Theo awake, and sitting at his drafting table. Just inches away from where I am now, on the other side of the wall.

Theo, whose words still sting in my ears—*you can't be fixed.*

Theo, whose evasions still bother me, whose secrets don't make sense to me, whose secrets I didn't even imagine existed.

In spite of all this I need to tell him what happened with Mr. Dannenberg. I owe it to him, and more than that, I *want* to tell him. There is nobody else who would understand what it means.

Standing in front of his door I raise my hand to knock but the door swings open at the first rap of my knuckles, before Theo has a chance to decide whether to answer the door or not.

He is sitting at the drafting table. But he's not working, he's staring out the window. His bad leg is propped on a footstool. He looks tired; he looks like he hasn't slept since I left him in this room yesterday.

"Edda," he says, startled, looking over and seeing me standing in the doorway.

My name is filled with hope, I can tell, at what I might have come here to do. Apologize? Forgive him? Press my fingers to his mouth?

"It's finished," I tell him, before either of us have time to think about what else I might be doing in his doorway. "I—I wanted you to know. It's over. I solved the caller."

For a moment he reacts as he would have reacted just yesterday, before we had the fight. He heaves himself out of his chair, rushing over toward me, face filled with amazement.

"You solved—who was it? Tell me everything. Was it the man with two sons?" Now his eyes fly to the list of names, which we'd tacked on the wall, quickly skimming through the families we'd never crossed off. "You shouldn't have gone to see him alone, Edda," he continues without giving me a chance to explain. "It was dangerous, and I would have come with you, I would have—"

"It was Mr. Dannenberg," I interrupt. "It wasn't the DuBois or the Shea families; I didn't even meet them. It was Mr. Dannenberg."

I can see from his facial expression that it takes him a few seconds to even place who the Dannenbergs are, that our visit to their house four days ago was already eclipsed by everything that happened in the days since.

"The family who needed the gravestone?" he repeats slowly. "I don't understand. Hadn't we ruled them out?"

"We had, but we shouldn't have."

I explain to Theo everything that happened, how I figured this out. The visit with the neighbor, the telephone company, the conversation at the train yard. The way that Mr. Dannenberg knew more about the circumstances of his son's death than we thought he had.

"But did he confess, then?" Theo asks. "Did he explain what he meant when he said that time was running out? Do you know what he would have done if you hadn't found him?"

"He didn't confess, and in a way he did?" I tell Theo. "I think he confessed as much as he is ever going to. I think I learned as much as I am ever going to. He was angry about the fact that his son had even gone to war; he was angry at all the people who sent him there, and all the people who gave the orders that led to his death."

"But did he specifically mention telephone operators?" Theo asks. "Did he specifically mention 'Brightwood'?"

He sounds stunned even as the words are coming out of his mouth, unable to grasp the idea that this is over, suddenly, before we expected it to be. He looks in shock. I think I'm still in shock, too.

"No, but—" Mr. Dannenberg hadn't mentioned Brightwood. Had he?

"Maybe if we go back together, then—"

"No." I interrupt Theo more firmly this time. "I am not going back again. I am not exposing that man to any more pain."

Nor myself. The telephone calls are going to stop. That is what I have to focus on. The telephone calls are going to stop, and I am going to have to keep going.

"Edda, this is—" Theo makes a gesture as if his brain has exploded. "I thought it was going to be impossible. If you'd asked me five days ago, I would have said the chances of you solving this mystery were nonexistent, and—how do you feel?"

I stop to think about his question. To really think about it, because for the first time in a while I am not sure whether I have an answer.

I feel relieved. I feel resigned. I feel restless but more at peace than I felt twenty-four hours ago. I feel incomplete and like I will never feel complete.

"I feel tired" is what I finally say. "I've been awake all night."

"I was going to knock on your door later," Theo rushes. "Edda, I wanted to say—"

"I think I might try to go to bed now," I interrupt him.

Because I'm not sure that I need to hear what he wants to say. I'm not sure that I have the energy to hear what he wants to say.

Being here in Theo's room, I can't stop thinking about the way he demanded to know who Luc was. The fact that it dragged up the memories I wanted to bury, but more than that—the fact that he felt entitled to know. I don't feel angry at Theo the way I did when we were arguing yesterday. Mostly I just don't *feel* toward Theo the way I did. Mostly it's hard for me to know how to feel at all.

"Maybe when you wake up," Theo begins, but I interrupt him again.

"I don't know. I don't think so," I tell him. And then, to soften things: "I wouldn't have gone back to the Dannenbergs' if you hadn't suggested the idea of paying for the headstone," I tell him. "And so in a way, I have you to thank. I'll always owe you a debt of gratitude."

The *always* in that sentence sounds final, I know it does. It sounds like a farewell. Theo hears it, too, and I think that's why the smile he puts on quivers a bit at the corners.

"I think I liked it better when you owed me a debt of cigarettes," he says, trying for the joking tone that used to define our conversations with each other.

"I should get back to my room," I tell him. "I cleaned it."

He nods then, again trying for a bright smile. I turn toward his door, which I don't have to exit through because I never really entered, and I think our conversation is over. But once I'm out of eyesight but not out of earshot, I hear Theo calling me again.

"Edda. Please wait."

When I turn around he's followed me, as far as his own doorway, and his eyes are shiny.

"What is it, Theo?"

He twists his hands helplessly. "I just—I wanted to tell you that I wasn't like some of the other soldiers over there, who had never shot a gun. I had a lot of shooting experience. Pheasant-hunting—it wasn't something we were going to do just because I was going off to France. It was something we did almost every weekend. I was around shotguns, and rifles—my father took it as a matter of pride. From the time I was a small child my father had me practice loading and unloading them."

"Yes?" I wait for him to go on, aware that what I'm hearing is some kind of unburdening. A thing Theo hasn't said before and never planned to tell me.

"What I'm trying to say is that if you were as familiar with rifles as I was, it would have been nearly *impossible* to accidentally shoot yourself the way that I did. If a soldier like me injured himself the way that I did, it—it wouldn't have been an accident. It would have been on purpose."

The way he's looking at me now is more intimate than even the way he looked at me when he held my face in his hands and came so close to kissing me that I could feel his breath on my eyelashes. This is Theo, stripped down to the nakedness that can only ever come from vulnerability.

"I was so scared," he continues. "When my number was called, going was what I was supposed to do. Be a man. Be the first brave man in the family. I wanted to go but I was so scared to go, and I would have done anything to not go. And then I got there and I did. Do anything. I did anything I could do to come home again. Do you understand?"

He doesn't wait for me before he continues; everything comes out in a rush now.

"I knew how guns worked," he repeats. "I knew exactly what I was doing, and I did anything I could do to come home again."

"Theo—"

"But once it had happened, I couldn't bear the idea of coming home. To a hero's welcome—wounded in the war." He chokes here, on the word *hero*, he spits it out like it tastes bad. "My family all cheering me on for being the first Graybill to go actually go off to fight instead of paying someone else to do it. And meanwhile all along I would know what the truth was.

"I'd like to say I would take it back, but if I had the chance to do it over again, I would still do anything to not go over there. I would still pay for a substitute to take my place, if that were legal the way it was in the Civil War. I would still…" He looks at his leg. "I would still do everything that I did.

"That's the thing about it," he continues. "Sometimes you're forced to make a decision that shows you who you really are, and it turns out who you really are is a coward."

Theo lets out a long breath, slow and controlled, like blowing the wisps off a dandelion. When he's finished, he jams his hands into his pockets and he tries again for a smile—self-mocking, this time, as if he's trying to give me permission to think as little of him as he currently thinks of himself.

"Anyway," he says finally. "I wish that I could just owe you a cigarette. Can't we go back to that?"

Can we? I'm not sure how to answer the question. Not even two days have passed since we had that, since we had skimmed along the surface and never went deep. It should be easy to go back to that. It should be easy to undo forty hours. Except that I've spent two months trying to undo events that were mere seconds, and it hasn't been easy at all.

I don't answer him. I let that request hang in the air, and I know that my silence becomes a kind of answer in itself.

What I want to tell Theo is that he and I feel like an unfinished telephone call, one where the call gets dropped when static hadn't compromised the line. Sometimes you can pick up the call again, sometimes it's as easy as lifting the receiver and waiting for an operator to connect you. Sometimes you can't.

He looks so earnest, in his doorway, eyes still puffy, smile still lopsided.

"Maybe our decisions don't show who we really are," I tell him. "But just who we were forced to be in the moment that we made them. But either way I don't think it's possible to move backward," I say, hand on the door, ready to shut it. "Because time only moves in one direction even when you would give anything for that not to be true."

30

ANDERS VAN DYKE

I'm barely back in my room—I've only just sat on my bed—when there's another knock at my door.

I know it's not Theo, I know he wouldn't do that right now, and sure enough, Aunt Tess's voice immediately follows the rapping.

"Are you awake? Edda?"

"Come in."

She's barely stepped in the door when she registers how different my room looks than it normally does: the swept floors and made bed, and the morning light now streaming in through the window. Once she does notice, it changes something in her posture, and she chooses her next words carefully.

"It looks very nice in here."

I can tell she wants to say something else here, either a reproach or a further suggestion about something I've missed, but whatever it is, she bites it back.

I now notice something myself—that Aunt Tess isn't wearing her customary whites and beiges, but is dressed in an all-black ensemble I didn't even know she owned.

"The funeral is this morning," she says by way of explanation. "Family only, but her roommates are holding a small reception at her apartment."

The funeral. *Jack Albertson. Carmen Barbosa. Gerry Champlain. August Danneman.*

But none of these make sense—Aunt Tess said *her.*

"Louisa," my aunt supplies. "I don't suppose that you'd want to come?"

Of course. Louisa Safechuck's funeral, the colleague I never knew.

"I don't have anything to wear," I say truthfully. "Everything that would be respectful is dirty."

"You can borrow something," my aunt says. "I have other dresses that would fit you."

"Are you sure I should go? I've already told you that I didn't—"

"I know, you didn't know her," my aunt interjects. "But I like to think she'd welcome my support nonetheless. And I'm sure you won't be the only telephone operator there."

And so I let her lead me down to her bedroom, I let her choose a somber navy dress, I let her brush out my hair and pin it back. I let her groom me and tend to me and it feels good, to feel her hands rest on my shoulders occasionally, to hear her hum under her breath.

"That should do," she says finally, when I'm more presentable than I've been in weeks or months. She glances at the clock on the wall. "And now we should go. It takes a good thirty minutes to get to Louisa's flat."

Downstairs we hail a taxi. The one that comes isn't an automobile but a horse-drawn carriage. I climb in after Aunt Tess and then lean my head against the doorframe, feeling the rhythmic clop of the horses' hooves down Massachusetts Avenue. The opposite direction of Central Dispatch, which makes sense—of course people don't live where they work. But since my only association of Louisa is as a telephone operator, I realize that in my mind I had thought we would be traveling to Central.

"Packed in like sardines," Tess says, our knees bumping against one another in the small cab. "At least with automobiles, the cab can be bigger than what a horse can pull."

Charley was claustrophobic. He hated small spaces.

That's what Mr. Dannenberg had said. His son had hated small spaces and Mr. Dannenberg was haunted by that when he learned Charley had died.

Something about that sentence is bothering me. Knocking on my brain. But I don't open the door. I don't let that thought in.

Aunt Tess leans out the window to verify the address of our

destination with the cabbie. I pull the window shade down, block-ing out the light. My hair is done and my clothes are pressed and my room is tidy and I am feeling the tiniest bit like myself, and also feeling as though I will never be myself again. The cabbie clicks on the horses and I close my eyes, grateful for the clopping of the horses and the numbness in my head.

31

DAVY WAGNER

Thirty minutes later we pull up to an apartment building. It's four stories of gray stone with a double wooden entryway, the kind of basic place I could afford to live if I weren't subsidized by my aunt's largesse.

Louisa's flat is on the third floor, a railroad layout whose inhabitants have done what they can.

Girls from Central are here as well; reliable Helen has ably taken over the kitchen, washing guests' teacups as soon as they dirty. There were two men when Aunt Tess and I first arrived, clean-shaven and gawky, but they left and all the other attendees are women. Miss Genovese is at the café table in the corner of the living room that passes for a dining room, quietly nursing a cigarette. I'm mildly surprised; I've never seen her smoke in the retiring room before, but maybe that was just her wanting to maintain a professional remove from the people who report to her.

"That's my supervisor," I tell Aunt Tess. "I should say hello."

"That's your supervisor? I'll come, too."

When we reach the table it's my aunt who speaks first. "I'm Tess St. James." She extends a hand. "With the Equal Justice League? I left a message to speak with you at your place of employ." Miss Genovese nods in recognition; she received the message even if she didn't return it. "But this isn't the place to talk about workplace conditions," Aunt Tess adds hastily. "I'm sure you came here to mourn your employee."

"As it happens, I didn't have to come here," Miss Genovese says dryly. "I live here already; Louisa was one of my roommates."

"Then I'm especially sorry for your loss," Aunt Tess pivots smoothly. "Are you leaving her room empty, or?"

Miss Genovese looks slightly irritated by the forwardness of the question. "We can't forever. I shared a room with Louisa and now I'm in with Sara and Joy. It's rather cramped."

Charley was claustrophobic. He hated small spaces.

This is why those sentences had bothered me. Mr. Dannenberg said that the circumstances of his son's death were especially painful to him because he was a boy who hated tight spaces and who died in the trenches. But he didn't die in the trenches. He died on a boat, in open water. Did Mr. Dannenberg not know that, after all? Why hadn't I immediately noticed that?

Because you were exhausted, I tell myself. *Because you were overcome with emotion.*

It's warm in here, warm and close, and I don't know why I'm still thinking about Charley Dannenberg. *Stop it*, I instruct myself. *You're here to pay your respects for someone else; stop it.*

But I can't seem to stop it. Now all the other unspoken things about that conversation with Mr. Dannenberg are again bothering me. Mr. Dannenberg talked about the people he faulted for his son's death. And he did mention the army. But he spent just as much time talking about the classmates who had bullied Charley.

"Isn't it, Edda?" my aunt is saying, her hand firmly on my elbow, trying to draw me back into the conversation that I have abandoned.

I wipe my hand across my brow. I feel sweaty and suffocated.

We had a whole conversation, but is it possible it was different from the one I thought we were having? Is it possible he thought that I was someone else? Is it possible he thought I—

"Isn't it?" Aunt Tess repeats, the words now coming through gritted teeth.

"Isn't it what?" I manage.

"It's a lovely neighborhood that Ms. Genovese lives in. I haven't been to this part of the city in years, and I believe the last time I was here the neighborhood had a different name? I can't remember what it was, though."

Miss Genovese takes one last drag on her cigarette before stamping it out on the ashtray sitting on the table.

"Brightwood," she says.

And I have heard that voice.

I have heard that voice say that word to me on the telephone.

32

HORACE WHITLEY

My skin is pricked through with electricity. Shooting down my arms, numbing my fingers and toes. My face is aflame, my whole face. I have forgotten to breathe and only realize it when I gasp, sucking in the close air of the little living room.

"You." I say the word so softly I'm almost mouthing it.

"Edda, do you want a tea sandwich?" my aunt asks, oblivious to the shift that has happened in the room, gesturing to the small buffet. "I'll get you one," she offers when I don't answer, and then walks off purposefully toward the food.

I have heard that voice, saying that word, on the telephone. I can't yet fathom what it means. I can't even fathom how it's possible. I can barely fathom that it's happening at all.

But I'm not imagining it. I'm here in this kitchen. I can hear, around me, the clinking of silverware and china. I can still see my aunt. I'm not dreaming, I'm here in this apartment and this is all real.

"It was you," I say again.

This time Miss Genovese's eyes flick up. She meets my eyes briefly before rising to her feet and turning away. I think she's going to completely ignore my question, not even give me the dignity of a response, when she looks back, her head in profile.

"I need another cigarette. Let's go to the fire escape."

The gathering indoors seems to move in slow motion, as if underwater, as we walk toward a half-open window and slide our bodies onto the iron grating three stories above the street below. Outside, I wait as she produces a slender enamel case from her pocket, as she reaches in again for a book of matches, as she taps the cigarette on the railing.

"It was you, there's no point in stalling or trying to deny it!" I say.

She hasn't tried to deny it, of course, but I'm certain that she's delaying as she tries to figure out how she might. I am certain she is just going to torment me further, until she finally raises a cigarette to her lips and I notice a tremor.

And for the first time I realize she is stalling because she is nervous.

"I'm not trying to deny it. I'm trying to figure out what to say."

How odd it is to hear Miss Genovese's clipped voice here, on this fire escape, instead of in the switchboard room at Central. How odd it is to realize that her voice doesn't sound clipped at all, actually. The woman I am sitting with—the girl who is only a few years older than I am—is a different person than the woman who supervises me every day.

"How did you know about what happened?" I whisper. "How did you know about what happened that night?" *How could she possibly have known about the boys from the Forty-Eighth, the boat, the call, my error. She was hundreds of miles away, thousands, she wasn't in the room.*

She flicks off a piece of ash, she looks out over the cityscape. We are on a hill, and from this fire escape I can see all the way to the spires of the National Cathedral. Miss Genovese keeps her eyes focused there, on the spires, as she starts to speak again.

"I was very honored," she says. "When I learned that the army was going to send women overseas as part of the Signal Corps, and that they had chosen Washington's Central Dispatch to study the art of telephone operation. Do you understand? I thought that this was the way I could be of service to my country. Teaching some officer from the army how telephone switchboards worked."

"Please don't try to change the subject," I beg her, wondering whether she's about to launch into a speech about how I failed my patriotic duty.

Now she looks at me. "I'm not trying to change the subject," she says. "I'm answering your question. I am telling you that I know what happened that night because it was my job to welcome the officers from the army who were going to liaison with the Hello Girls abroad. It was my job to make sure they were well cared for."

The American girls are always plucky. When I trained at the capital they were tougher than schoolmarms.

I heard those words the first night I arrived in France. I remembered those words when I came home from France and needed to find a job—that the switchboard operators in Washington were the best in the country. I heard those words from him.

When he said he'd trained at the capital, somehow I'd assumed he meant he trained in Paris, the capital of France. But that isn't what he meant.

Still, I feel the need to confirm it. "Are you talking about—"

"Yes," she says.

"He trained here," I continue. "This is where he trained, before he went to France to work with the Signal Corps."

"Yes."

We still haven't said his name. We both know of whom we're speaking but we still haven't said his name.

"Luc," I say it now. His name feels bitter on my lips.

According to Theo, I called it out in my dreams. But other than that, I didn't. I crossed an ocean and I didn't say it. I moved back into my parents' house and I didn't say it. I fled to Washington and I didn't say it. For months I didn't say it, tried not to even think it.

This is the first time I have said Luc's name since I stumbled out of the switchboard room in France.

"We had the newest switchboards," she says. "The newest technology; it made sense that they would send him here. I assigned him to shadow my best operator. Louisa."

This still doesn't make any sense. She heard about what I'd done to the boys in the Forty-Eighth from Luc? But she couldn't have. The one thing I am absolutely certain of is that she wouldn't have heard about it from him.

"Luc said that Louisa was a wonderful teacher," she continues. "He said that he had many things to teach her as well—that he had connections and could help her go far in her career. He said he wanted to return the favor for the way she had helped him."

She lifts her eyes.

Now she looks at me. She really looks at me, more than just a passing glance, and with her stare she is trying to communicate volumes of information.

All at once I understand.

When Miss Genovese says she knows what happened that night, she doesn't mean what happened to the boys of the Forty-Eighth.

She means my part of the story.

She means what happened that night to me.

"What did he do to Louisa?" I ask.

"What did he do to you?" Miss Genovese says. "I assume it was the same thing."

The table in my back, the fingers in my underthings, the shower of stars in my line of vision. Gasping, gasping for breath, praying someone would walk into the room and help me.

"He didn't." I swallow hard. "What he did to Louisa, he didn't do to me. But he tried to. It wasn't for lack of trying. How did you know?"

She hesitates. "I don't like any of the words: women's intuition, a gut feeling. But you left France early. Before the end of the war. And you came with that recommendation. From him."

I had. I had carried a recommendation from that man across an ocean, even when the thought of carrying something he had touched made me sick. Even when I feared that using the recommendation would make it seem as though what he did was permissible or that he could pay for it by helping me get a job.

But what else could I do? I did need a job.

"The recommendation said you were a good girl. And that was the phrase he used for Louisa when he was here, training," she finishes quietly. "His last day. He told me I was lucky to have such a good girl on my staff. When she told me later what had happened, the phrase made me vomit. Because it was my fault. I was so *proud* of the work we were doing. I was so proud to be able to introduce Louisa to him, thinking we were helping and being of use. I was so proud and so, so *wrong*." Her voice breaks on that last word, breaks in two, and what comes out is not only grief but shame.

The fire escape we are sitting on leads to the kitchen, where we exited from, but I notice now that it also leads to another window: a bedroom, with two neatly made single beds, a few books on the nightstand, a robe hanging on the closet door. Louisa's room? Is this where she lived and slept and wrote in her diary and—was Luc in this room, too? Is this the room where he attacked? Is this the room where she died?

I had no idea you were back there!

That's what I had said to Luc, the day I passed my final test in France, the day I met him when he appeared from behind the switchboard. *Switchboards can work this way?*

They could work that way so they could be used for training. They could work that way so supervisors could reach us in the middle of our workdays. Neither time that the voice called had I been paying attention to which line was asking to be connected. It was an internal line all along.

"You terrified me," I sputter. "Do you have any idea how scared I was to get those telephone calls?"

"I needed you to *do something*," she says, defiant and unapologetic. "You know what he is capable of. He could have done it again. You had a duty to try to stop him, to tell everyone the truth about who he is." She looks at me as if she thinks this should be obvious. "The war was ending. We had just learned he was going to come back here, and I didn't want him anywhere near my girls again. You had a *duty*."

"Why didn't *you*?" I ask. A *duty*, I can barely fathom the word. It was all I could do to keep myself dressed, fed, make it to my job. I already felt responsible for the boys of the Forty-Eighth. "Why didn't you come forward," I ask, accusing and begging her at once. "Instead of trying to get me to?"

"I couldn't come forward because it hadn't happened to me and because I would have lost my job," Miss Genovese insists. "Allowing something like that to happen under my supervision. Not properly disciplining Louisa for her indiscretion. And Louisa couldn't come forward because she—because."

Because she is dead. It's what Miss Genovese doesn't say and doesn't have to.

"But *you* could," she continues. "You could tell everyone what happened. What kind of man he is."

"I couldn't—"

"You *could*. I would have backed you up. But you had to go first, don't you see? It doesn't work to have just one girl's word against a man. You need two. You need twenty." She rubs her eyes. "Maybe twenty still would not have been enough. Maybe none of them would have been enough."

"Do you think there were twenty?" I ask her. Such a number never occurred to me. I thought he targeted just me. I thought I was alone. And then I thought he targeted just me and Mae. I thought we were alone.

"I don't know if there were more than twenty," Miss Genovese says. "But I believe there were more than two. Someone who does that doesn't just do it once or twice."

"I still don't understand."

"What?"

"That word. *Brightwood*. I don't understand why you used it."

That's what has been nagging at me. If Miss Genovese was trying to make contact with me not because of what I had done but because of what had been done to me, then she wouldn't have had any reason to find resonance in the term *Brightwood*. She would have had no way of knowing that it was the code name I had forgotten. And even if she'd known, she wouldn't have cared. It wasn't where her attention lay.

"Was it merely meant to draw me to this neighborhood?" I continue, trying to piece out what doesn't make sense. "Did you hope that I would come to this neighborhood and ask around for Louisa?"

"No, of course not. I mean, I did know that Brightwood was the old name for this neighborhood," she continues. "But if I wanted you to come and find me, why would I use the name of a neighborhood that no longer existed?"

"You wouldn't." I shake my head. "But if that's not why you said that word, then what were the reasons?"

"He said that was his name," Miss Genovese says, confused.

Now I'm the one at a loss. "But you know it wasn't his name.

If he worked at Central, surely you were told his name was Luc L'Enfant."

A long pause and then Miss Genovese speaks haltingly. "He said...he said it was a nickname. A private joke, something from the military. Captain Brightwood. I assumed it was the name Luc used with his girls. I assumed it was a name you would know him by." Worry rises on her face as she realizes for the first time that her calls were not only alarming to me, but utterly baffling as well. "Was I wrong?"

She's waiting for me to answer, and meanwhile I'm fixated on the way she pronounced his first name. Not *Luc*, the French way, but *Luke*, the accented pronunciation of someone who couldn't hear any better.

"You don't speak French, do you? Did Louisa?"

"Neither of us, no."

Captain Brightwood.

It's so simple. It's so simple it almost makes me laugh, in a sick and obscene and bile-producing way.

A firework incident in the Fontainebleau.

That's what he'd said, the day I passed my exam. His nickname came from a firework incident in the Fontainebleau, the famous forest southeast of Paris. An explosion would have made the woods light up.

Bright wood.

Bois clair.

To Louisa and Miss Genovese, who didn't speak French, he would have used the easy grade-school translation, maybe, the one for American ears. But when he first spoke that name to me, in my final examination to become a Hello Girl, he spoke it in French. Captain Boisclair.

My mouth gapes in disbelief. From the very beginning. From the very first telephone call. If only I had realized what was happening, if only I had realized which pieces were missing.

Another thought creeps into my mind, so overwhelming I can barely hold it. That night on the telephone. That night when the officer screamed at me to get him Brightwood, to connect him to Brightwood immediately. Is it possible that he was never asking to be connected to the Forty-Eighth regiment? Is it possible he was asking to be connected to the man who had just attacked me?

There is so much about that night that I will never, ever understand. I was so focused on the story of the boys who were hurt and lost at war that I missed the story of how I was hurt and lost at war. I missed part of the story. I missed my own part of the story.

"Miss Genovese," I say, realizing something. "You called me *before she died*. If you did this to avenge Louisa—your first telephone call was before she had even died. And it was before the war was over. A few minutes ago you said the war was ending and you wanted to make sure Luc didn't come back to hurt any of your other girls. But the newspapers didn't announce the armistice until later that afternoon and you reached me at five o'clock in the morning."

The timeline doesn't make sense, no matter how many times I turn it over in my head.

"She knew he was coming home." Her eyes are beginning to fill with tears. "The war ending confirmed it; the war ending is what made her—what made her do what she did. But she *knew*, even before the war ended, that he would be coming back. I don't know how, but she'd come to me that morning, just before her shift, to tell me that she'd heard from him. That he'd managed to contact her. She said there was a letter?" Miss Genovese shakes her head; this is something she hasn't been able to figure out for herself. "It doesn't make any sense. She said he had managed to contact her— he had written her—but I'm the one who always got the mail here at home, and I never saw a letter come through. And I would have known if he'd tried to write her in care of Bell System. It didn't make any sense."

This is something she hasn't been able to figure out for herself, but it's clear she hasn't stopped trying. This preoccupies her, it's her own mystery that she hasn't been able to solve.

"But I believed her," she continues. "Or at least, I believed that she believed it. She believed Luc was coming to find her, and when she told me at 4:55 that morning she was nearly out of her mind with panic."

The precision of the memory. It's clear that Miss Genovese has spent a lot of time going over the outline of this morning, scrutinizing every detail of what happened for clues. "She arrived for her shift like she always did. She went to her locker like she always did. And then, just a few minutes before she was scheduled to start her shift at her switchboard, she came running to me and said that Luc had managed to send her a message that he'd be joining her at Bell System. She was frantic; it almost sounded like she thought he'd gotten in the building."

She arrived just before her shift at five. She went to her locker first. She thought she got a letter from Luc.

"Joining her at Bell," I repeat, the words a bitter syrup on my tongue. "I just want to make sure I understand. Before her shift started, on the morning of the day we learned the war was ending, on the day that Louisa Safechuck died, she said she had a letter where Luc L'Enfant said he would be joining her at Bell System, those were the words?"

"Yes, that's what she said."

Join you at Bell.

The scrap of the reference letter left on the floor of my locker. The locker I shared with girls on the other shifts. The girls who had names like mine, in the same place in the alphabet. Edda St. James. Louisa Safechuck.

It is my great sadness that my interactions with Edda St. James have come to an end. But without reservations, I recommend that she join you at Bell System, the letter had read—the letter that ended up crumpled in my pocket, and then disintegrated in pieces on the floor of my locker.

300

Join you at Bell.

To Louisa Safechuck, those fragments wouldn't have read like a recommendation. Appearing out of the blue, without warning, in her personal locker with the signature of the man who assaulted her, they wouldn't have read like a recommendation. They would have read as a threat.

And then it is time for me to reach the end of my story. The end of my story of France, and Luc, and cause-and-effect, and what happened to me during the war, which it turns out is part of the same story of what happened to Louisa during the war, and ultimately part of the story of what happened to her after the war, too. "That letter wasn't for her," I tell Miss Genovese. "It was for me. That was my recommendation letter."

"I want him to be brought to justice," she says. "For everything he did."

"He can't be brought to justice," I tell her. "You can't have the ending you wanted. I can't have the ending I wanted. None of this can end how we wanted it to."

"I know that, but I thought—"

"You don't understand. He can't be brought to justice. He is dead."

33

Barry Wyndham

The commanding officer knocked on the door of our living quarters, Mae's and mine, the morning after Brightwood, the morning after what happened. Mae was with me. We were letting the soldiers man the switchboards because I hadn't been able to face the idea of going back into that room. I assumed that was why the officer had shown up—to find out why I was absent.

Instead he stood awkwardly in the doorway, looking obviously uncomfortable to be surrounded by the personal effects and intimate possessions of women. "I have some news," he said. "You may want to sit down."

I did not want to sit down. I did not want the officer to be there at all. I was too busy replaying every moment of the night before, the week before, the month before. Had Luc planned that moment in the switchboard room, the pinning and the pushing and the sour taste that disintegrated in my mouth? Did it just happen? Did it happen because I'd asked for it to happen, because I went into his office day after day and asked for new vocabulary and said that I wanted to learn more, do better? So eagerly I had shown up, every day, asking him to help me more, telling him I would do what it took. Was I supposed to know that that was what it took? Was I supposed to know what to do now?

Because I didn't. I didn't know what to do now.

"We are fine standing," said Mae, finally responding to the officer's suggestion that we might like to sit. He looked unconvinced.

"I know you are made of sturdier stuff than most women, but—"

"I think," Mae continued, "that we are made of exactly the same amount of sturdiness as most women. What is it that you have to tell us?"

This time he nodded; he wouldn't offer again.

"Captain L'Enfant," he said. "This morning, Captain L'Enfant didn't report for duty; he'd mentioned earlier that he was going to have a letter he'd written professionally typed. About thirty minutes ago, some troops returned from inspecting a bridge near Metz that suddenly collapsed—structurally damaged during the invasion. There was a body in the rubble, still wearing his tags. The body belonged to Luc L'Enfant."

He said this with such a grave and practiced tone, the kind of voice accustomed to delivering bad news to people who are unaccustomed to accepting it.

"What do you mean?" I asked, at the same time that Mae said, "Are you saying he's dead?"

"The bridge collapsed," the man repeated simply, in the way of someone who wants to make sure there is no ambiguity. "The body was under the rubble."

There was a ringing in my ears. He continued with what I assumed were more of the particulars. The ringing in my ears was the loudest thing in the room, and so I couldn't say for certain what he said.

"I know how much he meant to all of you girls. I know how much he championed you and looked after you," the officer said, and then he kept talking and then eventually there was a pause and I realized it was because the commanding officer had said something directly to me.

"—think it was his final act," he was saying.

"Pardon me?" I asked over the ringing in my ears. He looked at me sympathetically. He assumed it was my grief that had struck me silent.

"This is why I thought you might want to be sitting down," he said. "When we searched Captain L'Enfant's person, a letter was found in his pocket—presumably the document he went to go and have typed. It was a letter of reference for you, Miss St. James, to be given to your future place of employment. He said you were an excellent operator."

He reached into his breast pocket and produced a plain envelope, soiled around the edges, and held it out to me reverentially, as if it was an important artifact. "L'Enfant was so devoted to his work, to his girls," the officer said. "His last act—making sure you would have a letter of recommendation."

So I wouldn't tell, I thought. That was the real reason he suddenly needed to have that letter typed. What he'd tried to do to me was what he'd already done to Mae, but now she and I both knew about it, and Luc must have wondered whether we were going to tell. His letter of reference was a bribe for my silence.

"I couldn't," I said, recoiling. "I couldn't possibly take this letter."

But my revulsion was mistaken for sadness and the officer didn't tuck the letter away. "He would have wanted you to have it," he said, extending it again my way. It stayed there, in the chasm between us, rustling in his hand.

"I don't want the letter." I repeated the sentiment. "Luc was—you should know that Luc did something—"

The letter dropped half an inch as the officer waited for me to finish. "Luc did something?" he asked. His eyes weren't impatient and they weren't unkind. But I couldn't imagine knowing how to finish my sentence. Not then, not when what had happened was so fresh and so horrible and when I wasn't even sure I knew what had happened.

And so I simply didn't finish the sentence. I closed my mouth. I took it. I took the horrible letter and since I couldn't bear to have it close to my own body, I folded it into a book instead and set the book on top of my trunk.

The officer dipped his head and left the room.

And then I thought of the oddest thing. I thought of the word le séchoir, *which means "clothesline." But which in the war, in the French terminology of the war, meant "barbed wire." It was the slang that everyone used, and that I used a hundred times at the switchboard. I had ordered le séchoir. I had warned troops to avoid le séchoir. I had done all of this—I had known the word to begin with—because Luc L'Enfant taught it to me. He had made sure I remembered it. He had made me a better operator. He had seemed sincere in that. Whether his kindness had been a ploy, a plot, or whether it had been sincere, the effect was the same. He made me better at what I had come to France to do. I had saved lives because I knew to say le séchoir, I know I had.*

"This wasn't supposed to happen," *I whispered to Mae. And I could have been referring to so many things. Luc dying. Luc attacking me. In the moment, what I think I meant was that everything now felt unfinished. It wasn't supposed to happen that Luc should die, because a brave man's death meant that what he did to me died with him. I could never speak out now.*

"This is war," *Mae said.* "None of it is fair."

"What happened to me in the dispatch office wasn't war," *I told her. I didn't know what it was, I didn't have the words.*

I would have had the words if I believed Luc was evil, but I didn't know if I believed that. Even though it would have been easier to. Even though I wanted to.

"You are a young woman," *Mae told me.* "War looks different for women."

But now, my throat was still burning from how I had tried to scream. My thighs could still feel the memory of his belt buckle. My nose could still smell the peppermint schnapps that I knew, right then, would make me immediately vomit if I ever smelled it again.

"What do you want to do?" Mae asked me.

What I wanted was to go backward and erase the night before. What I wanted to do was place the call to the Forty-Eighth Regiment, to Brightwood. What I wanted was to never have come to France. What I wanted was for Luc to be here so that I could try to understand what had made him do what he'd done. So that I could make him pay. Or forgive him. Or confront him. So that I could choose.

"I want to go home," I told her. "I want to go home and I want to never think of this again."

34

CLARENCE ZIMMER

"What do you mean he died?" Miss Genovese says, disbelieving even though she has just heard my story, my whole story: how I arrived in France and succeeded in France and was foolish in France and how I feared for my life in France and how I eventually left France broken. I have been telling her about the firing lines, and the water in the basement of the hostel, and how when Luc attacked me it almost felt as though we were dancing, but we weren't. Dancing was just the only reference point I had.

The sun is directly above us here on the fire escape. We must have been out here for an hour or more.

"He doesn't get to just die." She stubs out her cigarette in anger, mashing it into the metal railing. "He doesn't get to just have that ending."

"But he did have it," I tell her. "That was the ending."

"No, it was—"

"It was."

There is nobody who has spent as much time as I have wishing for that not to have been Luc's ending. Nobody whose mind has done as much work as mine has trying to ignore that ending in favor of one that would have been more just.

Miss Genovese slumps against the railing, grounding the heel of her hand against her forehead and squeezing her eyes shut. When they open again they're red at the corners. She looks up at me.

"I wish Louisa had been able to do what you did." With a flick of her wrist she manages to catch a tear before it runs down her face. "I wish she had been able to never think of it again."

She's wrong, though. She's right and she's wrong. I thought of it even when I told myself I wasn't thinking about it. I thought of it every day. Every minute of every day. No matter how much I wanted to believe I could make myself forget it.

"It was always in my mind," I tell her. "I just didn't speak of it."

I didn't speak of it any more to Mae when she came into the room, even though she clearly knew what had happened; it had happened to her.

I didn't speak of it when I went home to Baltimore and I stopped bathing and my hair grew lank and my parents knew that the daughter who had left for France was not the daughter who had returned.

I didn't speak of it when I moved in with Aunt Tess and drew the curtains and never emerged, even when she asked me directly if I would tell her if things weren't all right. I didn't speak of it with Helen, even though her friendly overtures must have been prompted in part by knowing something was wrong.

I didn't speak of it when Theo told me I cried out in my sleep. Even when he told me that what I cried out was "Luc."

Luc.

My own pain was there all along, even if it was below the surface, even if it wasn't as visible as the pain I had caused others.

"Why didn't you?" Miss Genovese asks. Her question seems both genuinely curious and also pleading. Because she deeply and desperately wishes I had.

I could answer her in a dozen ways. I could explain how I felt too much guilt and shame. I could explain that my job was to answer telephones and there were boys over there whose job was to die. The horror over what had happened to those boys was so much more tangible and easy to explain than what had been done to me. "I don't know," I tell her. "I guess I just wasn't ready. I wish I could have, for Louisa."

I wish Louisa could have, for me.

"It wasn't supposed to end this way," Miss Genovese says, sadly.

And she is right. But also, I think that is life. I think that life means things end in the ways they aren't supposed to and yet we still have to find a way to move on.

35

Edda St. James

A funeral. We are having a funeral at last. Not an official one, those happened weeks or months ago, and they happened with loved ones, with family and close friends. We, the attendees of this funeral, are not the loved ones. We are the outsiders, the periphery. We are the breakers or the broken ones, the people whose lives were touched by the widest periphery of deaths.

We hold it not in a cemetery but my aunt's backyard, standing around a pile of stones, a memorial of sorts, a memorial with discreet glasses of gin. Gin in the backyard, drunk out of cups barely bigger than thimbles.

Miss Genovese is here to mourn Louisa, and so is my aunt, though she didn't know her at all.

I am here to mourn the boys who died, always to mourn them, but also to mourn myself, the girl I left behind in the war and the girl I will never get to meet because of it. We stand in a circle around a backyard fire, like a trio of spiritualists.

"Louisa and I started the same week at Bell," Miss Genovese begins a loosely planned eulogy. "She'd come to the interview straight from the train station, still carrying her suitcase, and she owned just one dress. It took months before she would buy another one, even after we got our paychecks. She had *eight* brothers and sisters back home in West Virginia and she was sending every penny back to them. Every night in our apartment she would wash the dress in the sink, and drip it dry overnight, and—" Miss Genovese's throat catches. "And we could never get her to come out to dinner with us, because if she didn't wash her dress immediately after her shift then it wouldn't have time to dry before the next morning."

She smiles a watery smile. "That's how I'll remember her. In her nightgown by six p.m. eating toast for dinner and curled up in bed with a book, telling us all to go on without her; she could always come out to dinner later, there would always be more time."

In my hand I clutch a letter from Mae, sent to my parents' house first and then forwarded to me. She'll be coming back to the United States. She wants to know if I want to see her. *To catch up on our memories of the war*, she carefully worded it. *But only if you have the time and inclination.*

"Visitor," Aunt Tess says, nodding toward the house. Theo

awkwardly stands in the frame of the back doorway, looking as though he's not sure whether to come out. I haven't seen him in weeks; he'd left on a research trip with a professor. Now he raises a hand in greeting, to all of us, though his eyes linger only on me. "Go ahead," Aunt Tess tells me. "Christina and I can put the fire out on our own."

It's still odd to remember that Miss Genovese has a first name, and that I am now in the circle of people with permission to use it.

Theo sees that I've responded to his wave and am coming toward him. Watching him leaning in the doorway makes me think of all the other times Theo has leaned in my doorway. How careful he was to remain on the border, how he never invited himself in. How his eyes are a beautiful cloudy gray. How I have been angry with him and also missed the shape of him standing there, his silhouette. How both of those things are true at once. How I still don't know what I want from him, or when I'll want anything, from anyone.

When I reach the back veranda he clears his throat.

"I wondered," he says, once I get closer. "I wondered whether you might come with me for a walk tomorrow afternoon."

"I can't," I tell him—and then add on, because I don't want him to think I'm turning him down only because I'm not interested, "I'm visiting the Hornadays."

"Really?"

"I'm visiting all of them, actually. One every week."

The list of names Theo and I had made, the list of all the boys' families and all their addresses—I still have that list. It's what I carry in my pocket now instead of the newspaper clipping. And every Saturday for the past three weekends I have gone to a different house, knocked on a different door, and told the truth:

The day your son died, I was on the telephone in France, and I was trying to save him. Lots of people were trying to save him, and all the other boys of the Forty-Eighth Regiment. I heard the franticness in their voices; I heard the urgency. I moved as fast as I could and I wish I could have moved faster. We were all doing our best. I just want you to know that. On that day, we were all doing our best and all trying to save your son, and since then not a day has gone by that I haven't thought of him.

That is what I have told the parents and sisters who have answered the door, and what I plan to tell all the other families. It might take a long time. A lot of things might take a long time.

"I understand," Theo says quickly. "I wish you the best of luck. Really all I wanted to tell you is that I'm leaving. I'm moving, tomorrow."

This pangs a little because it's unexpected. I thought there would be more time for us to decide whether or not our awkward silence was a permanent state of affairs, to figure out how to move forward since we can't move back. Instead I have to untangle all my feelings right now, and figure out how to transform them into a goodbye.

"I hardly know what to say—I wish you all the best, and I—and I—" My voice grows surprisingly emotional, but before I get too far Theo cuts me off.

"A mile," he says quickly, and his eyebrows raise in a little bit of his trademark impishness. "I should have clarified that from the beginning. I'm moving one mile away. To live with my parents in Foggy Bottom. They insisted and I didn't protest—easier to pay for school, fewer chilblains in the winter.

"But I will miss some aspects of this boardinghouse, though. The people. One person in particular, actually." He sighs, deeply. "Mrs. Pettibone. I'm really going to miss Mrs. Pettibone."

I smile, but just a little. "Obviously."

He starts to turn but I call out before I can second-guess what I'm doing. "Theo?" I say. "I'm not free tomorrow afternoon, but I am free tomorrow night. It's my day off work. If you can find your way to overcoming your profound sadness over leaving Mrs. Pettibone, you could stop by and borrow a cigarette."

His face breaks into a cautious smile, but one so earnest that it makes me smile, too. "Cigarettes are nasty things. I'd never smoke one."

"Didn't say you had to smoke it," I tell him.

"Didn't say I wouldn't accept it," he shoots back. And then, more softly, "Didn't say I wouldn't accept any invitation you gave me. So I'll drop by tomorrow night, and see if you're still around?"

And then he is gone, disappearing back into the house, and the fire in the yard is dying, and the breeze in the air is cooling and time is passing. In a few months, I will have been home from France for as long as I was in France. It is astonishing to think how much a few months can change a person. Or one month. One minute. One word.

Brightwood.

And it is astonishing, too, to think of how long life is—how much longer life is than that one word, one minute, one month.

Life gets bigger.

That's what August Danneman's sister had said to me on the front steps. *It's not that grief ever gets smaller, it's that life gets bigger around it.*

The girl I took to France isn't the girl who came home from France. But the girl I took home from France isn't the girl I will be tomorrow.

"You're going to be late." Christina has checked her wristwatch and now taps it, showing me the time.

My first reaction is to tell her she's wrong, I won't be late, it's barely noon. But then I remember that I have been promoted to a day shift. I work one p.m. to nine p.m. now, and I really do need to get ready for work, for the telephone calls connecting the problems of the people all over the city.

I am no longer wondering what endings can be made. I am wondering whether endings exist at all, or whether life is merely a series of pauses, breaths we take in before we move on, things we lose and things we carry. Life that gets bigger. Life that grows big enough to carry it all.

A NOTE FROM THE AUTHOR

I was neck-deep in revisions for what I thought would be an entirely different book set in 1918 when my husband stumbled upon some information about the Hello Girls and asked me what I knew about them. The answer was nothing. I'd never heard of the Hello Girls. I had no idea that, at a time when women could not legally vote, dozens of them crossed an ocean to go operate switchboards in the Great War. I had no idea that Grace Banker led a team of these women, equipped with gas masks and helmets, through perilous conditions only minutes from the trenches. I had no idea that when these women returned home, they initially had to fight for recognition because they had never officially been soldiers. I stopped what I'd been writing, and I never looked back.

If you find yourself as compelled as I was by the story of the Hello Girls, I highly suggest reading *The Hello Girls: America's First Women Soldiers* by Elizabeth Cobbs—a nonfiction account of the women who volunteered for duty. Some other books that I found fascinating in helping me understand the context of the United States in 1918 include: *American Culture in the 1910s* by Mark Whalan; *America Calling: A Social History of the Telephone to 1940* by Claude S. Fischer; *The Social Impact of the Telephone*, edited by Ithiel de Sola Pool; *Once Upon a Telephone: An Illustrated Social History* by Ellen Stock Stern and Emily Gwathmey; *The Great Influenza: The True Story of the Deadliest Pandemic in History* by John M. Barry; and *The Woman's Hour: The Great Fight to Win the Vote* by Elaine Weiss.

AT&T has a fascinating collection of video archives, many available online, which include recruitment materials for operators in the 1910s and 1920s, and short films about the daily life of an operator. They are available on AT&T Tech Channel's YouTube account and absolutely worth getting lost in. My favorites are the tutorials that were made for the general public, introducing them to the concept of the telephone in an era where private lines were only beginning to become standard. Sheldon Hochheiser, an archivist at AT&T, spent a patient hour on the phone with me, answering my questions about the technology and working conditions that operators like Edda would have been dealing with at the time. I hope that he can forgive any creative license I took as an author.

Finally, as a journalist by training, I would be remiss if I didn't also acknowledge how reading Washington and New York newspapers from 1918 enriched my understanding of how Americans were living their lives as a war raged and then ended across the Atlantic Ocean.

Thank you to my husband, for a career's worth of support, and to my daughter, whose birth arrived midway through my writing of this book. She is the best reason to blow a deadline, and her presence has made me a more empathetic writer and thinker. Thank you to Lisa Yoskowitz and Lily Choi, whose notes on early versions of this manuscript were the clear-eyed guidance I needed, and to the rest of my longtime family at Little, Brown Books for Young Readers. Thank you to my agent, Ginger Clark, and to the rest of her team at Ginger Clark Literary.

A book ends up with one name on the cover, but it was a team effort from beginning to end to tell the story of this chaotic period in American history, in which men were dying and women were trying to hold the country together while fighting for their own rights. I am staggered by the bravery of a generation.

CASSIDY DUHON

MONICA HESSE

is the *New York Times* bestselling author of *Girl in the Blue Coat, American Fire, The War Outside,* and *They Went Left,* as well as a Pulitzer Prize finalist columnist at the *Washington Post.* She lives outside Washington, DC, with her family. Monica invites you to visit her online at monicahesse.com.